POISON'S KISS

Books by Breeana Shields

Poison's Kiss

Poison's Cage

POISON'S
KISS

BREEANA SHIELDS

EMBER

Text copyright © 2017 by Breeana Shields
Cover photograph of snake copyright © by Mark Laita
Cover ornament copyright © by Transia Design/Shutterstock

All rights reserved. Published in the United States by Ember, an imprint of Random House Children's Books, a division of Penguin Random House LLC, New York. Originally published in hardcover in the United States by Random House Children's Books, New York, in 2017.

Ember and the E colophon are registered trademarks of Penguin Random House LLC.

Visit us on the Web! randomhouseteens.com

Educators and librarians, for a variety of teaching tools, visit us at RHTeachersLibrarians.com

The Library of Congress has cataloged the hardcover edition of this work as follows:
Names: Shields, Breeana, author.
Title: Poison's kiss / Breeana Shields.
Description: First Edition. | New York : Random House, [2017] |
Summary: In an alternate world based on the mythology
of India, a girl trained since birth as a "poison maiden"
in the Raja's service is ordered to kill a boy she loves.
Identifiers: LCCN 2015038606 | ISBN 978-1-101-93782-2 (hardcover) |
ISBN 978-1-101-93783-9 (hardcover library binding) |
ISBN 978-1-101-93784-6 (ebook)
Subjects: | CYAC: Assassins—Fiction. | Poisons—Fiction. |
Love—Fiction. | Mythology, Indic—Fiction. | Fantasy.
Classification: LCC PZ7.1.S517 Po 2017 | DDC [Fic]—dc23

ISBN 978-1-101-93785-3 (pbk.)

Printed in the United States of America
10 9 8 7 6 5 4 3 2 1
First Ember Edition 2017

For Justin
You're My Huckleberry

CHAPTER ONE

I'm not a bad person.

At least that's what I tell myself over and over as I wend my way through the marketplace, past the vendors selling spiced meats and bright fabric, incense and rare birds. *Not a bad person. Not a bad person.* It's a mantra I'm hoping will loosen the knot of dread that has been twisting in my stomach all afternoon.

It's not working.

I lift my hair off the back of my neck and yearn for a breeze that fails to materialize. It's hot today; far too hot for my waist-length mane, but Gopal took one look at my hair this morning coiled in a tight knot at the back of my skull and groaned. "No, Marinda," he said. "The boy will favor the hair down." His sudden concern about the preferences of any boy—especially this boy—struck me as laughably ironic, but I didn't argue. I just took out the pins and let my hair tumble around my shoulders. "Better, *rajakumari*," he said. "Much better."

The meeting is supposed to happen near the fruit vendor on the other side of the market. The streets are thick with people—women balancing baskets of laundry atop their heads, men pulling heavy carts loaded with bags of rice and tea, children chasing each other between vendors.

I feel a tug on my skirt and whirl around. A fortune-teller sits on a bright blue carpet surrounded by cards. Her hair is braided in intricate coils, and gold hoops dangle from her ears. She shows me her teeth—it's meant to be a smile, but it looks more like a challenge. "Let me read your future," she says, her fingers still clasped around a fistful of my sari.

"No, thank you," I tell her, and I have to take a step back before she lets go. Gita says that most fortune-tellers are frauds and a waste of good money. Even if she's wrong, it doesn't matter. I have no interest in knowing anything about my future.

I continue pressing through the crowd and I start to think about the boy I'll find waiting for me at the fruit stand. It's a bad habit, one I'm trying to break. I hope I don't like him. It will make it so much easier to walk away without feeling guilty. And I'm always the one to do both—the walking away and the feeling guilty. I wonder what he's been told about our meeting today. What does he expect from me? What does he know?

A quick glance at the sky tells me I'm early. I've been walking faster than I realized. I slow in front of the spice merchant to admire the neat rows of pails overflowing with the rich colors of the earth—spices in hues of deep brown, clay red and golden yellow. A woman with lime-green fingernails scoops the spices into brown paper bags and balances them against a small stone on a copper scale. It reminds me of the ancients who believed we get ten tries at life and then, after our final death, our hearts are measured to determine our worthiness—weighed on a giant scale, balanced against a feather. If the heart is as light as a feather, the person can enter the afterlife. If not, the heart is fed to a wild beast.

My heart will sink quickly even against a brick.

I move to the next vendor to reach for a colorful scarf and I notice my hands are trembling. I need to stop thinking. If I'm nervous, I will ruin everything. I clasp my hands behind my back and teach them to be still while I study the tapestry hanging at the back of the booth. It depicts the Raksaka—the kingdom of Sundari's four guardians—bird, tiger, crocodile and snake. The giant bird, Garuda, hovers in the sky above the others, her jewel-toned wings spread across the entire length of the tapestry. The tiger and the crocodile face off in the center, each of them looking ready for battle. The snake is coiled at the bottom, and no matter which way I tilt my head, his beady eyes seem to follow me. A shiver prickles at the base of my neck, but my hands are steady now and so I release them back to my sides and move on.

I arrive across the street from the fruit vendor with a few minutes to spare, so I duck into the shade of the stone archway and watch for the boy. Gopal said I would find him near the mangoes, but I don't know how I'll ever spot him in the throng. The fruit stand is crowded—boys, girls, men, women, children, dogs. But I shouldn't have worried. He turns up, and he sticks out like a fly in a bowl of soup. He is dressed too formally for a market day, and he shifts his weight from foot to foot without moving anywhere. He is lingering near the mangoes, picking them up, sniffing them, putting them down. All the while his gaze darts from side to side.

He's looking for me.

I walk casually toward the fruit stand and stop a pace or two from him. I pick up a green mango with a hint of blush on its cheek and hold it under my nose. The sweet fragrance stands in sharp relief against the smell of meat, incense and sweat that permeates the rest of the market. I press my thumb against the fruit and it yields slightly. That's how you know something is ready to be devoured, when it gives just a little under pressure. It's the same with people.

I can feel the boy staring at me, but I keep my face toward the fruit bin and watch him from the corner of my eye. I have to be sure. Finally I glance up and our eyes lock.

"Do you have something for me?" he asks.

I open my mouth to answer, when a small girl presses against his leg. Her clothes are little more than rags and her face is pinched with hunger. She holds out her grime-covered hands cupped in front of her. "Please?" she says in a scratchy voice. He looks down at her like she's something he's just scraped from the bottom of his shoe.

"Go away," he says. The knot in my stomach loosens and I am flooded with relief. I don't have to feel guilty for walking away. I turn my attention to the little girl, who has backed off, her expression a mixture of fear and disappointment.

"Come, *janu*," I tell her. She takes a step toward me, and I drop three fat coins into her palm along with a mango I have plucked from the top of the heap. Her face lights up in a smile.

I turn back toward the boy, his lip still curled in disgust. "I do have something for you," I tell him. And then I do what I came for.

I kiss him.

He tenses up at first—they always do—but then he relaxes into me, his lips soft and welcoming. Ripe. And that's when I put my hands on his shoulders and push him away. It was a brief kiss, but a fatal one. His eyes are wide and he puts two fingers to his mouth as if he's not sure what just happened.

"Did you have something for me?" he asks again.

"I'm sorry," I say. "I don't."

His face twists in confusion and his gaze sweeps across the market. "Oh," he says. "I guess you're not who I thought you were."

No, I'm not. I'm not who he thought I was at all.

I turn and walk away, and though it takes all the self-restraint I have, I don't look back.

It won't happen right away. The poison will take some time to absorb into his skin where my lips brushed against his, to find its way into his bloodstream. To destroy him.

In one hour, his skin will heat. I can picture him taking off his black jacket, tugging at his yellow shirt, fanning himself with a newspaper. In two hours his nose will begin to run and his stomach will roil. In three hours his chest will tighten, his pupils will constrict, he will feel like he is being squeezed in the jaws of a giant snake. He won't be entirely wrong. In four hours he will have lost control of most of his bodily functions. He will drool. He will soil himself. He will lose his dignity. In five hours he will stop breathing.

I hope whatever he did to deserve this fate was truly horrible. Because in six hours my guilt will be almost too much to bear.

• •

When I return to the flat, I knock on the door—three sharp raps, which means I am safe and alone. Two knocks means I might have been followed. Four tells Gita she should open the door with a weapon in her hand.

The door swings wide and Gita's face is drawn, worried.

"Marinda," she says with a catch in her voice, "you're late." She's holding a dish towel that her hands have shaped into a rope. The gray at her temples seems more pronounced tonight, as if she has aged in the waiting.

"Am I?" I ask, though I know it's true. The walk back always feels heavy, like a chore.

I move past her and step inside. Our flat is small, just one room with beds on one side and something that passes for a kitchen on the other. A tiny bathroom is tucked in the corner with only a faded yellow curtain for a door. It isn't grand, but at least I don't have to live at the home with Gopal and the other girls.

Mani is curled up on one of the beds, already asleep, though the sun isn't fully set. His small body is curved around Smudge, who lifts her head to look at me, licks a paw and then presses her face against Mani's chest.

"How long has he been out?" I sit on the side of the bed and smooth the hair from Mani's forehead. His face is warm and the bitter-smelling vapors of his breathing treatments cling to his clothing.

"Not long," Gita says. She stops tormenting the dish towel, uncurls it and smooths it with her palms. "He had more energy today." I can hear the effort in her voice and I know she's stretching the truth. He is less exhausted some days than others, but he never has energy.

She yanks on a chair, its legs scraping loudly against the wood floor as she drags it toward me. She plunks it down beside the bed and sits. Mani doesn't stir.

I lean down and kiss the crown of Mani's head—far

away from his eyes or mouth and separated from my lips by a dark mop of messy curls. It's the most I dare, and for a moment I am angry that I am deprived of even this small privilege, to be able to kiss my tiny brother on his sticky forehead. Gita must see the flash of emotion on my face, because she clears her throat.

"I gave him his medicine earlier this evening," she says. "So he should be all set for a few days." It didn't need to be said—the acrid smell clings to the inside of my nostrils. I can practically taste it. So I take the statement for the reminder it is: Mani's medicine for my work today. One life for another.

I pull the blanket up around his chin. "Thank you," I say, though the words cut like glass as they leave my throat.

"So how did it go?" Gita asks, and the question makes me hate her a little. I know it is part of her job to find out, to report back to Gopal, to keep the operation running smoothly. But sometimes she stays for dinner before she reminds me that I'm just a task on her list.

And really, how does she think it went? I just killed someone based on nothing more than the fact that Gopal told me to. But it isn't her burden to bear and so she never feels its weight. "It went fine," I tell her. "No problems."

"Good," she says, nodding. "Good. And was he alone?"

My mind flashes to the boy shifting nervously on the balls of his feet, and my stomach clenches. "Yes," I say, "he was all alone." I want to ask her more, want her to tell me why he had to die, but I don't say anything. Questions are against tradecraft. But I know I won't sleep tonight, that I will see that boy over and over and wonder what he did, wonder what *I* did, and wonder which is worse.

Gita leaves then, promising to check in on me tomorrow. When she closes the door behind her, Smudge leaps over Mani and bumps my hand with her head. A not-so-subtle demand and I obey without thinking. She purrs softly as I rub the spot between her ears and worry that my only talent is compliance. But will I be talented enough to save Mani?

CHAPTER TWO

The next morning I wake to Mani perched on the edge of my bed, giggling. I rub my eyes with the heel of my hand. "What's so funny?"

He grins at me and points to my middle. "Your tummy sounds like a creaky door." I look down as if there were something to see. It's true, though. My stomach is making horrendous noises, and I realize I haven't eaten since the day before yesterday. I learned a long time ago never to eat on the day of a kill. I can't keep anything down anyway, and so my body runs on adrenaline and guilt instead of food.

Besides, I work better when I'm hollow inside.

I sit up and rumple Mani's hair. "Maybe we need to stop for pastries before we go to the bookshop today."

His eyes light up and he bounces a little. "I forgot it was a bookshop day," he says, and the excitement in his voice touches something raw inside me. He is so easily pleased. Life never gives him a full meal, but he is always so grateful for the table scraps. I wish I could be like that.

I help Mani get dressed and then I sit on the floor to braid my hair while he plays with Smudge. He waves a piece of yarn just out of her reach, and she flies through the air like a furry gymnast, sending Mani into a fit of giggles. They play until Smudge grows bored and saunters away.

Mani moves to the edge of the bed and begins swinging his legs, kicking the bed frame. The sound is grating; it thumps in time with the pounding in my head, but I don't tell him to stop. I spent most of last night staring at the ceiling, and I didn't fall asleep until pink light had already started seeping through the curtains, so I couldn't have slept long. I feel that weird detached feeling that comes from too little sleep and not enough food. Or maybe from killing a man.

But today will be different. Today I get to step into another world. One where people die only in stories.

I slide wide bracelets onto both of my wrists to hide the scars there—dozens of pairs of shiny marks to remind me of the price of poison—and then I stand up and hold out a hand to Mani. "Are you ready, monkey?"

"Ready," he says as he slides his small hand into mine. Holding on to him makes me feel substantial, like if he weren't there, I might just float away.

Mani begins to tire after only a few blocks, so I let him set the pace and it's a plodding one. But when he catches sight of the bakery, he tugs at my fingers and speeds up. The smell of butter and sugar hits us in the face, a blissful kind of agony that coaxes a happy little sigh from Mani.

I buy two fat pastries slathered with pale orange frosting. We sit at a little table outside and eat in complete silence but for the sound of Mani sucking on sugared fingers.

He knows what I am, what Gopal made me. A *visha kanya,* a poison maiden capable of killing with nothing more than a kiss as a weapon. I explained it to him two years ago, when he had just turned five. Right before we tried to escape. He tilted his head to the side, like a small bird. "Is that why you never kiss me?" The question gave me a lump in my throat and all I could do was nod.

Mani patted my hand. "It's okay, Marinda," he said. "They're bad guys, right?"

"They are," I told him. But I've never been sure it matters what kind of guys they are. I have to kill them anyway.

I finish my pastry before Mani and sit with my chin cradled in my palm and watch him. After he takes his last bite, I slide my chair back, but he shakes his head and holds up a hand. "Not done," he says, and I laugh as he licks his thumb and presses it against the waxy paper to trap the crumbs. There's so much I can't give him—parents, friends, a life free of disease. But I can give him this. There is so little that's sweet in our life to savor.

We don't leave until his paper looks brand-new again.

∙ ∙

The bookshop is cradled in the elbow of Gali Street, between a butcher shop and flower peddler. The contrast never fails to startle me: one window blooming with bright life, and the other filled with limp geese swinging from the rafters, pink and freshly dead. Life on one side and death on the other, with only stories in between. Little bells on the door jangle when I push it open, and Japa pops his head from behind a stack of books. "Marinda," he calls, "you've just made my day. I'm swamped." Japa has a full head of silver hair and the kind of eyes that smile even when his lips don't.

I shrug off my identity at the door and feel lighter as I step over the threshold.

Gopal doesn't approve of me taking a job here. It makes him edgy, my interacting with normal people, though he would deny it. "There's no reason for you to work, *rajaku-mari*," he said when he found out about the bookshop. "Do I not provide you with all that you need?" We have enough in the way of money, but he doesn't come close to meeting all my needs or Mani's.

"It's good tradecraft," I told him. "Haven't you always taught me I should blend in? Girls my age work, Gopal. Most of them are apprenticed by now."

He had no reply for that. He just grunted and shook his head. But he didn't forbid me, so I keep coming at least once a week.

"Good morning, Japa," I say. "How can I help?"

Japa folds me in a brief embrace, and I turn my head slightly so that the kiss aimed for my cheek lands closer to my ear. No reason to be careless. He motions toward the stack of books. "I could use some help shelving all of those," he says, and then spots Mani hiding behind my knees. "Ah, and I see you brought the best helper of all."

Mani's face scrunches up in confusion. "But I never help," he says with a hint of a wobble in his voice.

"On the contrary," Japa says, mussing Mani's hair. "A boy lost in a book is the best kind of advertising." Mani gives a shy smile, and a wave of gratitude washes over me. Mani scampers off to the corner of the shop to curl up on a fluffy purple cushion like a small prince; he will spend the day there having adventures in the pages that he is denied in real life.

Japa plucks an ancient-looking book from the top of the stack. "Take extra care with this one," he says. "My supplier claims it's from the Dark Days." His eyes are bright. "Isn't that wonderful?"

I try to keep the ignorance from showing on my face. I've heard of the Dark Days in passing, but my education has been on a need-to-know basis. If it can't be used as a weapon, it's not deemed worth my time. That includes history.

"It's incredible," I say. I try to sound appropriately awed, but hot shame climbs up my neck and licks at my cheeks.

Thank the ancestors Japa is too entranced to notice. He admires the book a few seconds longer and then pats me on the shoulder. "I'll be in the back if you need me."

The book is deep burgundy with a ribbed spine and

worn edges. I ease the cover open to find that each page is actually composed of four separate, narrow rectangles made from dried palm leaves and strung together with a slender leather cord. Some of the rectangles have writing in a language I can't read—probably ancient Sundarian—and some are illuminated with miniature paintings. It's breathtaking. I turn the pages carefully—the palm leaves feel delicate between my fingers, like they could crumble with the slightest amount of pressure.

One page has an illustration of a village being destroyed. Flames curl up the sides of buildings, and smoke hangs thick in the air. But what catches my eye is the source of the inferno: it's an enormous snake with fire bursting from its mouth. And the villagers are staring at it in slack-jawed horror.

I close the book. I really should get to work. I slide the volume onto the top shelf where Japa keeps the items for collectors and turn to the rest of the stack.

Shelving is one of my favorite tasks. Japa isn't fussy about speed, so I take my time admiring the books, caressing their soft leather covers with my fingertips, flipping through pages, falling in love before I slide each volume onto the shelf, snug between friends. Slowly the gaps fill in and my pile begins to shrink. I'm so absorbed that I startle a little when someone pushes the door open and the noise from the street spills into the bookshop.

I shake my head, disoriented. The sun is high in the sky now and I must have been here for hours, though it feels like it has been only moments. Mani is curled on his side, eyes closed, a book splayed across the bridge of his nose.

A boy a year or two older than me stands at the entrance surveying the shop like he can't quite remember why he's here. He's tall and broad with arms shaped like a workhand's and inky black hair that falls across his forehead in waves. He glances over and I realize I've been staring. My cheeks flame. I should be offering to help—Japa isn't paying me to stare at the customers. I start toward him, my mouth already forming a question, when Japa calls out, "Deven, how are you, my boy?" I snap my mouth closed, disappointed and relieved in equal measure. Deven. The name rolls around my mind as he follows Japa into the storeroom.

Mani yawns behind me and I realize that I am still standing in the same spot, staring at the door. I press my hands through my hair at the temples. I can't seem to hold on to time today. Mani stretches his arms out in front of him and arches his back like a cat. He has a page-shaped line across the left half of his face.

"I fell asleep," he says.

"I can see that." I flop down beside him. "Boring book?"

He looks at me as if I've just suggested we have mud for dinner. *"No,"* he says. "It has pirates." He waits a beat. "I just got really sleepy."

I run my fingers through his thick hair. "A nap was probably good for you," I tell him. And it's true. His cheeks have more color and his breath is coming with less effort.

"Can we stay longer?" He clutches the book to his chest like he's afraid I'm going to pry it from him.

I laugh. "Yes," I say. "I'm not quite finished." Mani flashes me a grin and leans against the wall, book propped on his knees. I return to the shelves, though my gaze keeps wandering to the storeroom entrance. I can't help wondering what Japa and his visitor are talking about that is taking so long. Is Deven family? Is he Japa's grandson? I can't remember ever seeing him here before, but then again, I'm not here that often.

I try to get reabsorbed in my project, but it's too late. The spell has been broken and my mind is jumpy and distracted.

The last few books are cradled in the crook of my arm when Japa comes back from the storeroom with Deven at his heels. "Marinda," he says, "you've done so much." This is generous, considering he must know I could have finished hours ago—that he has been paying me to browse through novels. "I want you to meet my young friend Deven." Questions pool at the tip of my tongue. How do they know each other? And for how long? How can they be friends with such a large age difference? But I have been trained to swallow my questions, so I smile instead.

"Nice to meet you," Deven says, moving toward me. I step backward without thinking and then cringe. It's a mistake to let my discomfort show so easily, and I try to cover with a light laugh that comes out more like a bark. Deven gives a half smile, just one side of his mouth lifting a bit like he's not sure what to think of me. Then he tries again, leaning to kiss each side of my face. This time I am more adept at subtly twisting my neck, making sure his lips land far from mine. I find myself longing for one of the cultures west of Sundari where people greet each other with extended hands—what a luxury to have the length of two whole arms between you. Or even better, one of the kingdoms where greetings come in the form of nods and bows and there is no touching at all.

"The pleasure is all mine," I say, though now it sounds like a lie. Deven smiles—a real one with both sides of his mouth—and I stop breathing for a moment. My face feels hot all over and I'm relieved when I feel Mani's hand on my elbow.

"Ah," says Japa, "this is Marinda's brother, Mani."

Deven kneels down to Mani's height. "What book do you have there?" Mani doesn't answer but twists his wrists so that the cover is facing out. "That's one of my favorites," Deven tells him.

Mani raises his eyebrows skeptically. "Really? What's your favorite part?"

Deven strokes his chin. "Hmm," he says. "That's a bit like having to choose a favorite pastry. But if you forced me to make a decision, I guess I would have to pick when the pirates find the hidden cave with the maps painted on the walls in blood."

Mani gasps. "That's my favorite part too."

Deven leans forward, his voice just above a whisper,

conspiratorial. "I could tell you were a smart one." Mani beams and Deven claps him on the shoulder like they're old friends.

I feel unsettled, like Deven has made a promise that he can't keep. "We'd better go," I say. "It's getting late."

Deven stands up. "I need to get going too. Can I walk you home?"

The question makes my throat burn. It's an utterly ordinary thing for a boy to say to a girl. But boys never say ordinary things to me. It hurts how much it pleases me that he wants to walk me home. It hurts even more that he never can.

A memory surfaces, one I try never to think about. I was seven years old, playing on the grass in front of the girls' home. Gopal almost never allowed me to be outside by myself, but that day he was in a good mood and had given me permission. I gathered up as many rocks as I could find and I built a village—rock houses populated with rock people. Rock mothers and rock fathers and fat rock babies held by adoring rock siblings. A boy walking past stopped and watched me for a few minutes. Then he came into the yard.

"Do you want to play?" he said.

I shrugged. I wanted to, but I wasn't sure it was allowed. The boy sat down anyway. He showed me how to stack the stones into a tower and then, when we grew bored of that, how to use the chalky rocks to draw pictures on the darker ones. We played all afternoon, and then Gopal stepped outside.

I stopped breathing and braced myself for a blow that never landed.

Instead, Gopal invited the boy inside, offered him a drink and let us play for the rest of the day. My heart felt like it had expanded to fill my whole chest. It felt too good to be true.

And it was.

At the end of the night, Gopal held the boy down and forced me to kiss him. Then he made me watch as the boy perspired and cried and seized and died. When I tried to turn away, Gopal grabbed my head and held it in place. "Watch, *rajakumari*," he said. "Learn."

When it was all over, I was hysterical. "He was my *friend*," I said between sobs.

Gopal pinched my chin between his thumb and forefinger and stared into my eyes. "You don't *have* any friends."

The memory sends a wave of nausea through me. I'm about to tell Deven that he can't walk us home, but he's already heading for the door.

"We're done here, right, Japa?" he says.

Japa nods. "Of course. Have a good evening." He gives a wave meant for all three of us.

I feel trapped. "You really don't need to . . . ," I start, but then stop as Mani slides a hand into Deven's and turns toward me.

"Come on, Marinda." Mani's eyes are bright, his expression so hopeful that it sends a spasm of pain through me, but I can't give in to him. Deven can't be seen with us, can't know where we live.

I don't move.

"Is there a problem?" Deven asks.

Japa looks up sharply, and suddenly I'm trapped between two bad options. Let Deven walk us home or draw attention to ourselves if we don't. I swallow hard. Maybe we can find an excuse to separate from him before we make it back to our flat.

"No," I say. "Of course not."

But I hope I'm not leading him into a den of vipers.

CHAPTER THREE

We slip outside and collide with a wall of heat and noise. The air is so thick, I feel instantly clammy. Gali Street is filled with shoppers—the kind who want to avoid the haggling and magic of the market and prefer to pay a fixed price with no strings attached. It's not as loud as the market, no one is shouting out prices or calling out fortunes, but the sheer number of people produces a racket all its own—hundreds of small noises blended together into a dull roar.

A group of boys race in front of us carrying pails that slosh water over the sides. The children giggle as they dip rags in the buckets and toss them toward one another, droplets flinging through the air before the wet smack of cloth against bare torsos and legs. In this oppressive heat, it's a game where losing is winning. I turn toward Mani, expecting to see yearning on his face, but he's not looking at the children. He has eyes only for Deven.

I slide between the two of them, taking Mani's hand. I can't let Mani get attached. Deven gives me a puzzled look, but he doesn't comment.

After a few minutes he says, "So how long have you been working with Japa?"

"Not long," I say. "A few months."

Deven doesn't say anything, doesn't even make one of those little noises to show he's listening. He just lets the silence stretch between us until it grows so uncomfortable that I'll say anything to fill it, even if it means violating tradecraft by asking a question. "How long have you known Japa?" I ask.

"Longer than a few months." I'm working up my courage to ask him to be more specific when he says, "I've never seen you at the bookshop before."

"Well, I've never seen you there either." My tone comes out with more bite than I intended. Both Mani and Deven look at me with identical quizzical expressions. I sigh. "I'm not there that often."

"And what do you do when you're not at the bookshop?"

Mani stiffens at my side. "You ask a lot of questions," I say, and this time the tone is deliberate.

He laughs and it sounds warm and rich like chocolate sauce. "I only asked two questions."

I can hear my heartbeat in my ears. Deven can't be seen with us. It's too dangerous. For us. For him. Maybe I can tell him that we have plans. It's been so long since Mani and I did anything for fun. We could stop for flatbread and take it to the park to feed the birds. Mani used to love to do that. He would rip the bread into tiny pieces to stretch it as far as he could. The memory makes me smile.

Mani lets out a chain of barky coughs and stops to put both hands on his knees. The park is an impossible fantasy; I need to get him home. I rub small circles on Mani's back until the coughing subsides and then look up to see Deven watching us, his eyebrows pulled together in concern.

"How long has he been like this?" Deven is staring at Mani's white shirt sucked against his ribs. More questions.

"A couple of years," I tell him, because this question is answerable. This question isn't about how I kill men in my spare time.

Deven emits a low whistle and rakes a hand through his hair. "That's a long time," he says, and then narrows his eyes at me. "Do you know what's wrong?" His tone is all wrong, more a challenge than an inquiry.

"He almost drowned when he was five," I say softly so that Mani can't hear. "His lungs haven't ever fully recovered." An image of Mani lying blue and lifeless on the bank of the Kinjal River rises in my mind, but I quickly slam a door on the memory.

Mani starts coughing again. His lips are white, his expression panicked from lack of air.

"Breathe, monkey," I tell him. "You'll be fine in a minute. Just breathe." I keep pressing circles on his back with the heel of my hand. His coughing calms and he manages to suck in a lungful of air. "Good, Mani. That's good."

Deven is still watching me. "It seems to get better for a while and then worse again," I tell him.

He gives me a curt nod and then turns toward Mani. "It doesn't seem like you're up for walking today, pal." He scoops Mani up and lifts him onto his shoulders. Mani gives a startled little yelp and then flashes me a huge grin from high above the ground. It looks all out of place on his face, still drawn tight and pale from coughing. The sleeve of Deven's shirt has bunched up under Mani's knee, revealing a small tattoo. At first I think it's the Raksaka, but it's not. It's just the bird by herself, her blue-and-green wings stretched in flight.

"Lead the way," Deven tells me, and now I have no choice but to let him follow us home. I am praying to all the gods I know that Gita isn't there when we arrive.

Mani leans his upper body on top of Deven's head and is soon asleep. Deven carries him like he weighs nothing. We walk in silence for a while, and then Deven clears his throat and starts talking. "I've known Japa for years," he says. "He's like family. I work for him running errands, delivering messages. He's a good man—loyal to the kingdom and to the Raja." He glances over at me like he's measuring my response. I wish I could tell him that I'm loyal to the kingdom too, that I work for the Raja delivering messages of a different sort.

But admitting that I'm an assassin—even for a kingdom

Deven obviously loves—would put him in more danger than he's already in by walking through the streets of Bala City with me, so I try to change the subject.

"Garuda is my favorite too," I tell him. His eyebrows rise in a question. "Your tattoo," I say. "I like it."

When I was a little girl, I once told Gopal that of all the Raksaka, the bird was my favorite. He narrowed his eyes at me. "Garuda is no songbird, *rajakumari*. The legends say she is big enough to fly away with an elephant clutched in her claws like it weighs no more than a mouse." He meant to scare me, but I only felt encouraged. I knew Garuda was only a myth. Still, if she could lift an elephant, maybe there was a force strong enough to carry me away from Gopal someday.

But now Deven is studying me with the same calculating kind of look Gopal gave me all those years ago, and I'm not sure why. He glances at his arm and then back up at my face. He doesn't speak for a few moments and finally says, "Thank you. I'm glad you like it." But then he tugs on his sleeve so that the bird is covered again.

We turn the corner and Deven follows me down the narrow alley that leads to my flat. I glance back at him and laugh a little. He looks like he's wearing a Mani hat. But then I remember that Gita might be home—or worse, Gopal—and the laughter dies on my lips.

My door is a dull red that always reminds me of dried blood. We stop and I give two short knocks. Nothing. But it's too soon for relief. I dig the key out of my bag and turn my back to the door. "Thank you for your help," I tell Deven. "I can take him from here." I reach out my hands as if to lift Mani from his shoulders, when it's clear to both of us that I'm not tall enough or strong enough to do that. But I'm desperate for him to leave.

Deven shakes his head. "Let me help you get him inside."

"No, really. I'll be fine. Please just—"

"Marinda." It's the first time he's said my name, and it feels intimate hearing it from the mouth of a stranger. "He'll wake if I set him down here. Let me lay him inside and I promise to leave right away."

I relent. "Fine." My hands shake as I slide the key into the lock, and my heart feels like it could break free from my chest. Gita could be inside. She didn't answer my knock, but it's no guarantee. I hold my breath as I push open the door. The flat is empty and relief stings my eyes, burns in my throat. Deven ducks through the doorway.

"You can lay him down there," I say, motioning to my bed. Smudge is curled on Mani's pillow and is unlikely to relinquish her position without protest. Deven gingerly lowers Mani to the bed and pulls a blanket over him. Then he stands up and his eyes sweep over the room. It must seem so drab to him. So plain. His expression is unreadable.

"Thank you," I say.

"Sure." He closes his eyes and pinches the bridge of his nose. His eyelashes are thick and long, and his nose—right where his fingers are resting—is a little crooked, like he might have broken it as a child. He opens his eyes and sighs. "Will you be at the bookshop tomorrow?"

I don't answer right away. I just want him to leave before Gita gets here. The possibility of her walking in is thrumming loudly at the back of my mind. Deven raises his eyebrows and I manage a nod. "Yes, I think so."

"I'll bring some fruit for Mani. It should make him stronger." He doesn't wait for an answer before he spins on his heel and strides away. I watch him until he turns out of the alley and disappears. I close the door and rest my forehead against the cool wood. Slowly, all the pent-up tension seeps out of me until I no longer have the strength to stand. I sink to my knees and escape the only way I've ever been able to—by closing my eyes and letting sleep claim me for her own.

•   •

I wake to noise and have to blink several times to adjust my eyes. I fell asleep slumped against the door, and now my back aches and my neck won't move properly. Someone is pounding outside; it's an insistent smacking sound—all palm and no knuckle. I peel myself from the floor and open the door.

"Finally," Iyla says with a groan. She shoves a large paper bag into my arms and makes a show of looking me over. "You look terrible."

"Nice to see you too," I say. I peek into the bag, and

the smell of spices makes my stomach grumble. The bag is filled with containers of thick sauces in deep red and nutty brown, loaves of flatbread, lidded cups filled with rice.

"You forgot to eat again?" Iyla flips her long hair over one shoulder and shakes her head. She is clearly dressed for a job. Her dress is snug but not indecent—just fitted enough to highlight where the contours are. Gold and silver bracelets jangle from her wrists, her lips and cheeks are painted crimson, and she smells like an exotic flower.

"I didn't forget," I say, pulling containers from the bag and spreading them out on the table. "I just hadn't gotten to it yet."

Smudge jumps from the bed and circles Iyla's ankles, mewing for her share of food. Iyla shoos her away. "Gita said you would forget. She thinks you can't even be trusted enough to feed yourself."

I roll my eyes, but I'm surprised that this small criticism stings a little. "Mani doesn't have much of an appetite and I've been a little preoccupied." I'm annoyed with myself that I'm justifying my eating habits to Iyla, so I change the subject. "Are you working?" I open the cupboard and pull out two plates.

She laughs. "We're *both* working."

My stomach goes cold. I set the dishes down with more force than I intended and they rattle loudly. "What? But I just finished a job. It's too soon."

Iyla narrows her eyes. "Your part takes two seconds. It's not exactly straining."

My fingers find the scars at my wrists and trace their contours. *Two seconds.* If only it were that simple.

"That's not fair," I say. I busy myself setting out napkins, pulling glasses from the cupboard—I'm afraid that if I look at her, she'll see how easily she can hurt me.

Iyla and I have been paired for years now. She does all the reconnaissance for my kills. Gopal has all his girls matched up this way, in neat little couplets—one part spy, one part *visha kanya*.

Iyla's job is getting information, and she's good at it. She could charm the sweet from honey without breaking a sweat. When Gopal gives us an assignment, Iyla does the wooing, the flattering and the seducing. She coaxes information from the mark with small touches, significant glances, compliments; she does it with finesse. And when Gopal has all he needs, I finish the job.

Iyla loves her part. I hate mine.

I finish setting the table and glance up just in time to see Iyla's gaze skitter away from my bare wrists.

"I'm sorry," she says. "I didn't mean anything by it." She's toying with her bracelets—pressing them together, twisting them around, taking them off and putting them back on again. Under all that gold and silver, her skin is as smooth as river stone.

"It's fine," I tell her, because I don't feel like fighting tonight. "What's the job?"

Her head snaps up. "You know I can't tell you that." It's another of Gopal's rules. We aren't allowed to know any specifics about what the other girls do. Iyla is the only other of Gopal's girls I've even met. We are kept separated so that we can't be linked to one another if one of us runs into trouble. But it seems so unfair that Iyla always knows all about my tasks, while I know nothing about hers.

I miss the days when we were small and there were no secrets between us.

I try to remember the last time it felt like we were friends instead of adjoining pieces on the Raja's giant game board. But it's been a long time. Since before Mani was born. Gopal was away on an assignment for the Raja, and so Gita took us to the Festival of the Beasts—a huge celebration to honor Sundari's history. Iyla and I were wide-eyed at the riot of color. Men and women with their entire faces painted in bold hues, dancers with brightly dyed skirts and tall headdresses, children twirling umbrellas shaped like stars and moons.

But it was the painted elephants that had us begging Gita for coins.

Their trunks and foreheads were decorated in various designs—delicate pastel vines that sprouted lotus blossoms, geometric shapes in purple and green, wide stripes of orange and pink. And it wasn't just the paint. The animals were swathed in shimmering silk, golden bands glittered from their tusks, and they wore anklets of silver bells.

It was the most majestic thing I'd ever seen.

We pleaded until Gita relented and dropped a handful of coins in each of our palms, and then we raced to get in line with the masses of children waiting for their chance for an elephant ride.

When it was finally our turn, Iyla and I climbed on the same elephant—a huge beast with painted flames racing up the length of her trunk and exploding on her forehead. She wore a red silk scarf over her head, and her floppy ears donned gold hoops.

"Wow," Iyla said, sliding her arms around my waist. "Being this high makes me feel so . . . so . . ."

"Powerful," I said.

"Yes," she breathed against my neck. "Powerful." The shift in perspective was intoxicating. It was like we could see the secrets of the entire kingdom.

Across the expansive crowd, people waved banners of the Raksaka, but the occasional group had a flag that featured only one of the guardians of Sundari. We watched as a scuffle broke out between two clusters of men, one waving a flag featuring Bagharani, the tiger queen, and the other wielding a banner with the Nagaraja, the Snake King. It started with arguing, but soon the men were shoving each other and throwing punches.

"Why do they even care?" I wondered aloud. What a foolish thing to argue over a preference for a legend. The animals were symbols of a kingdom in balance, not leaders to rally around.

Iyla sighed. "I think some people just want to belong so badly that they pick sides, even if it doesn't mean anything."

"So whose side are you on?" I asked her.

She rested her cheek on my shoulder. "Yours," she said.

But that day seems like a lifetime ago, and now I'm the one she keeps her secrets from instead of the one she tells them to.

"You must be able to tell me something," I say. Iyla presses her glossy lips together and tips her head toward the ceiling like she finds me exasperating. She sighs and glances toward the door as if Gopal might walk in at any moment and catch her violating tradecraft. "It's someone important," she tells me. "Someone big."

I raise my eyebrows. "That could describe all of them," I say. "You aren't telling me anything."

She shrugs. "That's all I've got." She combs her fingers through her hair and runs her palms over her dress, smoothing invisible wrinkles. "Wish me luck," she says, heading for the door. "I'm off to make your mark fall in love with me."

I shake Mani awake and we eat our dinner. Mani sneaks bits of chicken and bread to Smudge, and I pretend not to notice. I smile and make small talk, but my stomach is hectic with dread. Because Iyla looked beautiful tonight and there is no doubt that this boy will fall for her. And then, whoever he is, I'll have to kill him.

CHAPTER FOUR

I wasn't born lethal. I wasn't that unlucky. My misfortune came later, when my parents decided that they longed for money more than progeny.

Gita loves to tell the story of how I became a *visha kanya*. She says that my father presented me to Gopal swaddled in a blanket the color of a ripe tangerine. He watched while Gopal filled a small dropper with toxin and then drained it against the squishy pink inside of my baby cheek. "Bring her back in three days if she's still alive," Gopal said.

He never expected to see me again. Most of the babies didn't make it through the first night.

"But in three days he returned," Gita says. Her eyes are always bright during this part of the story, her voice filled with wonder. "You're our miracle."

The story gnaws at me; what does it say about me that I am a miracle to Gopal but disposable to my father? Even now, I wish it were the other way around.

• •

Deven is already there when Mani and I arrive at the bookshop the next morning. He and Japa are at a table in the corner, their heads bent together, talking so softly that I don't even hear the low murmur of conversation. Japa raises one hand in greeting but doesn't look up.

Mani scampers off to find a book and I stand at the front of the shop waiting for instructions. But it quickly becomes obvious that Japa and Deven won't be finished with their conversation anytime soon, so I grab the broom leaning against the wall and start sweeping, easing the bristles under the bookshelves and pulling out thick piles of dust. Japa obviously hasn't swept in ages. Working soothes me, the purposefulness of it, the sense of accomplishment.

The next time I look up, Japa and Deven have disappeared. I poke my head around the corner and peek into the storeroom, but there's no sign of them. Then I notice a swirling pattern of dust on the floor in front of one of the bookcases at the back of the shop. It's not a bookcase for customers—it's piled with an odd assortment of cleaning supplies and boxes of unsold merchandise—and the pattern on the floor suggests a gust of air coming from beneath the lowest shelf. I brush my hand along the bottom of the bookcase, and a cool breeze tickles my fingers. There's something back there. I stand up and see three shiny marks in the dust on the side of the bookshelf at about chest height. I turn my hand and match my fingerprints to the marks. A door, then. I wonder if this is the secret storage room where Japa keeps the more valuable manuscripts, but I don't dare test my theory. Japa probably wouldn't look kindly upon me barging into a meeting he's worked so carefully to conceal. But I can't help being curious. Why would they need to move their conversation so far away? Do I seem so untrustworthy? Or are they talking about something more important than priceless books?

I rub at the marks with my sleeve until they disappear—no use having a secret entrance that calls attention to itself.

I finish sweeping and then find a soft cloth in the storeroom for mopping. I'm on my hands and knees, scrubbing at the floor, a bead of sweat trickling down the back of my neck, when I hear Mani's name. A ping of alarm zips through my stomach, and my eyes flick to the far corner of the shop. Deven and Japa are back—Deven is talking and Japa is watching Mani, his eyebrows drawn together and down in V-shaped concern. I glance at Mani. He looks like he always does, absorbed in his book. Though his lips are pale at the edges and his breathing is labored. Deven glances up suddenly and I drop my gaze.

"Hey, pal," Deven says, and his voice sounds so loud

in the silence that I jump a little. "I brought something for you." He holds a pale fruit—almost white—with a blush of pink at the top.

I stand and join them, not sure I want Mani to accept anything from Deven. But I can't think of a good excuse to stop him. Mani takes the fruit and gives it a sniff. "What is it?" he asks.

"It's called maraka fruit. My father grows it in his orchard."

"Your father has an orchard?" Mani says, like this is the most remarkable thing he's ever heard.

Deven laughs. "Not a large one. Go ahead, give it a try."

Mani takes a bite and his eyes widen with pleasure. Juice dribbles down his chin, and he wipes it away with the back of his hand. "This is so good," he says, talking around a mouthful of fruit.

I glance over at Deven and he is watching me with the strangest expression, like I'm a puzzle he can't solve. "I heard you talking about him," I say, tilting my head toward Mani. Deven doesn't say anything, just raises one eyebrow a fraction and waits for me to continue. "What were you saying?"

"That he looks ill," Deven says. His voice is gentle, sad. I just nod, because there's no response. Mani does look sick.

"Why the fruit?" I ask after a moment.

"He looks like he could use something healthy," Deven says. I prickle at the suggestion that I'm not feeding Mani properly, but then I remember the pastries we keep eating for breakfast and I swallow my complaint. Besides, anything that makes Mani feel better is fine with me.

Mani finishes his fruit and licks his fingers one by one. "You better go wash your hands before you touch any books," I tell him. He hates anything resembling a bath, so I am expecting an argument, but instead he grins at me.

"Completely worth it," he says, before skipping off to the basin in the storeroom.

Deven touches my arm. "Marinda," he says. "Are you—"

The bells at the door jingle, and a man and woman walk in. "Customers," I explain to Deven before I head to the front of the shop. I can still feel his hand on my arm, can still feel the exact placement of his fingers as I ask the couple if there is anything I can help them find. They browse for a while before they bring their selections to the counter—two beautiful books of fairy tales, leather-bound, gold-tipped and stunningly illustrated. I wonder what child will be lucky enough to read them. I wrap the books in fine paper and reluctantly trade them for a handful of coins. The customers leave, and Deven is still standing where I left him, as if he's waiting for me to come back. I busy myself stacking coins. Each one has a sun in the center with four rays that shoot toward the edges, dividing the circle into four parts. Each segment depicts a member of the Raksaka. I stack the coins and then twist them so that the bird is closest to me and the snake is farthest away. It's a silly childhood superstition, but the snake has always felt like bad luck. By the time I nestle the coins in the wooden money box under the counter, we have, to my great relief, more customers. It's several hours before the shop empties.

Mani is curled on his purple cushion reading again, and Japa seems to have disappeared. I busy myself straightening books and hope Deven will forget I'm here. He doesn't.

He comes up beside me and touches my arm—in the exact same place, as if the physical contact is a vital part of whatever he has to say. My breath feels lodged in my throat, because I want to shake him off and at the same time I never want him to stop touching me. No one ever touches me. Not like this, all affectionate and casual and unafraid.

"Marinda," he says again. "Are you and Mani—are you okay?" I'm not sure what I was expecting him to say, but it wasn't this. The back of my neck feels hot and I can't meet his gaze. I thought for just a minute . . . I thought . . .

"We're fine," I say.

"Are you sure?" he asks. "Because you don't seem—it doesn't seem . . ."

I can't have this conversation. There are a dozen reasons why I can't have this conversation, and all of them are life-threatening. I have been careless and now Mani and I can't ever come back here again.

I touch Deven's arm in the same place he touched mine. He is warm and I can feel the curve of muscle beneath my fingers. A little pang of sadness shoots through me, but I force myself to smile, to make eye contact. "Really, Deven, we're fine." It hurts a little to say his name, because I've never said it out loud before and now this is goodbye.

Deven's brow furrows. "Marinda, you can trust me. I—"

"Time to go, Mani," I say cheerfully, cutting him off. Mani sulks as he puts the book back on the shelf. My heart is thudding against my rib cage. *Stay calm,* I tell myself over and over. *Calm. Calm. Calm.*

"Japa," I call with too much brightness in my voice. "I'm leaving now."

Japa emerges from the storeroom and looks around. "The shop looks amazing," he says. "I can't believe what you've done."

He's grateful for the cleaning, but his words hit me at an odd angle. Because I can't believe what I've done either. I embrace Japa more fiercely than usual before I say goodbye. And then Mani and I walk out of the bookshop for the last time.

* *

I hold it together until we get outside, and then I can't stop myself from shaking. What have I done? I let Deven notice me and he noticed too well, too much. I feel like a fool. What did I think? That he would ask me on a picnic? That he would invite me to dine with him under the stars? Stupid. I could tell as he looked at me and Mani that something felt off to him. I've piqued his curiosity, and that is the worst violation of tradecraft. I am supposed to be invisible. My life depends on it.

A sharp pain shoots through my jaw and I realize I've been grinding my teeth. I take a deep breath and slow down.

I've been rushing, moving way too fast for Mani. I glance over at him, but he's having no trouble keeping pace with me.

"Hey, monkey," I say, "how are you feeling?"

"Really good," he says, searching my face. "What's wrong?"

I try to force cheer into my voice. "Nothing," I tell him. "I'm fine."

"Your neck is all splotchy—that's what always happens when you're upset."

"Oh," I say. "Well, I was reading a book today with a very distressing scene, so maybe that's it."

He rolls his eyes. "Oh, *please*, I'm not four years old."

That startles a laugh out of me, which makes Mani giggle, and soon we are both cracking up. It's the kind of laughter that often follows tension—exaggerated, as if that can somehow compensate. I don't knock when we get to our flat, just slide my key into the lock and open the door.

I stop laughing.

Gopal is here. He stands in the center of the room, his hands clasped in front of him. Each of his thick arms is tattooed with a black snake, the tail starting at his elbow and the body coiled round and round his arm until the head of the snake bites the inside of his wrist with sharp fangs. "Hello, Marinda," he says.

Seeing Gopal always makes me feel like I have been caught doing something wrong. Mani's grip on my hand tightens.

"Nice to see you, Gopal," I say, though it isn't. He

smirks like he can see my thoughts, and a shiver dances up my spine.

"I need to speak with you," he says, and motions for me to follow him outside.

"But Mani—"

"Gita will look after your brother."

Gita is sitting silently at the table, her arms folded across her stomach. I didn't notice she was here. A small clay pot sits on the table in front of her along with the bottle that holds the medicine used to make Mani's breathing treatment—it's the same unspoken threat as always. We exchange a glance and she gives me a small nod. I kneel in front of Mani. "I have to go for a bit, but I will be back soon, okay?" Mani bites on his lower lip, and I can see the fear in his eyes. Gopal terrifies him, and Gita is only marginally better. I fold him in an embrace and whisper against his ear, "I won't be long, I promise."

I follow Gopal outside. He begins walking and I fall into step at his side, waiting for him to speak. He reaches for my hand, and it takes everything I have not to flinch. When I was a little girl, Gopal held my hand wherever we went, the head of his snake tattoo pressed tightly against my skin. It used to give me nightmares, imagining those fangs sinking into the soft inside of my wrist, sucking out blood and replacing it with venom.

Gopal's fingers close around mine. I try to focus on something else. A half dozen soldiers are gathered on the other side of the street. The deep tones of their conversation interspersed with occasional bursts of gruff laughter float over my head, though the actual words have faded away before they reach me.

They wear black uniforms with a bright orange sun representing Sundari on one shoulder and the Raksaka on the other. One of them glances toward us. I see his gaze travel from my face down the length of my arm, where my fingers are intertwined with Gopal's. The soldier's expression registers shock, and I realize how I must look to him, hand in hand with Gopal like we are lovers. I taste bile at the back of my throat.

The soldier whispers something to his comrade, and then they are both watching us—no, watching Gopal—with expressions I can't quite place. Then understanding washes over me. They must know him, must know who he is to the Raja.

It's fear on their faces.

Gopal sees them staring and yanks me around the corner, out of view. He continues walking. "The Raja is in need of your services," he says after we've put some distance between us and the soldiers. I swallow hard and stare at my feet as we walk. Iyla said another job was coming, but usually it takes weeks before I am needed.

"Of course," I say, because this is the correct answer and the only answer that will please him. "When?"

Gopal's jaw tightens as if even this question crosses a line. He sets the pace of the conversation, not me. "Tomorrow."

I gasp. "So soon?"

He stops walking and spins to face me. "Is that a problem?"

"No," I say quickly. "Of course not. I am just impressed that Iyla was able to close it out so quickly."

Gopal's eyes narrow and I realize I've made a mistake. "Iyla should not be discussing her work with you," he says softly.

I shake my head. "She wasn't. She didn't."

"Then how do you know when she started this project?"

"I saw her dressed up last night. It was nothing. She said nothing."

He presses his lips together and looks toward the sky. "Iyla will need to be dealt with."

My stomach goes cold. "No, Gopal, please—"

He holds a hand up to stop me. "It is none of your concern, *rajakumari*. I will handle it."

But I can't let it go. "Iyla didn't do anything wrong. She was just bringing me dinner. Please, Gopal, I really don't think—"

He grabs my wrist and twists it painfully. "We are finished discussing Iyla. Is that clear?"

I bite my lip and nod. I'll only make it worse for both of us if I say anything more. He lets go. "Good. Now on to the details. The meeting will take place tomorrow morning sometime before midday. The boy will approach you with a book titled *The History of Sundari*. You will dispatch him as quickly as possible and then report back to me. Do you understand?"

"Yes," I say, rubbing my injured wrist. "Where is the meeting place?"

Gopal smiles and there's something unsettling about his expression, something predatory about it. "That little bookshop you love so much."

All the breath leaves my lungs. He is punishing me. He knows I have grown fond of Japa, maybe he even knows about Deven, and now he's going to force me to make a kill in front of them. I feel sick. The bookshop was the one place where I didn't have to be *this*.

I try to keep my expression neutral, but I am shaking all over. "They know me there," I say. "Couldn't that compromise the mission?"

His laugh is humorless. "Nonsense. They will simply see you kiss a boy." He leans in so close I can smell his sour breath. "They won't know that the boy *dies* painfully later."

My cheeks heat with shame, and Gopal laughs again before he leaves me standing in the street all alone.

* *

It was years before I knew that the men I kissed died. When I was small, Gopal told me we were helping people. "Spreading the love of the Raja," he said, and he had all kinds of methods of getting me within kissing distance of his target. Once when I was about five years old, he took me to the marketplace for *jalebi*. At first it seemed to be one of our rare outings with no strings attached. He bought me my treat and we sat under a tree while I ate. Buttery sunlight filtered through the leaves, and the sky was the pale blue of springtime. It wasn't until I popped the last bite of warm fried dough into my mouth with syrup-sticky fingers that Gopal said, "Someone needs our help today, Marinda." My stomach tightened into a hard ball, and I had trouble forcing myself to keep chewing and then to swallow. I liked helping people, but it seemed that it always involved pretending, and I wasn't very good at pretending.

"I know a man who needs a kiss from you, *rajakumari*." I kept my eyes down, wiping my hands in the grass to try to clean them, but only managing to make a bigger mess— now my fingers were stained green and black and they were still tacky. "Look at me," Gopal said. His voice had a sharp edge to it, the edge that demanded I pay attention.

I looked up at him and he smiled, but it wasn't a very nice smile. "That's better," he said. "I'm going to buy you a balloon, and then you are going to go stand by a man—I will point him out to you—and let the balloon go. Then— and this is very important, Marinda—you must start crying, you must make the man help you. When he does, you can kiss him for being so kind."

I hated that I had to let go of a perfectly good balloon, but I hated pretending to cry even more than that.

Gopal pulled a small jar of lip balm out of his pocket, and I held very still while he slathered a bit of the ointment against my mouth with his fat finger. I hated how it made my lips feel—sticky and suffocated—but I knew better than to complain.

"What if I can't make the man help me?" I asked.

Gopal's face turned hard. "You don't want to find out."

And I didn't have to find out, because as much as I hated pretending to cry, I could do it. I could pinch the palm of my hand, hard, and think about how I didn't have parents or any siblings, how I was all alone, except for Gopal and Gita, who only sometimes seemed to like me. It worked every time.

The man Gopal pointed out had salt-and-pepper hair, like a grandfather, and a kind face. When I let go of my balloon, I already had my tears ready, but he had fast reflexes. He jumped up and snatched my balloon right out of the air and handed it back to me. Only a few tears had escaped. I gave him a wobbly smile and threw my arms around his neck. I kissed the corner of his mouth. "Thank you," I said, and I meant it, because now I got to keep my balloon with very little pretending.

He chuckled and said it was no problem and that I was such an affectionate child. I had no idea what that meant, but it sounded nice and it made me feel good.

Years later, when Gopal told me what I really was, when he explained to me (with a fair amount of glee) that my kisses killed, it was that man who popped into my mind and then haunted my nightmares for months.

"I don't want to be a killer," I told Gopal.

He laughed and laughed. "You already are, *rajakumari*. You already are."

CHAPTER FIVE

Gita shakes me awake the next morning before dawn. She presses a finger to her lips, but I don't need to be told not to wake Mani. My nerves are already coming unraveled and I know I can't handle a tearful goodbye.

I dress in the dark, fumbling with buttons and with shoes. With jewelry and perfume and thick bracelets to conceal my scars. I wear my hair down.

When it's time to go, Gita steps outside with me.

"Take care of him," I tell her, and even to my own ears my voice sounds hollow. Every part of me wants to run. If not for Mani, I think I would.

Gita nods. "He was so much better last night," she says. "He was full of energy."

For a half second I consider telling her that he had some fruit yesterday and that I suspect that's what made him feel better. But then I swallow the temptation. I don't need her help caring for Mani and I don't want to open up to her about anything right now. "Tell him I love him," I say. "Tell him I'll be back soon."

"I will," Gita says. And then after a pause, "I'm sorry, Marinda." She doesn't say for what. She doesn't have to. Seventeen years stretch between us, and *sorry* seems too feeble a word. I leave without replying.

Pale pink dawn creeps over the horizon as I walk toward Gali Street. The world is still asleep, and the slap of my sandals on the cobblestones sounds harsh against the backdrop of so much silence. I can hear myself breathing. Do I always breathe this conspicuously? It should be a comforting thing to hear your own breath, to have proof that you're alive, but right now it's disconcerting. I try to hold my breath, but then I can hear my pulse rushing in my ears, and that's even worse.

The bookshop won't be open yet, so I turn down a dirt path and make my way to a small wooded area in a park nearby. There's a flat-topped rock in a copse of trees that serves as a nice bench. I sit on the rock under the canopy of a devil tree and put my head in my hands. There's no escape.

I tried to run once when I was ten years old. I didn't have much of a plan—just a bag filled with food and clothes and a guilt compelling enough to chase away my fear. I was living at the girls' home then, though I wasn't allowed anywhere near the other girls. My bedroom was the last room in a hallway full of empty rooms. There would be no one to hear the window creak open, no one to hear me drop to the ground below. I had one leg halfway into the night when the door flew wide. There was Gopal with a baby in his arms. The sight was so unexpected that I froze, hand splayed against the glass, bag slung over my arm, mouth agape.

"Are you going somewhere?" Gopal said. I didn't answer him. I was too busy staring at the bundle wrapped tightly in the same tangerine-colored blanket Gita had described to me so many times. The baby must be a new *visha kanya*. Curly black hair sprouted from the top of her head. She had tiny rosebud lips and long lashes that brushed the tops of her cheeks.

"Who is she?" I asked.

Gopal laughed. "Not she, *he*. He is your brother, Marinda."

My heart flip-flopped, and I climbed back into the room, set down my bag, closed the window.

"I have a brother?"

It didn't occur to me then, as it would later, that Gopal could be lying, that Mani could be any baby—not really my brother, but a trick to keep me from leaving. But by the time this thought crossed my mind several months down the road, it was too late. Whether or not we shared the same set of horrible parents didn't matter. He had become my brother and I wasn't ever going to leave him.

The sun has risen higher in the sky and it's time to go. I unfold myself from the rock and take a deep breath.

The walk to the bookshop doesn't take nearly long enough, even though I walk slowly, even though I try to wish it away. I can see Japa through the window. He sits at the reading table sipping a cup of steaming liquid and flipping through the pages of a book. He looks so content, so at home. I wonder if my face has ever known that expression.

After yesterday I never thought I'd be back, so it feels like a gift to see Japa for one more day. I feel a sudden rush of affection for him with his silver mop of hair, his easy smile and the papery crinkles around his eyes. He looks up and waves, and so I can't delay any longer. I have to push the door open.

"Good morning, Marinda," he says.

"Good morning," I say. I try to smile, but it feels tight on my face. Japa's expression falters for just a moment, and I wonder if he can see something in my eyes. Something that tells him I'm about to kill one of his customers. Something that reveals me as a monster. But then the moment is gone and his smile looks just as firm as it always does.

"You've been here almost every day this week," he says. It's true. Before, I came only once or twice a week, and now I've been here three days in a row. Japa scoops up his teacup and drains it in one swallow. "You cleaned the shop so thoroughly yesterday that I hope I can find enough for you to do today."

A spark of panic shoots through me. What if Japa sends me home? What would Gopal do to me? This was foolish of him to arrange a kill in a circumstance that I can't control.

Reckless. He is trying to send me a message that he owns me. That he has power to take anything from me, that I should have stayed isolated and not dared to carve out this small space for myself. But what if he has gone too far?

Japa lays a hand on my forearm. "Don't worry. I received new books yesterday that need shelving." He has misinterpreted the concern on my face. He thinks I'm worried about money and I don't correct him.

The stack of books is small, so I move slowly. Each time the door opens, my stomach pitches forward, my hands begin to sweat. But so far no one has presented me with *The History of Sundari*. At least Deven isn't here. I don't want to have to do this in front of him.

The bells on the door jangle. I shouldn't have tempted fate. Deven walks in and gives me a small wave before he strides away. Probably to have another secretive conversation with Japa. I groan. His timing couldn't be worse.

I shove the books onto the shelves. Why is he always here? I am tense enough without having to worry about Deven, who seems to notice everything, lurking around the corner. The door opens again. My gaze snaps up, but it is only a mother with two small boys. I pace up and down the aisles and I feel like I'm pulled too tight, like a rubber band that could snap at any moment.

"You're going to worry a hole in the floor." I spin around to find Deven smiling at me with only half his mouth. He's infuriating.

"Don't you have somewhere to be?" I ask.

He raises one eyebrow and I wonder if only half of his face is capable of expression. "Are you trying to get rid of me?"

"No, I'm just starting to worry that you're homeless."

He laughs a big, full sound that makes me feel a little pleased with myself even though I wasn't trying to be funny.

"Are you always this charming?"

"No," I say, because I'm not. It's Iyla's job to be charming. I only know how to be likeable for a moment. A moment is all I ever need. All I ever get.

My vision is blurry with unshed tears, but I refuse to cry. I start taking books off the shelves, stacking them in a pile on the floor.

"What are you doing?" Deven asks.

I don't look at him. "I need to dust."

"You dusted the shelves yesterday."

"Not underneath the books."

He sighs, but he starts helping me. We make a waist-high stack, and then I wipe each shelf, moving in small circles, wedging the cloth into the corners to get every bit of dust. Then we replace the books and start on the next bookcase. The door bells jingle and I jump.

It's a man.

My mouth feels like I've swallowed a handful of dirt. I don't say anything to Deven. I just hand him the cloth and make my way to the front of the shop. I hope this will be quick. I hope Deven isn't paying attention. I watch the man walk up and down the rows of books, trailing a thin finger over each spine, like he might know the volume he's looking for by touch alone.

My vision is filled with those same fingers trembling later, wiping beaded sweat from his high forehead and his bushy eyebrows before finally falling still as he takes his last breath. I squeeze my eyes shut and try to picture something else. Anything else.

"Are you okay?"

My eyes fly open. The man is standing in front of me, holding his book. He has a look of concern on his face. I couldn't mess this up any more if I tried.

I give him a smile, as genuine as I can make it. "I'm fine. Just a little headache."

"Ah," he says. "I'm sorry. My wife gets headaches too. Horrible stuff."

A wife. He has a wife. My knees feel shaky and I'm sure that I have the wrong expression on my face. "It is," I say, and my voice sounds foreign and wrong. "Horrible."

He rubs the top of his head right where his hair is thinning, like it's a nervous habit, and I find myself wondering if you can handle your hair so much that it falls out.

"You should try yarrow root," he tells me. "Works great for headaches."

"Sure," I say, "I will."

Our eyes meet, and he smiles and sets the book on the counter. I feel like I'm going to be sick. He pulls coins from his pocket and bounces them in his palm while he waits for me to give him a total. I won't be able to reach him from where I'm standing. I'll have to wrap his book and walk around the counter to give it to him, to embrace him. To kiss him.

It's going to take some effort to end his life.

My hands shake as I pull out the paper wrapping and slide the book toward me. Then all the air whooshes out of my lungs. The title is *Dreams and Their Meanings*. A little half sob escapes my lips and the man looks at me, alarmed. "Sorry," I say as I take his coins.

He pats my hand and then picks up his book. "Yarrow root," he calls over his shoulder as he leaves the shop.

My whole body starts to shake. The sun is high in the sky, morning is gone. Was this Gopal's twisted idea of a punishment? To give me a target that never materializes? To make me suffer all day for nothing?

"Marinda?" Deven's hand drops on my shoulder, and I yank away so fast that the coins in my palm go flying, skittering across the floor like startled insects.

A crease appears between his eyes. "What's wrong?"

I ignore the question and kneel to gather the coins, but I'm trembling so much that they keep slipping through my fingers.

"Here," Deven says. "Give them to me."

I drop the money into his open palm and climb to my feet. Deven's gaze roams over my face, searching, questioning. I turn away from him so he won't find whatever he's looking for. He goes around the counter and pulls the wooden box from where it's stashed on a low shelf. As he deposits the coins inside, I take deep breaths and try to will my heart to slow and my hands to still.

It's just another of Gopal's games, I remind myself. *Only dangerous if I don't understand the rules.* But my body isn't so easily convinced. Chills race over my skin and heat licks at the back of my neck until I'm not sure if I'm hot or cold.

"Marinda?" The tender note in Deven's voice rips something loose inside of me, and my carefully cultivated self-control slides from my shoulders like a shawl. I risk a glance at him, and his eyes are soft and liquid. He reaches for my wrists, but I think of the scars hiding under my bracelets and yank my hands back. Deven's eyebrows rise a fraction, but instead of retreating, he steps toward me and pulls me to his chest.

Every muscle in my body freezes.

I start to pull away, but Deven doesn't let go. His arms—both of them—are wrapped tightly around me, and I've never been held like this. Not ever. Slowly my tension unwinds, and against my better judgment, I let myself relax against him. I can feel his heartbeat, fast and strong, thudding against my cheek.

Japa emerges from the storeroom. "What happened?" he asks.

Deven waves him away. "She'll be okay," he says, and I hope he's right. I rest my head on his shoulder and he strokes my hair until I stop trembling.

The pressure in my chest recedes a little, and suddenly I

feel like I need to put space between us. I pull away and busy myself smoothing out invisible wrinkles in my sari.

"What did that man say to you?" Deven asks.

"Oh," I say, surprised. But of course that's what it would have looked like—that the customer said something so awful to me that I melted into a puddle of nerves. "It's not—he didn't—it wasn't like that. He was kind." Even to my own ears I sound ridiculous.

Deven doesn't speak right away. It's one of the things I like about him, how he takes his time to respond, how he treats the conversation carefully, like it matters. "The kindness upset you?" he asks finally.

"A little."

"But why?"

It's a loaded question and I'm not sure I can answer. I'm not sure I want to. I finger the edge of my sleeve while I think about it. "I don't deserve it," I tell him, and it's maybe the most honest thing I've ever said.

He brushes a lock of hair from my cheek and tucks it behind my ear. "How could you possibly think that?"

If he knew me at all, he would know that there is no other reasonable conclusion to draw. Of all people, I don't deserve kindness. This conversation has gone too far and now I feel exposed. I don't even know Deven, not really. I shake my head. "Can we talk about something else?"

Disappointment flits over his face, but he erases it almost instantly. "Sure. What would you like to talk about?"

I shrug. I'm no good at conversation and my mind is

busy trying to puzzle out what kind of game Gopal is playing.

"You could tell me something about yourself," Deven says.

"There's nothing to tell." What I really mean is that there is nothing I could tell him that wouldn't make him hate me.

He sighs. "If you're going to be difficult, then I'll go first. I love wood carving."

"Wood carving?" It's the last thing I was expecting him to say. It's something that belongs in a real conversation, and I'm not good at those.

"Yup," he says. "I'd live with a knife in my hand if I could."

"What do you carve?"

"All kinds of things. Animals, spoons, chairs, face masks. I've been itching to carve patterns in Japa's bookshelves for months, but I don't think he'd appreciate it. Now your turn. What do you do for fun?"

I come here for fun—or I did before Gopal stole it from me—but I can't tell him that. "I like to read," I say, which is almost the same thing.

Deven motions toward the bookshelves. "Obviously," he says.

"Not *obviously*. I could just enjoy shelving books and never read at all. Or I could just need the money."

"Do you?"

My cheeks heat. "No, but that isn't the point."

"Yes, it is," he says. "Tell me something I don't know."

I'm an assassin. I was supposed to kill someone today, but he never showed. My brother might be dying. My throat feels thick. Is that all there is to me? I slide down to the floor and rest my head on the wall. Deven sits beside me, still waiting for an answer. "I like sunsets," I tell him, "and the sound of crickets chirping and looking up at the stars."

"You like nighttime," he says after a moment, and this strikes me as incredibly insightful to understand so quickly from so little. Night has always been safer than daylight.

"And I have a cat," I tell him just for good measure, just to make me seem more like a normal person. Normal people have pets, I think.

He laughs. "I saw the cat when I walked you home the other day." That's right, he did. It seems like forever ago. He leans his head back against the wall next to mine, and we both just sit there in companionable silence staring at the ceiling. Deven glances outside. "I was supposed to leave hours ago," he says. "I'd better get going." He stands up and offers me his hand. I take it and he pulls me to my feet. "I think we scared Japa away," he tells me. "I'll go tell him goodbye."

He walks away, and suddenly I feel sheepish that I've made Japa feel awkward about being in the main room of his own shop. I'm mortified that he saw me break down like that. I press a hand to my forehead. This has been such a long day and I can't wait to crawl into bed and go to sleep.

Deven comes out of the storeroom with his bag slung

over one shoulder. "It was nice talking to you, Marinda," he says.

I nod. "Thank you for ... well, you know, for everything."

He grins at me, with both sides of his mouth, and it feels like standing in a patch of sunlight on a chilly day. "Anytime," he says, plunking several coins down on the countertop.

I raise my eyebrows. "What's this for?"

He slips a book out of his bag. "I'm taking this one," he says. It's several inches thick and bound in jade-green leather. The cover illustration is one of the most beautiful I've ever seen. A majestic bird flying through the air with an enormous snake dangling from its beak. Below that are dozens of people, their faces tipped toward the heavens in awe. But it's the top of the book that makes my heart stop.

Because there, in big block print, are the words I've been dreading all day: *The History of Sundari*.

CHAPTER SIX

All the heat drains from my face. The room feels like it's spinning and I hold on to the edge of the countertop for support. *Not him!* my mind screams. *Please, not him!*

"Marinda," Deven says. "It's okay. Japa knows I'm taking the book."

Someone else knows he's taking the book too. Someone else thought he'd leave with it hours ago. I still haven't spoken. My mind is scrambling for what to say, for what to do.

"What's wrong?"

I try to pull myself together, to arrange my expression into something less horrified. "Nothing," I say, waving my hand in front of my face. "Just a long day."

"Are you sure?"

I nod. "I'm sure."

Three steps. It will take me three steps to get to him

and only a moment to put my arms around his neck, only a moment more to kiss him. It could all be over in a few seconds.

I don't move.

Gopal told me the men we were targeting were evil, a threat to the kingdom, enemies of the Raja. These small truths have been my only solace for years. But Deven—I think of the way he carried Mani on his shoulders all the way back to our flat, the way he held me while I trembled. I can't do this. I won't.

Deven squeezes my hand. "I'll see you soon," he says. He pushes the door open and is swallowed up by the crowd.

The relief that washes over me lasts only a moment. Deven is safe for now, but if Gopal wants him dead, he'll be dead. I'm not Gopal's only option.

I stay in the bookshop until closing, and Japa's face is lined with concern as he hugs me goodbye. "You're sure there's nothing I can do?" he asks me for what must be the fourth time.

"I'm fine, Japa," I tell him. "Really I am."

He shakes his head. "You're not a very good liar," he says. His tone is playful, but a chill runs through me. I'm a better liar than he knows. "But if you need anything, Marinda . . . if things are bad at home . . . well, know that I'm here."

Tears prickle at the backs of my eyes. He sounds so sincere, and for a moment I'm tempted to tell him everything and beg him for help. Help to hide, help to run, help to escape. But I know that if I don't show up at the flat soon, I'll never see Mani again, so I just nod. "Thank you," I tell him, and then I leave before he can say anything else. Before he can tempt me to trust him with the truth.

All the shops on Gali Street are closing and the crowds have thinned out. I walk as fast as I dare without drawing attention to myself. Suddenly I'm desperate to see Mani and make sure he is okay. I feel like I can sense Gopal's anger already, and I want to shield Mani from his wrath. I have never disobeyed a kill-order before. Not ever. Gopal knows I hate what he makes me do, but I've never refused to do it.

I arrive at our red door and rap three times. The door swings open. Gita has fire in her eyes. "Where have you been?" Gopal is standing behind her. He's almost never here when I return from an assignment. This one must be important to him. Suddenly I know what I have to do.

"The mark never showed," I say. I hope I sound annoyed.

"What do you mean he never showed?" Gopal asks. There's a challenge in his voice, but I try to keep my face passive. I kick my sandals off and sink down into a chair. At least I don't have to fake the exhaustion.

"He never showed. I waited all day and nothing." Smudge circles my ankles and I pet her in careful strokes with steady hands. She purrs contentedly.

Gita is looking anxiously between me and Gopal. "Maybe we had the wrong day?" she offers. "Or the wrong place."

His eyes narrow. "Or the wrong girl," he says softly.

My stomach is swimming with panic, but I hope my

face is calm. I think it is. *Gopal is nobody,* I tell myself. *Just another man I must make trust me.* It's a lie, but it's a good one and I feel steady.

I shrug. "Unless the mark was a mother with small children or a balding man with bad dreams, then he didn't show. I can't kiss someone who isn't there. Even I'm not that good."

Gita's face smooths out and I know I have convinced her, but Gopal just continues staring at me. "Are you playing games with me?" he asks. I look straight into his eyes.

"I've been wondering the same thing about you all day," I say. This part is true and I know that Gopal can see it in my face.

He looks away first and I feel like I've won a small victory. He makes it to the door in two strides. "I'll be in touch," he says, and then slams the door behind him.

Gita puts a hand to her chest and lets out a long sigh. She stands like that for a while before she meets my gaze. "I made some rice," she says, gesturing toward the table. Mani is sitting in front of an untouched bowl. He hasn't said a word since I arrived.

"Thank you, Gita," I say. "I can take it from here." A hurt look flits across her face, and I almost laugh that she thinks she has the right to be wounded. As if, after today, I should want the pleasure of her company.

Mani doesn't look up until she leaves, but then he hops off his chair and flings himself into my arms. "That was the longest day ever," he says.

I pull him close to me. "Did they hurt you?"

It's a senseless question, because their very existence hurts him, but he knows what I mean. *Did they use my tardiness to punish you?*

He shakes his head, but his eyes are shiny with the memory of two years ago, when we thought we could escape. I'd been planning it for months—squirreling away money beneath the floorboards under my bed, mapping the fastest route out of the city, gathering supplies in two small packs until we were finally ready.

We left under cover of darkness—the fear clutched around my heart like a fist. My breath hitched at every shadow and Mani startled at every noise, but the farther we got, the more the seed of hope in my chest grew—expanding my rib cage and making it easier to breathe. We just had to make it to the Kinjal River and the edge of the city, where freedom waited for us.

Instead we found Gopal.

All my hope bled away and I scrambled for an explanation that would stay Gopal's rage, but he didn't ask for one. He reached us in three steps, yanked Mani from my arms and hauled him to the edge of the river.

"Stop!" I shouted, chasing after him. "Leave him alone."

I grabbed Gopal's arm and tried to wrench Mani away, but my strength was no match for his. He grabbed Mani by the hair and plunged his face into the water. Panic choked my throat.

"No, Gopal, please." Mani's small feet kicked in a frantic

attempt for escape. I tried to reach for him, but Gopal kicked me hard in the stomach, sending me flying backward. He lifted Mani from the water, and the sight of my brother's face sputtering and gasping for air broke something loose inside me.

"Please," I begged. "Please, let him go."

Gopal thrust Mani back into the water. "You know better than to try to leave me," he said. Mani thrashed in Gopal's grip.

"Yes," I said. "I know better." Mani's movements were slowing and I was desperate. *"Please,* Gopal. I'm sorry." Those were the magic words, and Gopal's face broke into a wide smile.

"That's a good girl," he said. He lifted Mani from the water and tossed his body onto the shore. Mani was blue and lifeless. "Never again, *rajakumari.* I can find you any-where. And next time the boy dies." Gopal strode away without another word.

I knelt beside Mani and lowered my cheek to his nose, praying to feel his breath stir across my face, but there was nothing. His chest was motionless. If he didn't get air soon, he was going to die. Without thinking, I lowered my mouth toward his and then, at the last moment, caught myself and pulled away, horrified. What was I thinking? My lungs were full of the air he needed, but I couldn't give him any. I couldn't try to save him without killing him. I put my hands against his breastbone and pressed with all my strength. "Please, Mani," I said. "Please don't die." I pounded on his small chest until, finally, a huge amount of water gurgled from his mouth and he sucked in a lungful of air. I held him close to me and rocked him back and forth. "I'm so sorry," I said over and over. "So, so sorry."

Mani's lungs were never the same, and I always wondered if things could have been different if only I'd been able to lend him my breath.

The memory sends a wave of nausea through me, and I bury my head in Mani's hair and rock him back and forth as if the near drowning happened two minutes instead of two years ago. My hatred for Gopal burns in my stomach like an iron in flame. I have to do the impossible. I have to find a way to protect both Mani and Deven. And I have to do it without bringing Gopal's wrath down on all of us.

* *

It won't be long before Gopal knows that I lied to him. I don't know if Iyla is his only source of information, but surely whoever told Deven to buy *The History of Sundari* will know that he bought it, that he was in the bookshop. And that he's still alive.

It's only a matter of time before Gopal sends another *visha kanya* to finish the job. The thought of Deven dying sends my stomach spinning, but I don't know how to protect him. Even if I tell him the truth, I can't tell him who to avoid. I've never met the other girls. And he probably wouldn't believe me even if I did tell him. Poison kisses sound like something out of folklore. He'll think I'm crazy.

I turn it over in my mind all night; it's a problem with no solution. Except one.

He would be safe if I could make him immune.

And that requires a visit to Kadru.

Mani and I arrive at the market late the next morning. His eyes are wide with wonder. I try to avoid bringing him here when I can—it's a place too full of painful memories—but this time I had no choice. After yesterday I don't dare leave him alone in the flat even for a few hours. Gita's voice pops into my mind. *Sometimes none of the options are good ones, Marinda. You just have to make the least bad choice.* I hate that her wisdom is following me today, when I am so angry with her. It's hard for me to reconcile the woman who told me bedtime stories and who taught me to read with the woman who helps Gopal control me. There are two versions of Gita, and my feelings about her are all tangled up.

Mani tugs on my sleeve. "Look at that!" I turn to see a small monkey on a leash juggling plums. He looks at Mani and smiles with sharp teeth. We keep walking past vendors selling pottery painted in bright colors, herbs meant to cure illness, gems to keep evil spirits away. But we don't stop until we get to the snake charmer. He sits on a faded brown carpet playing a lively tune on his pungi. A large cobra is coiled in a basket in front of him. The top half of its body protrudes from the basket taut and alert, hood flared. The snake's bright scales glint in the sunlight as it moves in response to the music. At least that's how it seems. But most snake charmers are frauds. This snake isn't mesmerized, only agitated. It lacks the outer ear to hear the music and is simply following the movement of the pungi as if it were a predator. The snake is ready to strike, but the charmer knows he's in no danger—he has stitched his serpent's mouth shut, except for a tiny opening just large enough for the tongue to flick in and out. The forked tongue is good for show but harmless. The real danger is in the fangs. I would know.

I guide Mani past the crowd that has gathered to watch the snake dance. I'm looking for the one snake charmer I know is not a fraud. Her tent is a short walk off the main path, and as it comes into view, my mouth goes dry. The tent is large and dull brown. Flashy colors would attract the attention of the market goers, and Kadru isn't interested in customers.

I was four years old the first time Gopal brought me here. The toxin from the droppers had only served to make me immune. It would take something far stronger to make me poisonous. Kadru seemed kind at first. She had big eyes, elaborate hair piled on top of her head, and rings on every finger. She was gentle as she lifted me onto her lap. "Hello, Marinda," she said. Her voice was almost a purr. "This is a special day and you are a very lucky girl." She traced a finger along the inside of my arm, down the blue-green vein that curved toward my hand. "Hold very still," she said, her breath hot against my ear. Her grip on me tightened, and without warning a white snake dropped from somewhere behind her and sank its fangs into my wrist. Hot pain shot through my arm and I screamed, flailed, cried. But her grip on me didn't loosen until the snake had released me and slithered away. "Shh," she cooed. "See? That wasn't so bad."

After that I wasn't so stupid. The next time we visited, Kadru had to hold me down.

A few years later, when I understood what Gopal was trying to accomplish, I begged him to find another way. "What about poison lip balm?" I asked. I knew it existed. I had worn it as a backup in the early days, when the toxin was still weak inside me. "Couldn't we just use that?"

He shook his head. "No, *rajakumari,* the most effective poisons—the deadliest ones—always come from the inside."

And so we made ten trips a year for ten years, until I was finally lethal enough to satisfy Gopal. The night before every visit, Iyla and I would sleep in the same bed, our foreheads pressed together, our hands entwined and clasped between us, prayer-like. "You're not afraid," she would say, over and over. "You're not afraid."

But I always was.

The snakes got bigger with each visit, and then they multiplied—two snakes at a time and then three. The last time, four huge white snakes feasted on my wrists and ankles while I screamed until I blacked out.

It's been years since I've been here, but the visceral reaction in my gut is so familiar that it feels like yesterday. I'm not sure I can do this. But Deven won't survive if I don't.

I kneel in front of Mani. "I want you to go sit underneath

that tree," I tell him. "Don't move until I come back for you."

Mani folds his arms across his chest. "I want to come with you."

"No, you really don't," I tell him. My voice comes out with a tremble and Mani's eyes go wide. He doesn't argue.

"Will you be very long?"

"I don't think so, monkey." I ruffle his hair and try to pretend a calm that I don't feel. Mani plops underneath the tree with a book and an apple. I've been trying to add more fruit to his diet—I've plied him with grapes, mangoes and pears—but it hasn't given him as much energy as the day Deven gave him the maraka fruit. Gita always says that just because two things happen at the same time doesn't mean that they're connected. It was probably just a coincidence that he felt better, and it had nothing to do with eating fruit. But where Mani is concerned, I specialize in false hope.

I cast one more glance over my shoulder before I approach the tent. There's no way to knock, so I clear my throat loudly at the entrance.

Kadru sticks her head through the flap of the tent. "Marinda?" she says. Her voice still sounds like warm honey, all soft and inviting. "It's been so long. Come in." I step over the threshold and go rigid. White snakes are everywhere—dangling from bamboo poles, coiled under tables, lounging on the sumptuous furniture. Some of them are small and some are as thick as small tree trunks. I feel as if a giant hand has reached through my chest and squeezed my lungs together. I can't pull in enough air. My heart is slamming against my rib cage and my whole body has gone cold.

Kadru laughs. "Oh, darling, relax. They won't strike unless I tell them to." But I don't think I can take another step forward. I feel like I'm five years old again and too small to run. I squeeze my eyes closed. I can do this. I can. I just have to go somewhere else in my mind; it's the same way I cope after a kill—*don't think about the boy.* Don't think about the snakes.

I open my eyes and keep my gaze glued to Kadru. She is dressed in white from head to toe. Her bodice is embellished with tiny pearls and small mirrors, and her flowing skirt just brushes the tops of her ankles. Shells are woven through her hair. Her feet and her midriff are both bare. The pale clothing against her dark skin is stunning. She doesn't look a day older than the first time I saw her. If anything, she is even more beautiful than I remembered.

"What can I do for you?" Kadru asks. Her expression is a mixture of amusement and curiosity. I try to keep my gaze on her face, try to ignore the snakes, but I'm still having trouble breathing.

"I need venom," I say finally. She laughs.

"Oh, darling. You're the last person in the entire kingdom who needs venom. You're positively overflowing with it."

I shake my head. "Not for me." I suck in a breath. I can't get out more than a few words at a time. "For someone else. I need to make him immune."

She arches her eyebrows. "How interesting. Well, now you have my attention." She saunters to an oversized chair and sits, tucking her feet underneath her. She snaps her fingers, and a large white snake drops from overhead and slinks its way around her shoulders. She often wears them like scarves. A shiver runs through me.

"Can you help me?" I ask, though I know she can. She made Gopal immune before she ever made me deadly. Gopal often reminds me that he is dangerous to me, but not the other way around.

Kadru runs her index finger over her bottom lip like she's considering. "Venom isn't cheap."

"I have money," I tell her. And it's true. I save almost everything Gopal gives me. Her eyes harden and the snake around her shoulders stops moving.

"You know it's not money I want."

If not money, then what? She must see the confusion on my face because her eyes widen. "Did Gopal never tell you the payment?" She laughs again, but there's a cruel edge to it. "The old man is even more depraved than I gave him credit for."

I think back to all the times I've been here before and try to remember a payment ever changing hands or a price ever being discussed, but I don't remember anything except pain and fear and dread.

"What is the payment?"

"Years," she answers.

At first I think I've misheard her. "Years?" I ask.

She nods but doesn't speak.

"What do you mean? It takes years to make a payment? I have to work for you for years?"

"Years off your life."

I have no response for this. I'm not sure what she means and I can tell from her expression she's waiting for me to ask. She's enjoying this.

"Does ingesting the toxin take years off your life?" I ask. If that's true . . . I shudder. I have so much venom running through my veins that I won't live to see adulthood.

"Of course not," Kadru says. She snaps her fingers again and the snake slithers off her shoulders and disappears behind the chair. She walks over to me, slow and catlike, and runs the back of her hand across my cheek. "Gopal would never do anything to shorten your life, darling. Not the way he adores you." I blink. Gopal doesn't adore me; he needs me, and that's not the same thing.

Kadru leans forward and kisses me on the cheek. "But you may make a different choice if you wish. The price for one vial of venom is five years from your life."

This pulls me up short. I can't imagine what she means. "I don't understand."

She smiles. "How old do you think I am?"

I haven't ever thought about this before. Kadru simply *was,* and I avoided thinking about her whenever possible. But now as I study her face, I realize she has an ageless quality. Her skin is smooth and supple, but she doesn't exactly look young either. "I'm not sure," I tell her.

"The truth is, I've lost count. But it's at least two hundred."

I gasp. "But that's impossible."

"I assure you, it's not. And if you want to save this boy you've grown fond of, you're going to make sure that I live at least five more." A prickly sensation races up my neck. I haven't told her about Deven. I never said I'd grown fond of anyone. I feel dizzy and look for somewhere to sit, but the snakes are draped over every surface. I try to swallow my fear.

"Did you take some of my life each time Gopal brought me here?"

She sighs as if my question taxes her energy. "Did you not listen, darling? Gopal wouldn't drain your life. You mean too much to him." Some of the tension in my shoulders loosens. Thinking of my life being slowly drained away is horrifying. "Of course," she says, "I didn't work for free." My head snaps up and a lazy smile spreads across her face. She reminds me of a cat toying with a mouse before killing it. But I need the toxin, so I'll play along.

"You drained Gopal's life?"

She snorts. "Gopal would never agree to such a thing. I'm afraid it was someone else's life in the bargain, but those are his secrets to share."

I don't want to know any of this. Who? Whose life was drained away so that Gopal could turn me into a killer? So many lives already press on my conscience, and now this too. At least this time it will be my own life I give away.

"I'll do it," I say.

Kadru's gaze sweeps over me and I try to look brave. "Very well," she says. "Stay here."

She walks toward the back of the tent. "Come, my pet," she says, touching one of the snakes lightly on the top of its head. The snake turns and looks in my direction like it has understood the entire conversation and disapproves of my choices. Then it slithers to where Kadru waits. She pulls a curtain so I can't see anything, but I can hear her murmuring gently to the snake. And then she begins to sing. It's a different language, so I don't understand any of the words, but her voice is captivating. The music tweaks something inside me, dredges up an aching feeling of sadness, and when the song is over, my cheeks are wet.

Kadru emerges from behind the curtain with an opaque vial. I reach for it. "Not so fast," she says. She slides her hand underneath my hair and grips the back of my neck. "First a bit of youth for my trouble." Her fingernails cut into my skin and I feel a sharp sting followed by an explosion of pain that seems to start in my chest and then radiate to the rest of my body. Black spots rush into my vision, and the last thing I hear is Kadru saying, "Thank you, my pet." And I don't know if she's talking to me or to the snake.

CHAPTER SEVEN

I wake up after nightfall and my first thought is of Mani. He's probably frantic—I need to get to him. I sit up too quickly and my stomach pitches forward. I cover my mouth with the back of my hand and try to breathe through my nose. The nausea is only part of it. My head is pounding and I ache all over. A hand closes around my ankle and I yank away, until I see it's Mani sitting near my feet. His eyes are red and swollen, and his breath is coming in short, panicky gasps. He has walked right into my nightmare. This is the last thing I ever wanted him to see.

"What are you doing here?" I ask him as I gather him into my arms. My limbs feel heavy and slow. He tries to answer, but he's crying too hard, and he can only manage a word at a time.

"I." Shuddering breath. "Got." Shuddering breath.

"Scared." He lays his head against my shoulder and I feel like a terrible person. Of course he would come looking for me, and he must have been terrified to find me here, unconscious and surrounded by snakes.

Kadru is curled up in her chair watching us with an amused expression. I give her a hard look and she shrugs. "I offered him something to drink, but he declined." As if I thought her lack of hospitality was the problem. My legs wobble as I stand.

"May I please have what I came for?"

She holds out the vial and spins it so the liquid swirls inside the glass. "Of course, darling." She glances toward Mani. "Is it for him?"

"No," I say, snatching it from her fingers. "It's not." I've thought of trying to make Mani immune many times, but I haven't wanted to take the chance. What if it didn't work? What if I killed him? But Deven will die if I don't try— I have to take the chance with him.

"Even more interesting," she says. "You fascinate me." I don't care what she thinks of me. I just want to take Mani and go home. I hold up the vial.

"How much do I give him?"

Kadru runs a lazy hand over the snake on her lap, and I hear Mani sob from where he's hiding behind my legs. I turn to look at him and see his eyes are squeezed shut.

"One drop at a time over two or three doses should do it," she says.

"Well, which is it? Two or three?"

Kadru's eyes narrow, and when she speaks, her voice is icy. "Try kissing him after two doses. If he dies, it's three."

Anger flares in my chest, but I'm powerless against someone like Kadru and she knows it—a snap of her fingers and one of her beasts could devour me. I have no choice but to walk away. With some effort I hoist Mani into my arms. He's too heavy for me—he has been for a long time now—but there are at least a dozen snakes between us and the door, and he is already panicked enough. I can carry him a small distance. He buries his face against my shoulder and I move through the maze of white snakes, stepping over them, winding around them. Kadru could call them to her, could make it easier on me, but she doesn't. By the time I get to the front of the tent, I'm breathing heavily and I have to put Mani down. I lift the flap of the tent and Kadru calls out to me.

"I'll see you soon, Marinda." I turn toward her. She looks regal, like a rani on her throne surrounded by serpentine subjects. I don't doubt her power. But I never want to see her again.

"I don't think so," I say.

She laughs. "We'll see, *rajakumari*. We'll see." My arms break out in gooseflesh to hear her call me by Gopal's pet name. She must have heard him use it, but it still unnerves me. I take Mani by the hand and we walk away without another word.

We're halfway back to the flat before Mani stops trembling. "I'm so sorry," I tell him.

"Who was she?"

I sigh. I've tried so hard to protect Mani, not to burden him with more of the truth than he can handle, but I have a feeling that won't work anymore. "She's the one who made me a *visha kanya*."

"Oh," he says. And then after a long pause, "Then why did you go to her?"

We're back at the flat now and I don't answer him right away. I put a finger to my lips, slide the key into the lock and ease the door open. The flat is empty and I breathe a sigh of relief. Smudge jumps from Mani's bed and paws at his ankles, begging for affection. Mani sits in the middle of the floor and pulls the cat onto his lap. "Why did you go back?" he asks again. I sit in front of him on the floor.

"Gopal asked me to kiss Deven," I tell him. Mani looks up sharply.

"You didn't, did you?" His eyes are already shiny with new tears.

"Of course not," I tell him. Though I don't say that I thought about it. That I might have. That I almost did. "But Gopal will send someone else, and so I need to protect Deven by trying to make him immune. That's why I went to visit Kadru. To get venom."

"What's 'immune'?"

"It's when you give someone just a tiny amount of poison so that he is protected if someone tries to give him a bigger amount. It would make it so none of the *vish kanya* could kill him." Mani's eyebrows pull together.

"Am I immune?" The question knocks something loose inside me and it takes me a moment to answer.

"No, monkey, you're not immune."

"Oh." He continues petting Smudge and she starts purring loudly, a steady little hum that sounds like a small roar.

"She sounds like she's part lion," I say. Mani grins.

"Do you remember when we found her?" he asks. Of course I remember. She was just a kitten and she showed up at our flat several nights in a row. I let Mani give her a dish of milk, but I wouldn't let him keep her. I didn't need any more responsibility, no matter how tiny or adorable. And then one night she showed up with a dead snake in her mouth. It was just a little garden snake, but still, she'd killed it, and it made me feel connected to her in a way that all her mewing and begging had not. She'd proven she was one of us, and we let her in for good.

I scratch Smudge under her chin. "How could I forget? Our little hunter."

"Our small tiger," Mani amends. He's quiet for a moment and then says, "Marinda?"

"Yeah?"

"I really hate snakes."

* *

After Mani falls asleep, I check my face in the mirror. I don't look any older, and I wonder from which part of my life Kadru took five years. The end? The middle? Will I wake up one day and find a handful of years suddenly missing, or will I just die younger than I should? The terms of the price I've paid aren't entirely clear, but I don't have time to worry about it. My biggest concern right now is figuring out how to get the poison to Deven before Gopal goes after him again.

It's an ironic problem, my wondering how to poison a boy when that is the sole purpose of my existence. But then again, I've never had to poison someone only a little bit. Nothing I've ever done has demanded the kind of subtlety that slipping Deven three separate doses of toxin will require. The jobs Gopal gives me are straightforward—they require only one meeting, only a moment of interaction. But this—this will require something so much more delicate, and I'm not sure I can pull it off. Subterfuge is squarely in Iyla's skill set. So that's probably where I should go for help.

I run a brush through my hair and then crawl into bed. After the day I've had, I'm expecting it to take me hours to drift off, but the last few nights of lousy sleep must have caught up with me, because before I know it, the night is over and sunlight is spilling across my cheeks. For just a moment I feel safe ensconced in a soft blanket with warmth on my face. But then the events of yesterday come rushing back and carve a pit in the middle of my stomach. I wish I could go back and live forever in that peaceful moment between sleep and reality.

Mani is still fast asleep, so there's time to make breakfast. We don't have to leave for Iyla's right away, and I need some time to decide how I can convince her to help me. Iyla is stingy with sharing her tradecraft, but she's also the closest thing I have to a friend. I prepare a simple porridge of brown rice, almonds and dried figs. It simmers for over an hour, but Mani still isn't awake. I sit on the side of his bed and push the hair off his forehead. His color is worse than yesterday and his breathing is shallow.

"Mani, time for breakfast." I shake him gently and get no response, not even a grumble or a sigh. "Mani? Come on, Mani." I try to wake him for five minutes, and the whole time I'm wondering if this will be the morning when I can't.

Finally his eyes flutter open and I'm flooded with relief. "Hi, monkey," I say, and there's a little hitch in my voice that I can't quite cover up.

Mani rubs his eyes. "Was I hard to wake up?"

"Nah," I say, "not too much." If he knows I'm lying, he doesn't challenge me. "Do you want some breakfast?" This perks him up a little.

"You made breakfast?"

"Hey," I say, "don't sound so surprised. Sometimes I cook." Mani smirks and I swat him lightly on the bottom as he heads to the table. "Be nice or I won't share."

I wait until he is polishing off his second bowl of porridge before I tell him my plan to visit Iyla.

"I don't think we should ask her for help," Mani says.

"Why not?"

"She's . . ." Mani licks his spoon as he thinks. "Kind of sneaky."

"Yes, I know. That's why we need her, to help us sneak the poison to Deven."

"Why can't we just tell him the truth?"

I sigh. "I don't think he would believe us, Mani. Would you voluntarily take poison from someone you just met? Even if they claimed it would help you?"

He scrunches up his forehead. "I guess not."

"Our best chance to protect him is with Iyla's help."

Mani frowns at me. "If you say so. I'll go get dressed."

Iyla lives in a more affluent neighborhood than Mani and I do. Butter-yellow row houses with deep-red rooftops march along the street in groups of four. The lawns are expertly manicured and boast shrubs clipped into the shapes of animals. The first time I saw Iyla's house, I complained to Gopal. It didn't seem fair that Iyla was living so lavishly while Mani and I were stuck in a tiny bedroom at the girls' home. Gopal smiled at my complaint. "Oh, Marinda," he said. "Don't be jealous. Iyla doesn't concern me, but you ... you I want close to me always." I didn't care what Gopal wanted—I wanted a place that Mani and I could call our own. A few months later Gopal agreed to let us move into the flat, and I never said another word about it. But every time I see Iyla's neighborhood, it still stings that she is treated so differently. Iyla lives at the far end of her street in the last house on her row. Mani and I are almost there when I hear a door close and then the unmistakable sound of Iyla's laughter. She's not alone. I hold out my arm to stop Mani and we duck behind a huge topiary elephant.

"When will I see you again?" Iyla says.

"I'm not sure," says a male voice, "maybe a few days?"

"A few days! But that's too long to wait." Her voice is dripping with so much false sweetness that I wonder who would be foolish enough to think she's sincere. I inch forward and risk a peek around the hedge. My heart jumps into my throat.

She's talking to Deven.

I've thought about it several times since yesterday—Deven and Iyla, how they must have been seeing each other for weeks, for months even—but the thought was so distressing that I banished it whenever it appeared. But seeing them now sends a spasm of pain through me. She probably knows him far better than I do. I bite my lip. I shouldn't feel betrayed—this is how it works. This is how it has always worked. But how could Iyla spend any amount of time with Deven and still want to go forward with this plan? Can't she see that he is better than all the others? That he is good? A germ of doubt wriggles into my mind. No. I saw the way the last boy treated that child at the market. She was hungry and he shooed her away like she meant nothing.

Mani is looking at me with a question in his eyes. I press a finger to my lips and move so I can watch Iyla without her seeing me. Her hand rests on Deven's elbow and she is saying something too quietly for me to hear. Then she stretches up on her tiptoes and kisses him softly on the mouth. My heart breaks a little. I will never have the pleasure of kissing someone I love. Iyla's kisses might be a lie, but mine are a death sentence.

Deven walks away, and he's headed right toward where Mani and I are hiding. I grab Mani's arm and pull him even farther behind the elephant-shaped hedge. But Deven passes by without so much as a glance in our direction. His hands are in his pockets and his head is down like he's lost in thought. I have the absurd impulse to call out to him, which would be foolish. How would I explain my presence here? But then again . . . I slip my hand into my pocket and finger the vial. Maybe this could be just the luck I need. I wait until I hear Iyla close her door, and then I motion to Mani. We trail Deven from a distance, keeping close to the houses so that we can duck into a side yard if he turns around.

We follow him all the way out of the neighborhood and into a part of Bala City I've never seen before. It's an upscale shopping district without the mysticism of the market or the mundaneness of Gali Street. Small shops line the streets with window displays that feature a breathtaking array of merchandise: dresses, scarves and saris in silky fabrics, jewelry inlaid with gems of every color, wool rugs in colorful patterns. One shop has a live model shifting between poses, her back to the street to show off her intricate hairstyle. I'm so entranced that my gaze keeps wandering from Deven to the shop windows, and I'm startled when I hear my name.

"Marinda?"

I look up sharply. Deven has turned and spotted us.

"Hi," he says. "What a nice surprise. What are you two doing here?" There's not a hint of suspicion in his voice. Warmth rushes to my cheeks and I'm too flustered to respond. It's Mani who answers.

"We're just exploring," he says.

"Exploring, huh?" Deven says. "Well, how would you like to explore some lunch with me?"

"Yes!" Mani says. Deven laughs and looks to me for confirmation. This moment is bigger than lunch. It feels like cracking open the door on my tightly locked life and letting Deven in. It's dangerous. It's exhilarating. It's the only way I can think of to save him.

"If you insist," I say, and I hope it's not the wrong answer.

Deven leads us down a side street to a little café. The facade of the building is stone, and the windows and doors are trimmed in deep green. A menu is posted near the door, painted in swirling gold script. Inside, the aroma of roasted meats and spices hangs heavy in the air. At the back of the room, behind a tall counter, a thickset man shouts orders at cooks—half a dozen of them—who are chopping meats and vegetables, stirring thick sauces and sliding flatbread into clay ovens. Tall tables and chairs line the edges of the room, while short tables with cushions for seating fill the middle. Deven turns and touches my elbow.

"Do you want to take Mani and find a table? I can order for us." I glance at Mani. He does look exhausted.

"Thank you," I say.

Deven grins. "Sure. What would you like to eat?"

"I'm not picky," I say. My stomach feels so tied in knots that I'm not sure I'll be able to eat anything at all. Deven turns toward Mani.

"How about you, pal?"

"I want whatever you're having," Mani says. Of course he does. Deven is like a small god to Mani.

Mani and I choose a low table, and I sit on one of the cushions with my legs tucked underneath me. Mani sits beside me and lays his head on my shoulder. I've pushed him too hard this morning with all the walking. I pat his back while I try to formulate a plan. Once Deven comes with the food, it's just a matter of distracting him for a moment so that I can slip the poison into his drink. The thought of him catching me makes my pulse spike, but I won't get a better opportunity. I wish I could just tell him the truth. But if he didn't believe me, he'd be in more danger than ever.

After a few minutes Deven arrives with steaming platters of meat pies with green dipping sauce, chunks of tender chicken skewered on wooden stakes, and fluffy white rice. He slides the platters onto the table and says, "I'll be right back with the drinks." Why couldn't he have brought the drinks first? There's no way I can poison anything on the platters. How can I be sure what he'll eat? My hands grow moist and I dry them on my skirt. Deven returns with three cups full of creamy, dark liquid. Mani examines his cup skeptically.

"What is it?" he asks.

"It's called a Hot Sweetie," Deven says. Mani giggles at the silly name. "It's good. Try it." I take a sip—it tastes like extra-creamy hot chocolate spiced with cinnamon and cloves.

"Delicious," I say. My voice is steady, but my hand is shaking so badly that some of the liquid sloshes out. A dark stain spreads over the white tablecloth, but if Deven notices, he doesn't say anything. I glance over at Mani, who is happily slurping his drink, a thin film of chocolate coating the area above his upper lip.

"Don't forget to eat," Deven tells him. The food looks and smells amazing, but I can barely taste it as I chew. I keep staring at Deven's drink. It's over half gone, and if I don't do something soon, I'll miss my chance. My mind wanders to Iyla and something she told me once. "It's easy to get boys to trust you," she said. "You just have to use their best traits against them." What is Deven's best trait? And then I know. I pick up my cup and take a sip and then deliberately set it near the edge of the table. When Deven looks away, I nudge it with my elbow. It tumbles to the floor, splattering dark liquid all over the polished hardwood. Deven is on his feet in an instant.

"I'm so sorry," I say, dabbing at the spill with my napkin. My cheeks are hot with deception.

"It's okay," Deven says. "I'll go get you another one." I have only a few seconds. I pull the vial from my pocket, yank out the stopper, and tip the container forward until a single pale drop falls into Deven's cup. Then I replace the stopper and shove the vial back into my pocket. I glance at Mani, and his face sends a pang of regret through my chest. He's looking at me like I'm a traitor, like I've just poisoned his friend. I put my arm around his shoulders and start to reassure him, but then Deven's back and holding out a cup to me. I snap my mouth closed. Explaining will have to wait until later.

"Thank you," I say. "I'm sorry for being so clumsy." I can feel Mani glaring at me.

"No problem," Deven says. He keeps eating and chatting—asking Mani about what he's been reading, peppering me with questions about my childhood that I have to answer with half-truths. I feel like I'm going to explode with tension and I want to pick up his drink and force it down his throat.

"Do you want more?" Deven asks.

I look up, startled. "What?"

"You're staring at my drink. You can have the rest if you'd like."

"*No,*" I say too emphatically. Deven raises an eyebrow. "Thanks," I say, "but I think one is all I need. It's awfully sweet."

"You just have to build up a tolerance," he says, and I wince at the wording. He tilts his head. "You know, for the sugar." I laugh, but it comes out tight and forced. Of course I knew what he meant, but building up a tolerance is exactly what I'm trying to do for him—except for poison and not sweets. When he finally picks up his Hot Sweetie and drains it in one swallow, I can breathe again.

"So what have you been up to today?" I ask. Deven smiles and I realize it's the first question I've asked, the first time I've engaged in the conversation at all, past distracted comments and brief answers.

"Just work," he says. An image of Iyla kissing him pops into my mind.

"Work? That's it?"

He plunks his cup down. "Yup. That's why I was so happy to see you and Mani. I needed a break." My stomach feels tight. Why is he lying to me? Why not just tell me that he spent the morning with his beautiful girlfriend? Who, no doubt, seemed astonished to see him, since she thought he'd be dead. But then again, why would he tell me anything? It's not like he owes me an explanation—we're just friends, if even that. He probably invited us to lunch only because he doesn't think I take care of Mani very well. My eyes burn and I'm furious with myself for caring. He's just a boy. A nice one, the kind who will invite you to lunch and hurry to replace your drink if you spill it. The kind you don't want to kill. But also the kind who is in love with your only friend and doesn't trust you enough to tell you about her.

Mani nudges my foot under the table and I realize I've been staring at Deven without saying anything for an inappropriate amount of time. I try to wipe my face clean of expression.

"I'm glad we could provide some relief from your busy day," I say.

Deven reaches for my hand across the table and squeezes my fingers. "We should do it again sometime." He holds my gaze and I don't look away.

"We *should*," Mani says, and both of us laugh at his enthusiasm. Deven walks us to the door, and my emotions are all tangled up. Part of me is upset that he didn't tell me about Iyla, and the other part never wants to leave his side. Maybe those are the same thing. And then there's the worry about the poison. Did I give him too much? Too little? Will it work?

"Thank you for lunch," I say once we step outside.

Deven bites the inside of his cheek and wrinkles up his forehead. "Are you sure? You didn't eat much."

"She *never* eats," Mani supplies.

Deven glances sidelong at me and I can tell he's suppressing a smile. "Is that right?" he asks Mani, who nods solemnly. "Well, I'll have to see what I can do to change that." Despite myself, my face melts into a smile. No one—except for Japa—has ever been so kind to us or treated us with so much respect. Mani is flush with pride. I look up to see Deven watching me with a curious expression.

"What?" I ask.

"I've never seen you smile before."

"That's not true," I say. Could that be true? Do I smile so infrequently?

He shakes his head. "Never. Not like that. Not a real smile."

"Oh, so you've seen some of my fake smiles?"

He shrugs. "A few. Mostly when you've been trying to get rid of me." Am I so transparent? Or have I just underestimated how much Deven notices? The thought both thrills and terrifies me.

"Maybe we can work on increasing the smiling along with the food?" he says. I can't help it; I smile again, and he smiles back and we just stare at each other for a moment. Then he turns to Mani and pats him on the back. "See you soon," he says. Before I know what's happening, he folds me in an embrace and kisses my cheek. It's not just a quick graze either; his lips linger there, soft and warm. Panic races across my skin. I didn't have time to turn, to position him safely. He pulls away and my fingers find the place where his lips rested. The spot is still warm and I can feel the contours of my cheekbone underneath my fingertips, so it's far enough from my lips. I sigh in relief and then clap my hand over my mouth. That sigh could so easily be misinterpreted. The way Deven is grinning, I see it probably has been.

"Goodbye, Deven," I say, carefully avoiding looking directly at his face.

"Bye, Marinda."

I take Mani's hand and we walk away. I resist the urge to look back as long as I can, and when I finally do, Deven has disappeared.

CHAPTER EIGHT

When Mani and I get back to the flat, Iyla opens the door. My stomach plummets. What is she doing here? She must know that I've been with Deven. She must have followed me or . . . and then I focus on her face. A fresh bruise blooms across her jaw—bright red bleeding into purple.

I gasp. "Iyla, what happened?" She meets my eyes and shakes her head, just a fraction. I understand her immediately. It's a signal as old as our pairing—*he's here, it's not safe to talk.* I look beyond her and, sure enough, Gopal is leaning back on one of the chairs, his hands clasped behind his head. I squeeze Iyla's fingers as I brush past her and step into the flat.

"Marinda," Gopal says, his voice dripping with sweetness. "So nice to finally see you." My mind is racing. What does he know? What did he do to Iyla? How can I avoid making it worse for her? For me? Mani is hiding behind my legs, a fistful of my skirt in his hands.

"I didn't know to expect you," I say. I try to keep my voice casual, airy, and I'm praying to the ancestors he can't read me as well as Deven can.

"Of course you weren't, *rajakumari*," Gopal says, letting the chair drop onto all four legs. "I just came to tell you that we sorted out our little misunderstanding."

"Oh?" I'm not sure exactly where he's going, and this is the most neutral response I can think of.

"Yes," he says, standing. "It turns out Iyla here was sloppy. Didn't tell me that our target regularly spends time in the bookshop." Iyla's expression is stony. "That could have made our timing rather . . . imprecise."

"What do you mean?" I ask. My heart is hammering. I'm not sure if Gopal really believes that Deven didn't show or if he's laying a trap for me. Either way, I have no idea what's next. Gopal starts pacing around the flat—he can cover the whole distance in just a few steps, and it's making me jumpy.

"Our young man showed up with the book—still very much alive—and when I discovered this, I was . . ." He pauses and searches my face. "Well, I was heartbroken, Marinda. I thought you had betrayed me." My mouth has gone completely dry. I *have* betrayed him and I'm trying desperately to keep any hint of it from showing up in my expression. I can feel the vial in my pocket, resting against my thigh like an accusation, and I have to resist the urge to touch it. The last thing I need is Gopal demanding I turn out my pockets. Gopal clasps his hands in front of his body and rocks back on his heels. "Then I talked to Iyla, and after some . . . *questioning* . . . she admitted that the boy visits the bookshop often. That he could have obtained the book outside the window I gave you."

Oh, no. What have I done? I've made Iyla look like a liar and now he's punished her. "I'm sure she didn't intend—"

"No, Marinda. Don't defend her. It was reckless and unprofessional." He throws her a hard look. "And completely unacceptable." Iyla lowers her head, chastened.

Bile rises in my throat. I don't know how to fix this, and I'm still not convinced that Gopal isn't playing some kind of game. If he knows that Deven spends time in the bookshop, it must have occurred to him that I might have seen Deven before, that I might know him.

"So," Gopal says. "We will try again, and this time Iyla is going to get it right." He turns to me. "And so will you." His gaze slides to Mani and then back. He lowers his voice to a whisper. "We wouldn't want your brother's health to worsen, now would we?" Something cold creeps down my spine. The medicine that Gopal provides for Mani is the only thing that is keeping him alive. If he took it away . . . "Are we clear?"

I nod. It's the only option right now—to promise compliance. Gopal draws his lips back from his teeth in what I think is supposed to be a smile. "Good girl," he says. "I'll let you two sort out the details, but I want that boy dead by the end of the week." He looks back and forth between me and Iyla, and he must be satisfied with the expressions on our faces, because he leaves without another word.

Mani lets out a shaky breath and I hug him to my side. Iyla is looking at me with daggers in her eyes.

"What is going on?" she asks.

"I was about to ask you the same thing." I'm stalling now. How much do I tell Iyla? How much can I trust her? I can't stop picturing her with Deven—laughing with him, kissing him. Iyla touches her jaw and I have a vision of coming back in the next life as a dung beetle. I'm being so insensitive—it's obvious what's going on with her. "Iyla, I'm so sorry," I say. "What happened?" She steps toward the edge of the bed to sit, but there's something wrong with the way she's moving; it's too deliberate, too careful. "What did he do?" I ask again. She meets my gaze and this time her eyes are shiny—it's the closest Iyla ever gets to tears. She turns her back and gingerly lifts her shirt. My hand flies to my mouth. Gopal hitting us to make a point is nothing new—my face has been discolored by his rage more than once—but this is something far worse. At least ten large welts climb up Iyla's back like a ladder. Some of them are crusted with dried blood.

He has whipped her.

"Oh, Iyla." My eyes fill with tears, but I blink them away. Mani is watching, his mouth hanging open in horror, and if I lose my composure, I'll only make it worse for him. I wish that he didn't have to see this, wish that I could protect him, but now it's too late. It was too late the moment Gopal placed him in my arms. I squeeze Iyla's hand. "I'll get something to clean you up." I go to the sink and return with a washcloth soaked in warm water and soap.

Sometimes I wish I could turn off my memories. Or better yet, erase them completely. Because this feels too familiar, sitting with Iyla, cleaning her wounds. Feeling guilty for her injuries. Trying and failing to bandage her body and my soul. It's happened more times than I can count. Once when we were twelve, Gopal broke Iyla's arm. He had given her a target—the father of a girl about our own age. Iyla was supposed to befriend the girl and spy on the father. It was meant to be practice for all that would come later. Three weeks into the mission, Iyla had gotten attached.

"I want you to promise me that you won't have him killed," she told Gopal one night at dinner.

He snorted. "I will do no such thing."

"Pari has already lost her mother. If you kill her father, she'll be an orphan." I flinched because Iyla had used the girl's name. There was no faster way to enrage Gopal than by referring to the targets like they were people.

He fixed her with a cold stare. "You aren't in a position to ask for promises and you won't get any from me."

"Then I won't spy on him for you," Iyla said. Her face was cold and defiant. My whole body froze, taut with alarm.

Gopal dabbed the corners of his mouth with his napkin, as calm as if Iyla had asked him to pass the pepper. He stood and placed the napkin precisely at the side of his plate. And then in one swift motion, he grabbed Iyla's forearm and snapped it over his knee like it was a twig.

Iyla's eyes went big and all the color drained from her face, but she didn't cry out. She didn't make a sound. I did, though. I cried enough for both of us as I held her and rocked her back and forth.

And I was still sobbing later as I made her a sling from an old sari and tied it behind her neck.

"Why aren't you crying?" I asked her. "Why do you *never* cry?"

She didn't answer right away. But finally she said, "If I cry, then he thinks he controls me."

"He broke your arm, Iyla. He does control you."

"No, he doesn't," she said. But we both knew it was a lie.

Her arm healed fine. It was a clean break—the kind that comes only with practice.

And now I feel like we're right back where we've always been. It takes me twenty minutes to clean her wounds. I work slowly with as much gentleness as I can. Iyla stares straight ahead and only flinches twice.

"Thank you," she says when I've finished. She turns and studies my face for a moment and then says, "Did he really not show?" My heart falls into my stomach. How can I tell her that this is my fault? I press my lips together and close my eyes.

"I couldn't do it," I say finally.

Iyla goes very still. "Why not?"

I open my eyes. "Because I know him, Iyla. And he's not a bad person."

She fixes me with an icy stare. "That's never been your call, Marinda. Never."

"You know him too. Do you think he deserves to die?"

She's quiet for a moment. "It's not for me to say," she says softly.

"Iyla!"

She shoots to her feet. "No. You don't get to do this. You don't get to moralize to me. I have known all of them. Every single one. And you've never asked me what kind of people they were or if I thought they deserved to die. Then you get cozy with *one* boy and you suddenly decide you're in charge of this whole operation? You put all of our lives at risk?"

I'm too stunned to speak. I've always thought I had the bigger burden, the greater guilt. I've never thought about what it must be like for Iyla. To know them all. To care about them.

"Were they all like Deven?"

She sits heavily on the bed and winces. "Not all of them. But a lot of them, yes."

I feel like I'm going to be sick. I sit down and put my head in my hands. "I can't do this anymore."

"We don't have a choice, Marinda."

I hesitate. What will she do if I tell her the truth? Can I afford to confide in her? Can I afford not to? Mani catches my eye and shakes his head. He can see I'm close to telling her and he doesn't want me to. He doesn't trust her. But Mani doesn't easily trust anyone and he doesn't know Iyla like I do. Before Mani was born, she was the closest thing to family that I had. Choosing to love her, choosing to believe that there was at least one person in the world I could rely on, was the only thing that kept me sane for the first ten years of my life. She can be cunning and cruel, but my life has been in her hands before and she's always kept it safe. I lift one shoulder and hope Mani understands—I don't know what else to do.

"We do have a choice," I say. "I want to make Deven immune."

Iyla looks up sharply. "What are you talking about?"

"I visited Kadru."

Iyla blanches and her eyes go wide. "Why would you do that?" There's a tremble in her voice, and I remember how much Iyla hates Kadru—even more than I do.

"To get venom. For Deven. If I can give him a little at a time, he'll be immune. He'll be safe."

"You love him," she says. It's not a question.

My cheeks heat. "No. No, that's not it. I just don't want him to die, Iyla. Not by me and not by any of the other *vish kanya* either."

Something dark passes over her face, but it's gone so quickly that I think I must have imagined it. She shrugs. "But Gopal will still expect him to be dead. Poison kisses aren't the only way to kill a man."

The threat in her words hits me like a slap. If I won't

kill Deven, she will. All the compassion I had for her bleeds away and I'm left only with rage.

"The *vish kanya* make good assassins because we don't leave evidence behind—nasty things like stab wounds. So if you think you can win Gopal over with your newfound loyalty and a sharp knife, I'm afraid you're going to be very disappointed."

Iyla's eyes flash. I've hit a nerve. But then her expression goes forcefully blank and her voice turns dismissive. "I have no desire to win him over," she says. "But I'm also not going to be punished because you've suddenly grown a conscience."

I'm losing her. She'll go to Gopal, and Deven will be dead before sundown. And probably Mani too, once Gopal knows I betrayed him. If I can't convince her to keep quiet because it's the right thing to do, I need to find another way. But Iyla is almost impossible to manipulate. How do you control someone who doesn't care about anything except not being controlled?

I force out a hard laugh. "I guess he finally owns you."

"What are you talking about?"

"You were always so sure you'd never belong to Gopal," I say. "It always disgusted you that I let him control me. And yet look at us now—I'm defying him and you're following his orders like a well-trained puppy."

She flinches and I hate that I'm hurting her. But I've found a weak spot and I need to put pressure on it—it's the only way to wrest the power back. "When you run to him to tattle on me, make sure to do it with a newspaper between your teeth. Like a good dog."

Her jaw tenses. "Gopal doesn't control me."

I take a step toward her. "Then who does, Iyla? Or are you really that cold that you just enjoy seeing innocent people die? Has it started to be fun for you? Maybe you're not obeying Gopal as much as you're turning into him."

She opens her mouth like she's about to say something and then snaps it closed. I've never seen her look so unhinged. "Fine," she finally says. "What's your plan?"

Some of the pressure lifts from my chest. It's not a truce—not even close. But at least she's listening.

"We can't openly defy him," I say. "So you do exactly what he asked you to. Set up the meeting. But try to give me a few days so I can get Deven two more doses of venom."

Her head snaps up. "Two *more*? You've already poisoned him?"

I swallow hard. It's more than I intended to tell her. "Yes. Mani and I had lunch with him today."

For just a moment Iyla's detached mask slips and there's something raw and vulnerable in her expression. "How did you get him to take it? Does he know about you?"

I shake my head. "I slipped it into his drink when he wasn't looking."

Iyla gives a low whistle. Her face is back to normal again, cool and impenetrable. "Impressive. You're more devious than I gave you credit for." It's not clear whether she means this as an insult or a compliment. She stands up and her movements are stiff. My gaze wanders to the bruise on her cheek, and my stomach twists with new guilt.

Iyla tilts her head to one side, watching me like an inquisitive bird. "Ah, Marinda. Do you feel guilty for getting me beaten?"

My face falls. "Of course I do."

Her smile disappears and her expression goes hard. "Good."

A shiver runs through me. I know that voice. It's Iyla at her worst. "I never meant for—"

She laughs and waves a hand in front of her face to stop me. "Lighten up," she says. "I'm only teasing." But she's not. She blames me. For each welt, for every bruise. Not Gopal, who wielded the whip, but me because I refused to kill. She's angry with me. It makes her a dangerous ally, and suddenly I wish I hadn't told her anything.

She eases her bag over her shoulder, careful to avoid her back, and starts to walk away, but I reach out and catch her fingers in mine. She freezes and our eyes meet. Just for a moment I'm taken back to our childhood, when it was us against Gopal, us against the world.

Now it's just us.

"I'll make him pay for this," I say, softly so that Mani can't hear. "One day Gopal will be the one to bleed."

She lets go of my hand and looks away. "I'll let you know when I have the meeting place."

Her hand is on the doorknob. "Iyla," I say. "If you hurt

Deven . . ." She turns and raises her eyebrows in a question. "If you hurt him, I'll kill you myself."

Our gazes lock and I refuse to be the first to look away. After a long pause she nods once and then slips out the door, closing it softly behind her.

I glance over at Mani and he's glaring at me. "I didn't have a choice," I tell him.

"That's what you always say."

"Mani—"

"I don't feel good," he interrupts. "I'm going to have a rest." He crawls under the covers and turns his back on me. His rejection stings. I can think of only a handful of times Mani has ever been angry with me, and all of them were years ago. Like always, he falls asleep almost immediately, and I have only my thoughts to keep me company. And they are gnawing a hole in my middle. What if Mani is right? What if it was a mistake to tell Iyla? Though for the life of me, I can't come up with an alternative. Gopal knows Deven is still alive, and he's forcing another meeting. At least now there's a chance I'll have Iyla on my side, a chance she'll help me save Deven, help me protect him from more than just the *vish kanya*. But she could just as easily go to Gopal. I want to trust that she still cares about me, that she still has a shred of humanity left, that she's still the girl I knew all those years ago who got her arm broken to try to save a playmate from the heartache of losing a father. But if I'm honest with myself, I haven't seen that Iyla in a long time.

Mani sleeps for hours, waking only briefly to eat a light dinner and then promptly falling back asleep. He says just four words to me while he's awake: "A little," when I ask if he's hungry, and "I'm full," when I ask if he wants more soup.

I have so few people in my life and nearly all of them are mad at me: Mani, Iyla, Gita, Gopal. The only one who isn't angry is Deven, and he would no doubt be furious if he knew what I've done, what I am. I think about the days before I had a brother—how lonely it was, how all I thought about was finding a way to run. And that's exactly how I feel now, like running away and never looking back. I watch Mani's chest rise and fall. His hands are tucked beneath his cheek, and dark curls fall over his forehead. He looks even smaller in sleep, even more vulnerable. He would never make it if we tried to leave. But if I can find a way to make Mani well again, I'll do a better job of escaping. I'll take him and run so long and so far that Gopal will never be able to find us again.

CHAPTER NINE

I drift off curled in a chair by Mani's bedside, but my sleep is choppy, plagued with nightmares of huge snakes, dying boys and snapping whips. But when I wake gasping, reality is no comfort. Remembering the previous evening sweeps me up in a wave of regret. Why didn't I ask Iyla where Deven lives? Gopal wants him dead by the end of the week, and that gives me only six days to slip him two more doses of toxin, and I have no idea where to find him. Why didn't I ask Kadru how far apart the doses need to be? I don't know if one day is enough or if I need to move more slowly. And it may all be a moot point if Gopal sends another kind of assassin after Deven—he must have them, other assassins who kill people in more traditional ways. But there is one question that haunts me the most: *What did Deven do that the Raja wants him dead?*

At some point during the night the sky grows angry and a torrent of rain pelts against the metal roof of our flat in an unrelenting rhythm. The sound is so loud it drowns out my thoughts, and sleep finally finds me.

When I open my eyes, the room is dark. It could be midnight or morning—it's impossible to tell.

"Marinda?" I can tell it isn't the first time Mani has said my name. It must have been his voice that woke me.

"Hmm?"

"Someone is at the door."

I bolt upright. At first I think Mani's wrong, that it's only the rain, but then I hear it. *Tap, tap.* Pause. *Tap, tap.* It's not a pattern that I recognize—not Iyla or Gita or Gopal. I look over at Mani and hold a finger to my lips. His eyes are wide and he's trembling, but he nods. He can be quiet. I wrap a blanket around my shoulders and creep to the window. My heart is thudding against my rib cage and I'm half expecting Gopal to be on the other side of the door with a whip in his hand to finish with me what he started with Iyla. I push back the edge of the drapery, just a fraction, just enough to see who is there.

It's not Gopal.

Deven stands outside, a bag in one hand and a bouquet of marigolds in the other. He's dripping wet. His dark hair is pasted to his forehead, and tiny droplets cling to his lashes. He wears a hopeful expression, like it's a holiday and he's just been handed a present. It's a strange kind of pleasure to watch him without his knowing. He looks younger without an audience, less confident somehow. Warmth spreads through my chest. I spent the whole night worrying about how to find him again, and here he is on my doorstep.

"Marinda?" Mani asks. His voice is colored with worry.

"Everything is fine," I tell him, dropping the drapery. I open the door and Deven's face breaks into a smile.

"Good morning," he says. Then he looks me over and frowns. "Oh, no. I woke you."

"No." I run my fingers through my hair, suddenly self-conscious. And then I remember my bare wrists and drop my hands to my sides. "You didn't. I just . . ." I'm still surprised to see him here and I have no words.

He laughs and steps through the threshold into the flat. "Yes, I did." He holds up the bag. "But I brought a surprise, so hopefully you'll forgive me?"

Mani bounds off the bed. "What did you bring?" The excitement in his voice stings a little after he gave me the silent treatment yesterday, but I'm glad to see him smiling again.

"This is for you," Deven says, handing the bag to Mani. "And I brought your sister some flowers." He presents me with the bouquet of golden blossoms held together with a white ribbon. Careful to keep the insides of my wrists facing me, I take the marigolds and press them to my nose. They smell sharp and woodsy, more like a boy than a flower. I close my eyes and try to capture this moment, and suddenly I feel apart from myself—like I'm standing to the side and watching a different girl's story. Because this isn't my life, not really, and this moment belongs only to the Marinda that Deven thinks he knows, not the real me. The boys in my life don't have flowers and sweet words. They have headaches, and tremors, and death.

"Thank you," I say past the lump in my throat. *Thank you for making me feel like a normal girl and not a poisoned one.*

Deven's eyes are soft. "You're welcome."

Mani tugs on my arm. "Look what Deven brought me," he says, holding up the same pale fruit he ate at the bookshop. "Maraka fruit. Can I eat it now?"

I ruffle his hair. "Sure, monkey, go ahead."

"Eat a few pieces," Deven says. "You're going to need your energy." I raise my eyebrows in a question. "The flowers weren't my only surprise. I came to kidnap you."

"What?" Mani and I say together.

"The three of us are going on an adventure today," Deven says.

"I don't know—" I start, but Mani interrupts me.

"Please, Marinda. *Please, please, please.*"

I glance over at Deven and he presses his hands together under his chin, imitating Mani. "Please, Marinda," he says in the same pleading tone.

I laugh. "You two are trouble," I say.

"So?" Mani asks.

"Yes, all right. Let's go have an adventure." Both boys grin and then they slap their palms together in a celebratory high five. I roll my eyes. "Breakfast first," I tell them.

"Of course," Deven says.

I dress behind the curtain in our small bathroom—black pants, hiking boots, a silky lapis-colored top and wide silver bracelets. I pull my hair back in a ponytail and tie it with a scarf. This is probably unwise, going off with Deven like this. A few weeks ago I wouldn't have even entertained the idea.

But Deven makes me reckless.

And just for one day I want to know what it feels like to be the girl he thinks I am.

After I finish dressing, while the boys are laughing over a game of dice, I warm two loaves of flatbread, smear them with butter and sprinkle them with cinnamon. Then I pour each of us a tall glass of orange juice.

I make sure Deven gets the poisoned one.

• •

We're a few hours into our hike up a steep mountainside blanketed in lush green trees when Deven reaches for my hand. "Close your eyes," he says. "I want this to be a surprise." He laces his fingers through mine and presses his other hand against my waist. I close my eyes and let him guide me forward.

"No peeking," he says. I can feel his breath on the back of my neck. It's exhilarating, the thought of him that close to me. But then panic seizes me. What if I can feel his breath only because it's labored? What if the poison I gave him is starting to kill him? I strain my ears, but all I can hear is the trill of a songbird. I focus on the feel of his hand in mine, check to see if it feels hot or clammy. It doesn't—it feels soft and strong. Some of the tension drains from my shoulders. He's fine. At least for now.

The ground is still damp from the earlier rainfall, and my boots sink into the soil as I walk. Cool mountain air bites at my cheeks, but it feels pleasant after the heat of the valley and after the exertion of the long hike. Mani is humming happily beside me. His eighteen hours of sleep yesterday must have restored some of his energy. He hasn't asked to stop for a break once. Suddenly Mani falls silent and I hear a sharp intake of breath.

"Wow," he says softly.

"We're here," Deven tells me. He drops his palm from my waist, but he doesn't let go of my hand.

I open my eyes, and my breath sticks in my throat. We're at the base of an impossibly blue lake nestled against the side of a sheer cliff. The lake is surrounded by thick green forest. A brilliantly white waterfall tumbles from the rocks into the water below. It's breathtaking.

"It's not the tallest waterfall in Sundari," Deven says, "but it's the most beautiful." This is the only waterfall I've ever seen, but I have no doubt that he's right. I'm completely mesmerized.

"What's it called?" Mani asks. His face is tipped upward and he's wearing an expression of such joy that it tugs at my heart. It didn't occur to me that the waterfall would have a name, but Deven is ready with an answer.

"It's called the Maiden's Curtain."

"Why?" I ask.

He turns to me. His eyes are bright. "It's from an old legend," he says. "Would you like to hear the story?"

"Yes," Mani and I answer in unison.

Deven laughs. "Okay, but let's get comfortable first." He pulls a large blanket from his pack and unfurls it on a flat, grassy area near the water's edge. We lie on our backs, gazing up at the waterfall, close enough that the mist dances over our cheeks. When Deven starts speaking, there's a melodic quality to his voice, like he's told this story many times before.

"The legend goes that this lake once belonged to a maiden who was renowned for her beauty. Stories of her were told far and wide, spoken around cook fires and whispered at bedtime. Eventually the tales reached the ears of a lonely prince who was determined to find a beautiful bride. He had courted many maidens, but none of them were lovely enough to satisfy him. So the prince set out to find the maiden of the lake. He searched for months until he finally found this water—the brilliant blue of a sapphire. The lake was so perfect that he was certain he had the right place. And sure enough, a little ways off, he saw a young woman bathing herself in the water. He crept closer, trying to catch a glimpse of her and see if the legends were true. The maiden was submerged up to her neck in the water, and her back was to the prince, so all he could see was her dark hair. But it was beautiful hair, so his heart swelled with hope as he waited for her to turn."

Deven stops talking and for a moment there's just the rush of the waterfall in our ears. "So what happened?" Mani asks.

Deven props himself up on his elbows. "Do you really want to know?"

I swat him on the arm. "Of course we want to know," I say. "No fair stopping in the middle of a story."

He shoots a stern look at me. "The first rule of legends is that you never strike the storyteller."

"Even if he is an obnoxious tease?" I ask.

His face breaks into a wide grin. He tries to force it from his face and assume a more serious expression, but he's not having much luck. "Even then," he says.

"*Dev-en,*" Mani whines. "Just tell us what happens."

"All right," Deven says. He clears his throat. "Finally the maiden began to turn. The prince held his breath, anxious for his first look at her face. But when he saw her, his heart sank. She wasn't beautiful at all."

"She wasn't?" Mani asks.

Deven shakes his head. "She wasn't. She was actually quite plain. The maiden saw him and asked, 'Why have you come?'

"'I came to see if the legends about your beauty are true,' the prince said.

"'And what have you discovered?'

"'I'm afraid I've been misled,' the prince told her.

"The maiden was so offended by his rejection that she used her magic to create a curtain of sweet milk that tumbled from the cliffs above to shield her from the prince's view. And then she continued to bathe. The prince turned to leave, but he hadn't gotten very far when he heard a sound so beautiful it made him ache inside with a longing he had never known before. The maiden was singing. The prince ran back to the lake, and as he listened, he fell in love—not only with her beautiful voice, but also with the words of her songs, which revealed her heart. Suddenly he thought she was the most beautiful woman he had ever seen. He called out to the maiden and asked her to remove the milky curtain. Although it added much beauty to the lake, it blocked her from his view, and he desired to court her. But the maiden refused.

"The prince was determined not to leave until she changed her mind, and so he made his home near the water and spent his days talking to the maiden—telling her the stories of his youth, discussing philosophy, reciting poetry.

"Gradually the maiden's heart softened and she fell in love with the prince. But still she wouldn't remove the curtain. Although the prince could not remember why he had ever doubted the maiden's beauty, she could not forget that he had once thought her plain."

"So what happened?" I ask.

"They died—each of them in love with the other, but never seeing one another again."

"They *died*?" Mani said. "That's a terrible story."

But I didn't think so. It was tragic, true. But also romantic and beautiful.

"Some people say if you listen very carefully, you can still hear the maiden singing," Deven says.

That makes us all fall silent. And for just a moment, in the rush of the waterfall, I think I can hear something that sounds like music.

* *

"Are you up for seeing something else?" Deven asks after we've lunched on a picnic of samosas and maraka fruit. The sun has risen high in the sky, chasing away the crisp mountain air, and now we are bathed in a pool of buttery warmth. I'm reluctant to leave such a beautiful place, and so I don't answer right away.

Deven studies my face. "Or we could stay here?"

"No," I say. "We can't have an adventure with only one stop. I just . . ." My voice is suddenly scratchy with emotion, and I have to pause and take a breath before I speak again. "I really love it here." And I do. I've never been anywhere so serene in my entire life.

His eyes are bright. "I knew you would." He smiles, but it's not his usual grin—this smile spreads slowly, like spilled honey. His face looks younger and less guarded, like it did this morning when he stood outside my door in the rain. I smile back and he holds my gaze until my cheeks grow warm, and I let my eyes slide away.

He turns to Mani. "What do you think, pal? Do you want more adventure?" But Mani is already on his feet, bouncing lightly on his toes. We all laugh. Deven slings his pack over his shoulder and holds out both of his hands—one for me and one for Mani.

Deven says the walk will take over an hour, but I almost wish it would never end. We hike under huge trees that filter the light into dappled patterns on our arms and legs. The air smells so fresh that I feel like if I could just breathe deeply enough to pull it all in, it might wash away all the darkness. A songbird flits in the trees above us. With a start I realize that it looks like a miniature version of the great bird—its wings are the rich blue of lapis lazuli, edged in emerald green. I can't pull my gaze away.

"Look," I say, tugging on Deven's hand, "it's Garuda." We stop and admire the bird for a few minutes before continuing on.

There's a warmth radiating from my chest, and the thought crosses my mind that this must be what happiness feels like. And then, for some reason, my mind wanders to my mother. Or rather the empty space where my memories of her should be. When I was a little girl, I wondered about her incessantly—her eyes, her hair, the timbre of her voice. But I stopped thinking about her years ago, the way you avoid stepping in a puddle after a rainstorm. Because why make yourself miserable on purpose? And yet somehow the beauty of this day, its simple perfection, pushes my nonmemories of my mother forcefully to the surface. It's as if my mind is trying to keep things in balance—like adding sour to sweet in a recipe. Gita's stories of me as a baby include only my father. I've never heard her or Gopal mention my mother—though clearly I had one, even if she did agree to sell me.

"What do you think?" Deven's voice pulls me from my thoughts and I follow his gaze. The trees have parted to reveal a small cove, closed in on all sides by mountains. Azure-blue cottages spill into the valley and spread out in every direction, the blue roofs rising and falling in waves. For a moment I'm too stunned to speak. It seems incongruous to see a village in such a secluded location. It's beautiful in a whole different way than the waterfall is, but just as breathtaking.

Mani finds a voice before I do. "What is it?"

"The Widows' Village," Deven says. His voice is full of awe, like this place is sacred to him.

"Widows?" I say. Widows are considered unlucky in Sundari—superstitions abound that if a wife outlives her husband, she must be cursed, and socializing with her is dangerous. Even stepping in a widow's shadow is said to bring seven years of bad luck.

Deven clears his throat. "Years ago the Raja heard reports about a settlement of poverty-stricken widows living in the far reaches of Sundari. He traveled there to see with his own eyes, and it was even worse than he thought. All of the women were destitute, dressed in rags and barely surviving off only a few meals a week. Their families had disowned them when their husbands died, and they had nowhere to go. It infuriated him that the women should be so poorly treated for something that wasn't their fault, so he had his men search the kingdom high and low for somewhere they could be secluded and start a new life in a place of their own. When his advisers showed him this valley, he knew it was perfect. So he had this village built for them, and now they live and work together without any stigma."

"That's incredible," I say. A wave of warmth washes over me. Gopal has always said that working for the Raja is an honor, but until this moment the Raja has never seemed like a real person, let alone a kind one. Maybe my work is noble after all. But then I remember that the Raja wants Deven dead, and the feeling drains away.

"Why are the houses blue?" Mani asks.

"Living under a blue roof is a symbol of dignity," Deven explains. "But the Raja didn't want to settle for just the roof. He wanted the entire house to be blue."

"It's beautiful," I say. A solitary blue house might look garish, but all of them together are like a work of art. I can't tear my gaze away.

"How did you find this place?" Mani asks.

A shadow passes over Deven's face and it takes him a moment to answer. "My grandmother lives here," he says finally.

"She does?" Mani claps his hands together. "Can we meet her?"

Deven laughs. "We'll have to save that for another day. If we don't head back soon, we won't make it before dark." I glance up and see that he's right. It must already be late afternoon.

On the way back Deven slides his hand into mine, and tingles race up my arm. It's a lie, our palms pressed together, our fingers entwined like we belong to each other. But it's a lovely lie, and I wish it never had to end.

* *

By the time we make it back to the flat, the sun is dipping beneath the horizon and the sky is blushing like a new bride. Mani is finally worn out, and he slumps against me as I fish for my key. When I swing the door open, he crawls into bed still fully dressed and pulls the covers over his head.

Deven leans against the doorframe. "Thank you for today."

"So typical," I say.

"What?"

"Thanking me when I've done nothing at all."

He smiles and tugs gently on my ponytail. "You came," he said. "I didn't think you would."

"I didn't think I would either."

"So why did you?"

I'm sleepy and content and it's working on me like a drug running through my veins, making me loose and fearless. I tell him the truth. "You make me do irresponsible things."

He laughs and pulls me against his chest. He wraps his arms around my waist and presses his lips to my forehead. "I hope to make you do more irresponsible things in the future," he says. I lay my head on his shoulder and relax against him. His fingers move up and down my spine, and my whole body comes to life. It steals my breath away, this sensation of being touched, of feeling alive. Deven's fingers twine through my hair, stroke the back of my neck. My nerves are singing. I lift my head—just for a moment—and he catches my face in his palms. His thumbs idly stroke my cheeks. I can't breathe. I can't think. He's looking at me like I'm the only person in the world. His eyes are deep brown, pools of melted chocolate, and I could drown in them. Deven leans toward me, lips already parted, and time seems to slow down. I want him to do it. I want him to kiss me more than I've ever wanted anything.

I put a palm on his chest and push him away. Deven's hands drop to his sides and a look of hurt flashes across his face.

"I'm sorry," I tell him, and I am. So sorry. "I can't. I . . ." I'm floundering for an excuse, for a way to erase the wounded expression on his face. I reach for his hand and squeeze his fingers. "It's just that Mani is here and I'm so tired."

"Oh," he says. "I'll let you get some rest, then."

I nod. "Thanks," I say, because it's the only thing I can.

He turns to leave and then stops. "Wait. I almost forgot." He pulls something from his pocket and drops it into my palm. "I brought this for you," he tells me. "It's a cricket."

And it is—a cricket just smaller than the length of my palm carved out of silky, dark wood. Every detail is perfect, from the tiny wings and slender antennae all the way down to the folded legs poised for jumping. This must have taken him hours of work, maybe days. No one has ever given me a gift before, and I can't stop staring at it.

"Do you like it?" he asks.

"I love it."

Deven leans forward and brushes my cheek with the pad of his thumb. "I couldn't work out how to carve a sunset, and a star seemed too ordinary." *You like nighttime.* On the day I was supposed to kill him, he was memorizing the things that I love.

"Thank you," I tell him. My voice is thick with emotion and I feel like something inside me has cracked open and I'll never be able to close it up again. "I can't . . . I don't know how to repay you."

He grins and presses another kiss on my forehead. "You'll think of something," he teases. "Good night, Marinda."

"Good night," I say. And it was. It was a perfect night. Yesterday I told Iyla that I wasn't in love with Deven.

I think I lied.

CHAPTER TEN

Deven needs one more dose of poison, but I haven't seen him in two days. Mani and I have searched everywhere—the park, the market, the café where he bought us lunch—but Deven seems to have vanished. I try to tell myself that he's just busy, that he isn't lying on the side of the street somewhere writhing in pain from the poison I've given him. But red-hot worry snakes through my veins and coils tightly around my middle. I run my thumb along the back of the silky-smooth wooden cricket in my pocket. This may be all I have left of him. Mani and I are running out of places to search.

Now my final bit of hope bleeds away as Mani and I stare at the CLOSED sign dangling in the window of the bookshop. I hoped that Japa would be able to tell me where to find Deven, where he lives. But the darkened windows feel like a bad omen. "Japa never closes the shop," I tell Mani. The worry in my stomach rears up and strikes with sharp fangs. What if he's by Deven's bedside? Or worse, at his graveside? But Mani's not paying attention to me. His gaze is fixed on a boy not much older than himself sitting in a booth across the street. A sign hangs above his head that says WISDOM FOR SALE. PRICES VARY.

"He's on the wrong street," I say. "That kind of foolishness only works in the market."

Mani looks up at me like I've offended him. "Maybe he can help us," he says. His expression is so earnest. He wants to find Deven as much as I do, but throwing away money will do us no good.

I soften my tone. "I don't think so, monkey. You can't buy wisdom."

"Of course you can," he says. He motions toward the shop. "What about books?"

"That's different."

"How?"

I put my arm around his shoulders. "Well, for one thing, most books aren't written by ten-year-olds."

Mani glares at me and moves so that my arm falls away from him. "Children aren't stupid," he says.

"That's not what I meant . . . ," but I don't get to finish because he turns his back on me and marches across the street toward the booth.

"Mani!" I call, but he doesn't turn and so I hurry to follow him. I catch up just as he's dropping a handful of coins into the boy's palm. The boy counts the money before he places it in a leather pouch fastened to his waist. He looks up at the sky and taps a quill against his cheek. His fingertips are stained with black ink and there's a dark smudge across his cheek. I open my mouth to speak, but Mani gives me a look so withering that I snap my jaw shut. The boy drops his gaze and levels both Mani and me with a long stare. Then he nods once like he's satisfied with his assessment of us. He dips his quill in the inkpot beside him and scribbles on a piece of parchment. His tongue pokes out of the side of his mouth as he writes, and it makes him look even younger. He sets the quill down and blows on the ink. Mani is bouncing on his toes, and his hands are laced together in front of him like he's restraining himself from snatching the wisdom from the boy's fingers. Finally the boy rolls the parchment into a loose cylinder and hands it to Mani.

We walk a few steps away before Mani unfurls it. As he reads, his brow furrows and he chews on his bottom lip. He hands me the parchment. Written in a script that belies the boy's age is this: *Suspicion is the only defense against betrayal.* My blood runs cold. I whirl to face Mani.

"What did you tell that boy?"

His face is twisted in confusion. "What?"

"Before I came up behind you, what did you say to him?"

"Nothing," Mani says. "I just said I wanted to buy some wisdom."

"Why would he write this?" I shake the parchment in

front of Mani's face. He takes a step back and I realize I'm scaring him. I pull in a deep breath.

"I'm sorry," I tell him, hugging him to my side. "It doesn't matter." But the words on the page have rattled me, and I walk back to the stall where the boy is still sitting, a look of absolute calm on his face.

"We want our money back," I tell him. The boy studies me for a moment before responding, his eyes roaming over my face as if searching for something.

"Certainly," he says finally. "But you will need to return what you've purchased."

I toss the parchment at him and it drifts to a stop near his inkpot. He glances at it but doesn't pick it up. "That isn't what I sold you."

"Yes," I say through a clenched jaw, "it is."

"Did you read it?"

"Of course I read it."

"Do you remember what it said?"

"Yes."

"Then you still possess the wisdom. If you can return that, then I will happily give you a refund."

"You know I can't do that," I say.

He picks up the parchment and holds it out to me. "Then I'm afraid I can't return your money." The hairs on the back of my neck prickle to life. This child talks as if he is a hundred years old. It's just a trick, I remind myself. I have seen it dozens of times at the market. Fortune-tellers, snake charmers, palm readers, each of them playing on the things that all of us have in common—love, loss, heartbreak. Their proclamations are so generalized that they seem personalized. But they are all charlatans who lie for money, and this boy is no different. Still, as I walk back to Mani, I can't help wondering: *Am I the betrayer or am I the betrayed?*

Mani takes my hand and we don't say anything as we leave Gali Street and cross into the wooded area nearby. We walk under the shade of the devil trees until we get to a small pond occupied by dozens of swans. Mani snatches the parchment from my fingers and drops it into the water. And we watch as the ink bleeds away, leaving just a blank page without any wisdom at all.

* *

"We could try Iyla's house," Mani says after we've spent an hour watching the swans swim in circles. The suggestion sends a shock of pain through me—to imagine Iyla and Deven together, to think that she might be the reason that I haven't seen him. But as unbearable as it is picturing him in Iyla's arms, it's better than the alternative, better than finding out I've given him too much venom and he's dead. The thought of killing him by accident is so much worse than the prospect of killing someone else on purpose. And thinking so makes me feel like a horrible person.

"It's worth a try," I say. I try to keep my voice steady, but I don't fool Mani. He squeezes my fingers.

"Don't worry," he says. "Deven likes you better."

But that's not the point. The pang of sadness comes from imagining that he cares for anyone else at all.

Mani and I don't speak on the walk to Iyla's house, and the silence that hangs between us is heavy and anxious. When we get to her neighborhood, my shoulders are tight with dread that we will come upon the same scene as before, that we'll have to crouch behind a hedge and watch Iyla and Deven embrace. But we don't see them, and oddly this worries me too. By the time we climb the steep steps to the front door, Mani's breathing is coming in small gasps. The cords in his neck are bulging and taut. I pat him on the back. "Breathe," I tell him. He puts his hands on his knees and sucks air slowly through his nose. Before I have a chance to knock, the door swings open to reveal Iyla, her face a mask of rage.

"What are you doing here?" she asks. Her gaze darts from side to side. "You're causing a spectacle."

Anger flares in my chest. "He can't breathe, Iyla." She looks at Mani and her face softens.

"I'm sorry," she says. "Come in." She ushers us through the door and quickly closes it behind us. I forgot how beautiful Iyla's home is. Plush white carpet stretches from wall to wall, and all the furniture is oversized and covered in brightly colored luxurious fabrics. A mosaic of the Raksaka made entirely of gemstones hangs on the wall—an amber tiger stalks through a jade meadow, the emerald head of a crocodile peeks from a sea of blue topaz, a sapphire Garuda flies against pearly clouds, and an onyx snake gleams from the ground, a ruby tongue flicking from its mouth.

Dozens of small candles nestled in glass jars are scattered on tabletops, and I'm forcefully reminded why Iyla lives in more lavish circumstances than Mani and I do. Our flat is meant to be functional. Her home is meant for seduction. A wave of nausea overtakes me as I picture Deven here with Iyla, her face bathed in candlelight.

She motions toward Mani. "What does he need?" she asks. He needs a breathing treatment, though I have a feeling Gopal will withhold one until either Deven is dead or he's convinced Deven can't be killed. Mani's breathing is calming, although it's still strained.

"He'll be fine," I tell her. "He just needs a moment."

Iyla's arms are crossed over her stomach. Her face is completely scrubbed clean and her hair is pulled into a messy bun at the back of her head. The bruise on her jaw has turned a sickly green color. She doesn't look like she's working today, and it makes me breathe a little easier. Iyla sees me studying her and narrows her eyes.

"What on earth would possess you to come here?" she asks.

"I can't find Deven." I try to keep my voice steady, but it comes out more like a supplication than a statement.

Her eyebrows disappear into her hairline. "You came here for that? Do you have any idea how bad it will be if Gopal finds out you're here?"

I narrow my eyes and force nails into my voice. "He'll only know if you tell him."

She groans and presses her fingers to her temples. "That's not true. He could've had you followed." Her gaze slides to Mani and I see the accusation in her eyes—that loving him makes me weak, that I'm less careful because of him.

"We weren't followed," I say. "I'm not stupid. Do you know where Deven is or not?"

Iyla sits in a chair with thick red and orange stripes. The colors flatter her complexion, and I wonder if they were chosen for that reason. She crosses one leg over the other and studies her fingernails.

"You won't find him today."

"Why not?"

She doesn't look at me. "He's unavailable."

My heart speeds up. "What is that supposed to mean?" I have the horrible thought that by "unavailable" she could mean dead, that my worst fear has been realized, that I've killed him in my attempts to save him. Or maybe she means Gopal has already chosen another plan, a different assassin. I sink down into the chair directly across from her. "Is he in danger? Just tell me where he is." I hate the note of pleading in my voice, hate the smug look it plasters across Iyla's face.

She swings her foot and avoids looking at me. "He's fine," she says, and the worry in my stomach uncoils, just a little. "But I can't tell you anything more."

Fear has been eating away at me for days, and Iyla is

as calm as a sea made of glass. She has all the knowledge, all the power and none of the worry. She can find Deven whenever she wants. I have the sudden urge to flip her over and shake her like a coin bank until her secrets spill out like silver treasure. "Iyla, stop playing games and tell me where he is."

She finally meets my gaze and fixes me with an icy stare. "The last few times I've shared things with you haven't gone well for me."

My fingers curl into my palms and I have to resist the urge to raise my voice. It's so unfair of her to blame me for the terrible things Gopal has done. "That's not how it was," I say. My voice is choked with emotion, despite my best efforts to stay calm. "I never intentionally betrayed your confidences." But the bruise is splayed across her face like an accusation.

"I know," she says. "Still . . . you'll understand if I'm not eager to give you information."

I rake my fingers through my hair. "I have to find him, Iyla. He needs one more dose of poison."

She shrugs. "Like I said, it won't be today." She studies my face. "Look, Marinda, I said I wouldn't tell Gopal and I won't, but that's all I can do. It's safer for you if you don't know where Deven is."

"If you hurt him—"

"Stop it," she says. "You don't have to threaten me. He's going to be fine." She leans forward and puts a hand on top of mine. "I promise." For just a moment I think I see something hard in her eyes, and a prickle of unease races across my skin. But then I blink and it's just the Iyla I've always known, squeezing my fingers and offering me a weary smile. It's not until we're almost to the door that I notice her earrings—delicate golden birds with small diamonds for eyes.

"Those are pretty," I say, lifting my chin toward her ears.

Iyla strokes one of the birds with the tip of her finger, as if she forgot she was wearing jewelry. Her cheeks flush and she looks away. "Thank you," she says, but she won't meet my gaze.

I wait for her to say something more—to tell me how she sweet-talked the jeweler at the market and got them for half price, or how she scored them for free from the little shop on Gali Street—but she doesn't. Iyla never misses an opportunity to brag. My stomach clenches.

The earrings must be a gift from Deven.

It shouldn't bother me, the thought of him giving her a gift. But somehow this is even worse than seeing them kiss. My fingers find the cricket in my pocket and trace small circles over its tiny wings.

Iyla insists on checking that the street is empty before she lets us leave. "Get out of here quickly," she tells us, and I wonder if it's Gopal she's worried will spot us or if it's Deven. Maybe he's unavailable because they have plans. The thought leaves a sour taste in my mouth, but he's alive and that's all that matters.

Mani slides his hand into mine as we walk away. He's quiet for several minutes, but then he stops walking and looks up at me with big, worried eyes. "Is Iyla going to kill Deven?"

"Of course not," I say.

"How do you know?"

I put my arm around his shoulders and pull him close to me. "Because Gopal didn't make her for killing, monkey."

"What did he make her for?"

There's no comfort in the answer, but I tell him the truth anyway. "He made her for lying."

CHAPTER ELEVEN

The next few days pass with excruciating slowness. Mani is growing sicker by the moment, and it's as if everyone in our lives has vanished. We don't see or hear from Deven, Iyla or Gita. There's no sign of Gopal either and no hint that he's ever coming back. He will—of course he will—but if Mani dies before he gets here, he won't find me waiting.

The need to find Deven fades into the background as Mani loses strength. He's too weak to leave the flat and has spent the morning curled on his bed staring vacantly into space, his pupils dilated, his eyes watering and his breath so shallow I have to strain to see his chest moving up and down. I've made three trips to the healers in the marketplace, and none of the potions I've purchased have done Mani any good—not the ones from the real healers and not the ones from the frauds either. I've seen

Mani's face this pale only once before, and I almost lost him then.

A few days after the incident at the river, Gopal showed up on my doorstep with a ceramic pot and a bottle of medication. "This should help your brother breathe easier," he said. This was Gopal's way—to create the problem and then insist on being treated like a savior for providing half a solution.

The breathing treatments helped Mani at first—enough that I was willing to tolerate the foul-smelling vapors that clung to our flat for days after each treatment. But after a few months, he stopped improving and I grew suspicious of Gopal's motives. The next time he showed up with a treatment, I told him I wanted him to breathe in the vapors along with Mani.

"Excuse me?" he said. "What are you implying, Marinda?"

"How do I know you're not making it worse? If the medication is harmless, then what will it hurt if you inhale it too?"

Gopal's laugh was brittle. "How quickly you forget the lessons I teach, little one." He stalked over to the bubbling water and dumped nearly half the vial of medication into it. A bitter mist rolled through the flat, and Gopal stood with his face pressed to the pot for a full minute, inhaling deeply and grinning like a madman. Then he stood up and tipped the remaining contents of the bottle into his mouth and grimaced as he swallowed.

"Satisfied, *rajakumari*?"

My stomach curled around the terrible mistake I'd just made.

Gopal tossed the bottle on the floor and it shattered into a hundred tiny pieces. "But if you are convinced that I'm trying to hurt the boy, then I'd best keep my distance."

The coldness in his voice was final and he was true to his word. He didn't return for ten days. Mani grew weaker and weaker, until his face was as pale as rice and he shivered uncontrollably. I held off as long as I could, hoping against all reason that he would improve on his own, but soon he was so ill I couldn't wait anymore. I ran to the girls' home and found Gopal. "He's dying," I said. "Please come."

Gopal looked at me with ice in his eyes. "Beg me, *rajakumari*. Tell me I was right."

Shakily, I fell to my knees. "I was wrong to doubt you," I said. "I'm begging you to give Mani the breathing treatment. Please."

Gopal reached down and stroked my cheek with the backs of his fingers. "See now? Was that so hard?"

Mani's health looks just as dire as it did that day, but I know Gopal won't give him the treatment until there's blood on my hands.

Several times I'm tempted to go to the bookshop to talk to Japa, but something holds me back. My emotions are taut, stretched to their very limit, and I worry if I see Japa's kind face, I will break down and tell him everything. If I thought he could save Mani, it would be worth the risk, but if there were a medication to heal his tiny broken lungs, I would have found it already.

Instead I curl myself around Mani and try to calm the shivers that have taken over his small body.

Finally, after days of silence, there's a knock at the door, and I open it to find Gita. Relief floods through me and I have to resist the urge to throw myself into her arms and beg her never to leave me again. But I remind myself that she's not here to offer mercy—she's here to exact Gopal's revenge. And I won't let her.

She offers me a weak smile. "I forgot my key," she says. She looks tired—blue smudges underline her eyes, and the wrinkles around her mouth have deepened.

"That's just as well," I tell her. "Because unless you have Mani's breathing treatment, you aren't coming in."

"After I deliver my message," she says. "After you follow Gopal's instructions."

"No," I say. "Now."

"Marinda," she says, a warning in her voice. "Don't start. Not today."

Rage shoots through me at her offhand tone, as if I'm four years old and we're discussing whether or not I need a bath. I take a step toward her and she stumbles backward. "Let me explain how this works. I'm not doing *anything* until Mani is better. Gopal can come here and kill me himself, but I'm not moving until Mani gets that medication."

Gita bites her lip. "I'm not supposed to give it to him until you've completed the assignment."

I put my hand on her chest and give her a little shove. "Then run back and tell Gopal you couldn't convince me. I'm sure he'll thank you for following his instructions so dutifully."

A hint of fear skitters through her eyes. "Very well," she says. "But then you must promise to listen to me."

I step away from the door so she can come inside. Right now I will say anything to get relief for Mani. "I promise."

I pace as we wait for the water to boil. When it begins to bubble, Gita drops the medication into the pot and then retreats to the far side of the flat. I scoop Mani into my arms and hold him over the burbling water, a blanket tented over both of our heads. The bitter steam fills the small space and Mani stirs to life, his head turning toward the pot like a flower reaching for the sunlight. My heart tumbles forward. He's going to live. I hold him in my arms until the pot boils dry, and by the time I finally lay him down on the bed, my muscles are screaming. Gita stands in the doorway with her hand over her nose and mouth to block the smell.

"Time to talk," she says. "Let's go outside."

I step out and close the door behind me. The air smells so clean out here that I pull in the deepest breath I can, let it expand my lungs until they feel ready to burst. Gita watches me with a pained expression. She reaches for my hand, but I pull away.

"Marinda." She says my name with such affection that it actually hurts a little. "Gopal asked me to come. Iyla has set up the next meeting."

I knew this was coming, but I still feel a pressure against my chest that makes it hard to breathe. I haven't given Deven the last dose of venom, and I'm not sure how I will protect him now.

"Where?" I ask. "When?"

Gita sighs and lays a hand on my arm. "Please listen to me," she says. "It is important that you do this thing for Gopal."

"This *thing*?" I ask. "You mean this murder."

Gita closes her eyes, as if I'm trying her patience. "I think we've had enough insolence for today." It's pointless to argue with her. She has a message and she's going to do her duty and deliver it.

"Just give me the details," I tell her.

She digs her fingers into my arm and shakes me. "Not until you pay attention." Her voice is colored with urgency and her eyes have gone wild. "Gopal is as angry as I've ever seen him. You must not defy him again."

I swallow hard. "Again?"

Her eyes narrow. "Gopal is not a stupid man, Marinda. He knows you haven't been truthful. This boy is not worth it, no matter what you think of him." She lets go of my arm and presses her palm to her forehead. "There are things you don't know," she says. "Decisions you're in no position to make."

My stomach is churning. Gita's words confirm my worst fears—that Gopal never believed me, that he whipped Iyla only to send a message. He intended for her to show me the welts on her back. That he would hurt her only to force me into compliance isn't surprising, but it still makes me feel sick.

Gita studies my face. "Don't put your safety at risk," she says. And then after a long pause, "Or your brother's safety." Her words send gooseflesh racing up my arms.

"Are you threatening to hurt Mani?" My voice comes out like a growl.

"Of course not," Gita says, though we both know she can hurt him simply by staying away. "But you would do well not to anger Gopal." She hands me a folded slip of paper. "The boy's address is written here," she says, tapping the paper. "You must go immediately."

"To his *home*?" This is unprecedented. The kills always happen in a public place, surrounded by people and noise. It's part of tradecraft, something that has been drilled into me since I was small. Never be alone with the target. Missions are completed in full daylight. My mouth goes dry. I have spent nearly the last week wishing I knew where Deven lived, and now I'm holding the answer in my palm. I unfold the paper and my mouth falls open.

"This is Iyla's neighborhood," I say.

Gita chews her lip and nods. It must mean something that they live near each other, but I can't think what. "Memorize the address," she says, holding out her hand. "Then I will destroy the paper."

It won't be hard to remember. I've passed this house

twice in the last week. I give the slip back to Gita and she tucks it away. "You go now," she says. "I will stay with your brother."

"No," I say. "Mani comes with me."

"Marinda, you can't—"

I hold up a hand to stop her, and fix her with a hard stare. "He comes with me or I don't go." After Gita's thinly veiled threat, I know I can never leave Mani alone with her again.

"Very well," Gita says. "I will allow you to be stubborn on this point." She grabs my jaw and forces me to look into her eyes. "But make no mistake: Gopal expects the boy to be dead by sundown."

* *

The only way to save Deven now is to tell him the truth.

I'm across the street from his house, leaning against a tree trunk. The knobby stump of a missing branch digs into my back, but I don't move. Mani sits at my feet, twisting blades of grass into a rope. His recovery was almost instant—a few hours after the breathing treatment and he walked here on his own strength. From the outside, Deven's house looks exactly like Iyla's—the same pale-yellow stucco, an identical red roof. But I have a feeling the inside will be completely different. I'm just searching for the courage to find out. I rehearse in my mind what I need to say, but I'm not sure I can make my mouth form the words: *Today I'm*

supposed to kill you, but I think you should run instead. There's
a good chance someone else will try to kill you soon, so don't trust
anyone. And whatever you do, don't let anyone kiss you.

I have the vial of poison in my pocket on the off chance I can convince him to take a final dose. It seems unlikely.

"You should just get it over with," Mani says. His gaze stays glued to the grass in his fingers.

"What's wrong?" I ask him. He's been unusually quiet since Gita left, and I'm not sure if he's just recovering or if something else is bothering him.

"Come on, monkey. Tell me what you're thinking."

His voice is so quiet I have to strain to hear him. "He's going to hate us." I close my eyes. Mani's right, but it hurts to admit it, even to myself. I crouch down and touch his shoulder.

"If he hates anyone, it will be me," I say. "He has no reason to hate you."

Mani looks up at me, his chin quivering. "Even if he hates only you, I'll never see him again." This makes my throat burn. Mani asks for so little, and I wish I could give him this—Deven as his friend.

"Maybe he won't hate either one of us," I say. "Maybe he'll be grateful I warned him." But we both know it won't matter. Whether Deven is angry with me or not, he will need to leave Sundari to stay safe. It's likely that neither one of us will ever see him again. I press a kiss on the top of Mani's head, take a deep breath and cross the street.

My hand trembles as I knock on the door. Three seconds

pass and then ten. I'm torn between hoping he's home and praying he's not—it's not clear which is safer for him. A full minute passes and I'm just about to walk away when the door swings open. My heart trips forward at the sight of Deven. He is dressed casually, with damp hair and bare feet as if he's just emerged from the shower. His face is open and friendly, and I feel the corners of my mouth lifting without my permission. But then he focuses on my face and his expression goes dark. It startles me so much that I take a small step back.

"What are you doing here?" He practically throws the words at me, slaps me with them. This isn't the same boy who held me to his chest, who kissed my forehead. He's not looking at me like I'm the perfect girl from his imagination anymore. This is an expression I recognize, one I know as well as I know my own face. It's the one I wear when I look in the mirror.

My throat feels strangled, but I force myself to speak. "I need to talk to you," I say. "It's important."

Deven shakes his head. "I have nothing to say to you." His tone has a finality that leaves no room for argument. He tries to close the door, and I have to press myself in front of it to stop him.

"Are you angry with me?" Even as the question leaves my mouth, I realize it sounds foolish.

Deven's laugh comes out like a bark. "Angry? You could say that."

My mind is racing, but I'm coming up with more

questions than answers. Deven has a hundred reasons to hate me, but I haven't explained any of them yet.

"May I ask *why* you're angry?"

His eyes narrow. "Marinda." He says my name softly, almost tenderly. "Have you been pouring poison into my drinks?"

All the air leaves my lungs and I have to hold on to the doorframe for support. "How did you—"

"So it's true?" For just a moment his hard expression softens to a wounded one.

"It's not like that," I tell him. "I can explain."

Deven rakes both hands through his hair. "I really doubt that," he says. His fingers curl into fists. "Did the people you work for hit Iyla? Did they whip her until she could barely walk?"

I can hear the rush of my heartbeat in my ears, and something inside me unspools. Tears prickle at the corners of my eyes, but I blink them away. I refuse to let him see me cry. Not when he's looking at me like that.

"Did they?" Deven asks through a clenched jaw.

"Yes," I say in a whisper.

"And did that have anything to do with me?" I open my mouth to explain, but before I can say anything, he asks another question. "Are you a killer, Marinda?"

I am completely undone. I wrap my arms around my middle as if I can hold myself together. I want to explain, to tell him my version of events, but it's too late. Iyla has fed Deven a tale that is completely true, and when I hear it spill from his mouth, I sound like a monster. He will never forgive me. I was right that Iyla's power for destruction is in her words, and her bruised face tells a better story than I can. But at least she kept her promise. I won't have to kill Deven—there is no chance he will ever let me get close enough again. My ribs ache with the loss of him, even though he was never really mine.

"I didn't want to believe it," he says. "Even when I realized what you'd done to Mani, I wanted it to be a mistake."

My head snaps up. "What I'd done to Mani?"

"Drop the pretense," he says. "Anyone with eyes can see that he's in the late stages of *vish bimari*. To work for the people you do—to kill for them—it's awful. But to harm a child? It's disgusting."

I feel as if I've been plunged into a black hole. Bile rises at the back of my throat. *Vish bimari*. Poison disease. It's what kills most of the babies exposed to the toxin. It's what failed to kill me. But that's not what Mani has—it's impossible. He got sick right after Gopal nearly drowned him. The timing of the symptoms would be too much of a coincidence. Unless . . . I think back to when Gopal pulled Mani from the river, when I nearly put my lips to his. Did I get too close then? My stomach curls into a ball of fear. Maybe that's why the breathing treatments only half work. Or maybe I'm more toxic than I think, and being with me is too much for his little body. I've tried to be so careful. I never kiss him on his face. We never share food or drinks. But maybe it's not enough. Am I slowly killing him?

"That can't be right," I say more to myself than to Deven. It seems so unlikely. A flicker of doubt passes over his face, but then his eyes are hard as flint.

"No more lies, Marinda." He starts to close the door.

"Wait!" I call out. He raises his eyebrows. "You really are in danger," I tell him. "Leave Sundari. Please."

He gives me a scowl. "Trust me," he says. "I can take care of myself."

And then he slams the door in my face.

I stumble back to Mani in stunned silence. He takes one look at me and throws his arms around my waist. "Don't worry," he says, like he's the older sibling. "It will be okay." But it won't. How can I tell him that I could be to blame for his illness? My chin is resting on the top of his head and I have to resist the urge to push him away from me. How much contact is too much? Am I leaking poison from my palms? My breath? Will I have to be separated from Mani for him ever to get well? Gopal once told me that my mouth was poisonous because of the many doses of toxin slipped past my lips. It made them the deadliest part of me—but he never said they were the only deadly part. Kadru's snakes feasted from my wrists and ankles. Maybe even holding Mani's hand leaches poison into him. A sob rips from my throat and Mani pulls away, alarmed. I'm scaring him. I pull in a lungful of air and try to calm my breathing. I scrub at my eyes and force a smile.

"You're right," I say. "Everything will be fine."

Mani bites his lip like he's not sure he can believe me. "Can we go home now?" he asks.

"Soon," I say. "We have one more stop to make."

* *

I pound on Iyla's door until my fists ache, until they're as red and raw as fresh meat, but she doesn't open her door. I hate myself for trusting her, for believing that she was my friend. And even more I hate that she didn't have to lie to betray me. She only had to arrange the truth in a clever way. The words of the boy selling wisdom are pulsing through my mind like a headache: *Suspicion is the only defense against betrayal.*

I was too trusting of Iyla.

Deven was too trusting of me.

I press my forehead against the door and squeeze my eyes shut. I'm desperate to talk to her, desperate for answers. Gopal will be furious when he finds out not only that Deven is still alive, but that Iyla has compromised our entire operation. She didn't help me, but she didn't help Gopal either. She could have refused to be part of my plan, or she could have told Gopal that I had lied and that Deven would need to be dealt with by someone else. It would have made it harder for me to save him, but it would have made it clear where her loyalties were.

But she knew I cared about Deven and she made him hate me. Does she despise me that much?

I slam my shoulder against the door so hard that the windows rattle, but still nothing. My shoulder is throbbing, but I don't care. I crash against the door again. Sweat trickles down my forehead and stings my eyes. I press the full weight of my body against the door, but it's clear that brute force—no matter how anger-fueled—isn't going to get the job done. I pull the pins from my hair to pick the lock, but my fingers are trembling, and it takes me three tries before the knob finally turns freely. I step into Iyla's foyer and Mani reaches for my hand, but I pretend not to notice and move away from him.

"Help me look for her?" I ask.

"Sure." Mani scampers off, and his small feet press footprints into the plush white carpet like tracks in freshly fallen snow. I turn in the opposite direction and call out Iyla's name. I move through her sitting room, her kitchen, her dining room. Everything is pristine, from the gleaming countertops to the polished tables. Nothing is out of place—no blanket thrown casually across a chair, no bowl left in the sink or sandals by the door. I wonder if Gopal provides Iyla with a maid.

"There's nothing here," Mani says, poking his head into the dining room, where I'm running my fingers across the table, marveling at the lack of dust.

I sigh. "She must be out somewhere. We'll just have to wait for her to get home."

Mani shakes his head. "No. I mean none of her stuff is here."

"What?" I race up the stairs to Iyla's bedroom and fling open her closet. It's empty. I pull open the drawers, search in the bathroom. Nothing.

Now I know why Iyla wasn't worried about incurring Gopal's wrath. She never intended to see him again.

CHAPTER TWELVE

An hour ago I didn't think it was possible to feel more betrayed, but I was wrong. This hits me like a punch in the stomach. I sink to the floor and pull my knees to my chest.

Iyla escaped. It's something we've dreamed about for years, something we planned to do together. But she left without me. Worse than that, she made Deven despise me, made sure Gopal would punish me, and *then* she left.

Mani sits on the floor next to me and lays his head on my shoulder. "I'm sorry," he says.

I rest my head on top of his. "Not your fault."

"At least she can stop hating me now," he says, his voice wobbling.

"What are you talking about? No one could ever hate you."

"No. She did. I kept you from leaving—both of you—and she hated me for that."

I turn my body toward him and hold his face in my hands. "That's not true."

Two fat tears slip from the corners of his eyes and I brush them away with my thumbs. Then I remember that I probably shouldn't be touching his face at all, and I let my hands fall into my lap.

"It is true," Mani says. "She told me once."

A little shock of panic goes through me. "What? What did she say?"

Mani's face crumples, and it takes him a few seconds to compose himself enough to speak. "She said that I wasn't really your brother. That I was just some random kid Gopal picked up off the street to ruin your life and that because of me you'd both have to work for him forever." He scrubs at his eyes. "I didn't mean to ruin your life."

My mouth falls open. "Oh, Mani." I pull him to me and cradle his head against my shoulder. "Iyla's a fool. You didn't ruin my life. You saved it."

And as I hold him, I realize it's true. Taking care of Mani—loving him—is the only thing that has held the darkness at bay. Iyla thinks he makes me weak, but he doesn't. He makes me human.

Mani gulps in breaths between sobs. I rock him back and forth. "And, Mani?"

"Yeah?"

"In a choice between you and Iyla, you win every time. Got it?"

He pulls away and looks me in the eye. "I know that. We're still together, aren't we?"

I give him a smile instead of an answer. Because if I'm the one making him sick, it's going to be harder and harder to keep it that way.

Suddenly I have a realization that knocks the breath from me: Gopal knows what's wrong with Mani. He must. If Deven knows what *vish bimari* looks like, Gopal knows too. How the venom works on the body is something he's studied his whole life. It has fascinated him, consumed him.

So why wouldn't he tell me that I'm hurting Mani by being with him? Why would he let me believe that Mani's lungs are damaged? But the answer is obvious—if he told me, I would find another home for Mani, and then Gopal wouldn't be able to use him to control me. He's letting Mani die so I don't run.

But what if it's even worse?

I race downstairs to Iyla's kitchen and fling open her cabinets until I find a clay pot. I fill it with water, and my fingers shake as I set it over the heat. Mani stands on the stairs watching me.

"Marinda, what's wrong?" he says, and I realize I've stuffed my knuckles in my mouth.

"Just give me a moment," I tell him. I keep my gaze fastened on the pot, and when it begins to steam, I pull the vial of venom from my pocket and let a single drop fall into the water. The smell that fills Iyla's flat is as familiar as it is repulsive. I throw my hand over my mouth. Gopal hasn't been giving Mani breathing treatments.

He's been poisoning him.

And he doesn't give him a drop at a time like I've given Deven. Gopal puts venom into the water by the spoonful. I squeeze my eyes shut. I should have known better. I should have trusted my gut when the treatments didn't work right away, but Mani nearly died when Gopal refused to give him the medication. It was the only thing that ever made him feel better.

Mani hops off the stairs and launches himself at me. "You got my medicine," he says, and the joy in his voice is unmistakable. "How did you do it?" He steps up to the pot, closes his eyes and breathes in the vapors like he's savoring the smell of chocolate.

It reminds me of a man we used to see in the marketplace when I was young. He was always either smoking poppy straws or shaking violently and begging for coins. Gita told me that he was addicted to the opium plant and that he'd smoked it so often that his body betrayed him by demanding the very thing that was killing him.

Mani has that same look on his face—like he's inhaling salvation.

Rage wells in my chest and I snatch the pot from the heat and fling it across the room. It slams into the wall in a spray of water and shattered clay.

We had an unspoken agreement when Gopal pulled

Mani from the river—my compliance for my brother's safety. It was the only thing that kept me inside the nightmare Gopal had created. And this entire time Gopal has been killing Mani slowly right in front of me. My stomach turns. He made me *beg* him to poison Mani, made me fall on my knees and plead.

I yank open Iyla's drawers and find a sharp knife to slip in my waistband under my sari.

"Marinda?" Mani says, his voice full of fear.

"We have to go," I tell him. Late-afternoon sun streams through the window. Gita is supposed to meet us back at the flat at sundown, just a handful of hours from now. We have only a small window of opportunity to escape. I won't be Gopal's puppet anymore. Saving Deven is no longer enough. There will always be a next boy and then a next. But I won't be the one to kill them. I don't care how necessary the Raja thinks the deaths are.

"Are you strong enough for another walk?" I ask.

"I think so," Mani says. "Where are we going?"

"Back to the flat for supplies," I tell him. "And then we're going to leave."

"Forever?"

The hope in his voice sends a spasm of pain through me, and I'm determined not to fail him this time. "Forever," I say.

We take a different way back to the flat than usual, and I stop frequently to duck into doorways and wait before continuing on. I'm nearly certain we haven't been followed, but Gopal has surprised me before. I touch the knife at my waist—this time if he's one step ahead of us, I'm prepared.

When we get to our street, Mani tries to run ahead, but I catch his hand in mine and pull him behind me.

"Me first," I say. Even though we're not yet at the deadline, there's always a chance someone could be here waiting, and I want my body solidly between Mani and Gopal's rage.

I slide the key into the lock and ease the door open.

My heart plummets.

The flat has been ransacked. Our drawers are gaping open like a mouth with missing teeth, and what few clothes we have are strewn about the floor. The mattresses are askew and the floorboards are ripped up. I know before I look that I won't find the coins, but I check anyway—nothing. The money I've saved for years, the money that was going to save us, is gone.

Mani makes a strangled noise behind me. I follow his gaze and stop cold.

On the other side of the flat, Smudge is stretched out in a sticky puddle of blood. Her belly is sliced open from her chest to her tail, and her entrails spill onto the floor. Her paw rests on the corner of a blood-smeared note written in script large enough that I don't even have to bend down to read it: *Mani is next. We look forward to your compliance.*

I grab Mani's hand and pull him out of the flat so I can retch in the alley. I can't stop gagging, even when there's nothing left in my stomach. I press my back against the wall, gasping for air. I think of Smudge suffering—of her tiny mews of pain or fear—and I start to heave again. It takes me several minutes to catch my breath, and then the full weight of the note hits me. I need to get Mani out of here. Gopal must already know I defied him, and that means we're out of time. I race back into the flat, grab a bag and fill it with as many clothes as it will hold. I wish that I could take the time to give Smudge a proper burial, but I don't dare stay longer. I crouch down and rub my fingers between her ears just how she liked.

"I'm sorry," I say softly as I stroke her fur. "I'm so sorry."

Mani is sobbing silently behind me. "Bye, kitty," he says, but he's not looking at her. His face is pressed against my back, his tears soaking through my sari.

I stand up and sling my bag over my shoulder. "Come on, Mani," I say. "Time to run."

• •

We sprint all the way to Gali Street. Now that we have no money and no supplies, it's the only place I can think to go. Last week Japa told me I could come to him if things were ever bad. I hope he's willing to keep his promise.

By the time we're standing in front of the bookshop, Mani's lips are blue. The shops have all closed, but I'm hoping Japa is still here. I haven't been back since the day I was searching for Deven and found the CLOSED sign dangling in the window. For a sickening moment I worry that Japa never came back, that he's gone forever. I hold my breath as

I rap on the door, and when it finally opens, I sigh in relief. But as soon as I see Japa, I know that Deven has already been here. Japa is eyeing me warily and his whole face is turned down. It's an expression I've never seen him wear before and it makes him seem years older. I swallow hard. "I'm in trouble."

His whole body is rigid and he doesn't answer right away. Then his gaze slides to Mani and his expression softens a little.

"Please," I say.

He sighs deeply and rakes his fingers through his silver hair. Finally he opens the door wider. "Come in," he says. "Hurry."

The bookshop looks different in the dim light. Long shadows climb the walls, and the same silence that is restful in daylight feels ominous now. Mani shivers beside me and I squeeze his fingers. Japa locks the door before he turns to us.

"What kind of trouble?"

I ignore his question and ask my own. "Have you talked to Deven?" It isn't my only question, just my least desperate one. There are so many things I want to ask: *Is he alive? Has he left Sundari? Do you think he'll ever forgive me?*

Japa scowls. "I'll ask the questions," he says tersely. "What kind of trouble?"

My head is pounding and I press my fingers to my temples. "Mani and I can't go home," I say finally.

"And why is that?"

"I can't tell you," I say. "But we're in danger. You said that I could come to you if things . . . if things were bad."

He shakes his head. "That was before I knew who you were."

I wince. I'm not surprised he said it, only surprised at how much it hurts. Until this moment I didn't realize how much Japa's approval meant to me. It takes me a moment to find my voice. "I know you must hate me, but Mani didn't do anything. Will you help him? I'll leave if you'll just promise to keep him safe."

"No," Mani says sharply. "You can't leave me." He grabs my wrist with both of his hands, but I ignore him and keep my gaze fixed on Japa.

"He's only a child," I say. "Please, Japa. He could stay in the room behind the bookcase. Just until I can gather supplies so we can leave Sundari."

At the mention of the secret room, his eyes narrow. "How do you know about our safe room? Is this something you learned from your contacts—something to help you kill Deven?"

"What? No," I say. "I know because you leave it dusty and there are fingerprints where it slides open. And the door clicks softly. And sometimes there's cool air that slides beneath the shelving."

His gaze is still razor sharp and so I keep talking. "You and Deven sometimes disappear—I knew you had to go somewhere. You're not as careful as you think. But I would never hurt you or him—no matter what you may have heard. Japa"—my voice breaks—"they'll kill us if we go back."

Mani begins sobbing and buries his face in my arm. Japa's eyes flick between the two of us, a tangle of emotions playing out on his face. Finally he presses his lips together and gives me a small nod.

"Follow me," he says.

He leads us to the bookcase at the back of the shop and then pauses to examine the shiny fingerprints on the side of the wood. He grumbles as he wipes them away. Then he pushes the bookcase aside to reveal a set of narrow stairs, which we follow down into a spacious underground room.

Shelves line one wall, and a desk piled with messy stacks of papers sits in the corner. Boxes of books fill half the room, and a map of Sundari is tacked to the wall.

"Mani can sleep here for a few days," Japa says. "But then we'll have to figure out something else." Mani's sobs have turned to wails now and my sleeve is damp with his tears.

"Please don't leave me," he sobs. "Please."

Japa pats Mani on the back. "Marinda isn't going anywhere," he says. My head snaps up, but Japa is focused only on Mani.

Mani sniffles. "She can stay?"

Japa meets my gaze. "For tonight," he says, then turns back to Mani. "But first I need you to rest while I talk to your sister. Okay?"

Mani nods. "Okay."

Japa rifles through a cabinet and produces several blankets and a pillow. He busies himself making a bed on a wooden pallet in the corner of the room. Mani has stopped crying, but he is still struggling to pull in enough air. I rub circles on his back and remind him to breathe. Japa stands up and watches the two of us without speaking. Gradually Mani's breath comes with less work. "You get some rest," I tell him, turning his shoulders toward the pallet. "I'll be right upstairs if you need me."

He crawls onto the makeshift bed and wraps himself in a blanket. Japa and I climb the stairs, and before I can even pull the door closed, Mani's breathing is beginning to deepen. Japa motions for me to follow him to the back of the bookshop. He leads me to a small table with two chairs. I sit down and put my head in my hands.

"Thank you," I say without looking up.

Japa slides a chair out and sits heavily. "Start talking," he says.

I'm exhausted. I can feel it deep in my bones—a weariness so complete it feels like resignation. I'm tired of worrying and sneaking and keeping secrets.

I sigh. "I'm an assassin." I expect Japa to look shocked or angry, so I'm taken off guard by the sadness in his eyes.

"For how long?"

My throat feels like it's closing up. "Since I was a little girl."

Japa sucks in a sharp breath. "But that can't be," he says. The expression on his face is shocked, but the hard angles have softened and he looks more like himself. It gives me courage to keep speaking.

"It's not a life I ever wanted," I tell him. "I never really had a choice."

Japa's eyes are wet. He rests a hand on my forearm. "Marinda, we always have a choice."

I shake my head because he doesn't understand. "When I was five, the Raja gave me the option: become his assassin or leave Sundari forever. Where would I have gone at five? It wasn't much of a choice."

"The Raja?" Deep lines have carved themselves into Japa's forehead. "At five?"

"Yes," I say. "I had to be loyal to the kingdom or leave."

Japa presses his lips together and stares off into the distance. "You had orders to kill Deven?"

"Yes," I say.

"And so you meant to accomplish that by poisoning him?"

"No," I say. "Of course not."

Japa's face is twisted in confusion. "Deven said you'd been slipping him doses of poison."

Tears prickle at the corners of my eyes. "I was trying to make him immune," I say softly.

"Immune from what?"

"From me. From others like me."

Japa raises his eyebrows in a question. I press the heels of my hands to my eyes. I don't want to say it out loud, but there's no other way to make him understand.

"My kiss is deadly," I say. "I was supposed to kiss Deven,

but I couldn't do it. He was too good and too kind. But if I didn't, I knew that my handler would send another girl, so I had to make him immune to protect him."

"A *visha kanya*?" Japa breathes.

My pulse quickens. "You've heard of us?"

"Only in legends," he says. "It's not possible. And the Raja would never . . ." He shakes his head. "It's just not possible."

"I wish that were true." We sit quietly for a moment, each absorbed in our own thoughts. And then I say, "Deven says Mani has *vish bimari*. Have you ever heard of that?"

Japa nods. "It's clear that he does—the trouble breathing, the lack of energy, the way his eyes are always dilated. That's why I told you to come to me if you needed help. I thought someone was hurting the two of you. I never suspected . . ." He trails off, but I can guess the rest of the thought. He never suspected it was me hurting Mani.

"It wasn't me making him sick," I say.

"You didn't give him poison?"

"Of course not. I would never hurt Mani." I lower my eyes to my hands. "I thought it was a problem with his lungs. But now—I think my handler has been slowly poisoning him over the last several years. Until Deven accused me of hurting him . . . I didn't think it was possible."

Japa shifts in his chair and scrubs a hand over his face. "You understand that I'm finding it difficult to trust you?"

"I do. I'm not asking you to trust me. I'm just asking

you to help me help Mani. None of this is his fault." My voice breaks. "I can't lose him."

Japa stands up and begins pacing around the storeroom. "So what's your plan?"

I trace circles on the tabletop with my fingers. "There's a village tucked away in a small valley high in the mountains—"

"The Widows' Village?" Japa interrupts.

"Yes," I say. "You know about it?"

"The question is, how do you know about it?"

"I . . ." Thinking about that day gives me a dull ache in my chest. I can almost feel the pressure of Deven's palm against mine, the cool mountain breeze on my cheeks. "Deven showed me," I say softly. "We went on a hike and he took me there as a surprise."

Japa's eyes go wide. "He did?" His voice is full of astonishment. "He must have cared about you a great deal more than I realized."

I bite my lip. It doesn't escape my notice that Japa used the past tense, and I try to push away the sting with a question.

"Do you think the widows would take care of Mani? If I can get him there safely?"

Japa nods. "It's a good idea," he says. "I think it's likely they would."

Relief fills my chest at the thought of Mani tucked away safe in the mountains. But there are so many steps between here and there. "I need to get him well first," I tell Japa. "Is there a cure? Do you know?"

Japa drums his fingers on the back of the chair. "I'm not an expert on *vish bimari,* but from what I understand, it can only be cured with an antidote," he says.

"So, where do I get one?"

He sighs. "Well, that's the tricky part. You have to know the exact source of the poison. I don't suppose you know where it came from?"

Kadru. I stand up so fast that my chair falls over. "I have to go," I tell Japa. "Keep Mani safe." I start toward the door, but Japa catches my wrist and spins me around.

"You can't go now," he says. "It's pitch-black outside. It's not safe."

"I have to. Mani needs me."

"Marinda, you promised him you'd stay. Get some rest. Wait until morning."

I chew on the corner of my lip. I want nothing more than to run all the way to Kadru's tent and demand that she help me. But Japa is right. Mani would be devastated to wake up and find me gone. "Fine," I tell him. "I'll leave at first light."

Before I go to bed, I take a damp cloth and wipe down every inch of the bookcase in front of the safe room until it gleams like all the others. I close the door behind me and wedge a rolled-up rug into the space at the bottom of the door to block any breeze from escaping into the room above us.

Mani doesn't stir when I pull a second pallet beside him.

As I crawl into my makeshift bed and close my eyes, a kernel of hope takes root in my chest—there's a chance I can find a way to heal Mani, a chance we can finally escape. It occurs to me that this is the first time in as long as I can remember that I'm falling asleep in a bed Gopal doesn't own. And even with the horrible day I've had, the thought makes me smile.

CHAPTER THIRTEEN

I stand outside Kadru's tent the next morning with my heart in my throat. All the way here I was full of fiery indignation, ready to make demands and insist on answers. But now the thought of facing the snakes has turned my resolve slushy. I wipe my palms against my sari and try to breathe through my nose. I love Mani more than I fear the snakes. I faced the snakes to get the toxin for Deven and I can do it again to find answers for the antidote.

"Kadru," I call out, and my voice betrays me by trembling. "Kadru?"

She opens the flap and greets me with a wide smile. "I told you we'd be meeting again soon," she says. I bristle at her self-satisfied tone, but I don't say anything. Kadru is dressed in scarlet today. Her hair is plaited in hundreds of tiny braids that are twisted into a wreath on top of her head. Rubies hang from her earlobes and neck. Her fingernails, toenails and lips are all painted the same bright crimson.

"Don't just stand there, Marinda," Kadru says. "Come in." She pulls the flap wider—white snakes cover every surface, and I have to swallow my fear to move forward into the tent. I keep my eyes trained on my sandals. I try to breathe deeply, but pulling in more air only intensifies the musky reptilian smell that makes me want to gag.

Kadru turns to face me. "Was there a reason for your visit, darling? Or did you just miss me?"

My stomach twists and I'm not sure if it's nausea or anger. I focus my whole attention on Kadru's face, try to pretend we're alone so that I can speak to her without distraction. "I need to ask you about an antidote."

"An antidote?" She laughs. "Oops. Did you give your boyfriend too much venom?"

I shake my head. "No, he's not my boyfriend and it's not for him. It's for my brother."

"Your brother?" Her confusion looks genuine. "Oh, you mean that little boy Gopal gave you for a pet?"

I go hot all over. "Mani is not a *pet*."

"I never said pets were *bad*, Marinda. Look around—I adore my pets." I refuse to look and she sniffs as if offended. "Either way, I can't help you."

"Why not?"

"Because I don't have an antidote."

She has to be lying. "How could you not? Look around." I throw her own words back at her but she just holds my gaze, and when she speaks, her voice is gentle.

"I tolerate the snakes the same way you do, my darling. I'm immune."

"You really don't have an antidote?"

She shakes her head sadly. "I really don't. I can't think of a single reason why I would ever need one."

"But . . ." I'm at a loss for words. If Kadru can't help me with this, there is no one else who can. I press a hand to my forehead. There must be something.

"What about the Raja?" I ask. "If you could tell me how to contact him—how to get through the guards at the palace—maybe he could help."

Kadru's eyes widen. "Surely you don't think you belong to *that* Raja."

My stomach goes cold and my pulse is beating out a warning. "What other Raja would there be?"

Her mouth pulls down at the corners and she strokes one of the snakes absently. Her jeweled fingers send light bouncing around the walls of the tent.

"What other Raja?" I repeat more forcefully. Kadru meets my eyes.

"The Nagaraja," she says softly. I take a step back.

"Nagaraja? The Snake King? No, that can't be right. Gopal always said . . ." I stop talking, trying to remember what Gopal said. Did he ever specifically say the Raja of

Sundari? I can't remember. Kadru is watching me carefully, studying my face in a way that sends gooseflesh racing up my arms. There's something almost sad in her expression.

"He really never told you?"

"He never tells me *anything* except that we are working for the Raja."

She sighs and falls into her chair. Two large snakes follow her and coil themselves at her feet. Another snake drops onto her shoulders from a bamboo pole above. "We serve the Nagaraja, Marinda. He specifically chose you. Surely Gopal told you that much?"

My fingernails bite into the tender flesh of my palms. "He told me the *Raja* chose me. The Nagaraja . . . the Raksaka . . . those are just stories." My heartbeat is roaring in my ears. This can't be happening. The only thing that has kept me from hating myself completely is knowing that I'm serving my kingdom, helping the Raja fight evil. If I've been killing for any other reason . . . I clap my hand over my mouth. I really am the monster that Deven thinks I am.

"I'm sorry to upset you," Kadru says kindly. "Gopal really should have told you by now. But now that you know, maybe it will make things easier."

"Easier? How would it make things easier? I will never kill for Gopal again. I won't serve a *snake*."

Kadru's eyes fly wide in alarm. The snakes at her feet turn their heads toward me and hiss in unison. Their eyes look like polished onyx. "Hush, Marinda," she says. "You're just upset. Of course you will serve the Nagaraja. Of course you will obey Gopal's orders." Her voice is soothing and sweet, but there's a warning under the surface.

"No," I say, my voice as hard as flint. "I won't. He can have one of the other *vish kanya* do his bidding."

She jerks her head back. "One of the *other vish kanya?*" Her face reddens and she flies to her feet, sending the snakes slithering away. "Gopal is a fool. Has he told you the truth about anything?" I just stare at her because how would I know that? Kadru begins pacing. "There are no other *vish kanya*, Marinda. The Nagaraja chooses only one."

"That's a lie," I tell her. This I'm sure about. We are arranged in pairs—both Gopal and Gita have been clear about that. Part *visha kanya*, part spy.

Kadru raises her eyebrows. "Have you ever met another one?"

My certainty falters. "Well, no. But only because it's against tradecraft."

She releases a breath through pursed lips. "It has nothing to do with tradecraft. You've never met another *visha kanya* because you are the only one. You have been for years. Gopal lied to you."

"How do you know that?" I shoot back. "Maybe he lied to you."

She laughs. "I know because *I* was the last *visha kanya*." The tent suddenly feels far too warm. My legs go spongy and I look for a place to sit down, but the snakes have claimed every surface. "I used to be you," Kadru continues. "And when the Nagaraja grows tired of you or when you become too deadly to be useful, you will become me."

My throat starts to close. I can't imagine a worse fate than being Kadru, stuck in a tent, surrounded by the snakes I detest. Holding children down while serpents feed on them and listening to their screams while their blood becomes toxic. Stealing years from girls who don't have any other options. Kadru and I are nothing alike.

She walks in a lazy circle around me, and the snakes follow her until I'm surrounded on all sides. I can barely breathe. "I don't see how I could be too deadly to be useful," I say through clenched teeth. I desperately want her to be lying.

"Oh, you will be," she says. "The poison is part of you now. And it will build and build until in a few hundred years you'll be able to kill with nothing more than a touch."

"That's not true," I say. It can't be.

"Do you remember the first boy you killed? How long did it take him to die? Five hours? Six? Darling Marinda, *my* kiss would kill a man in seconds." She throws her head back and laughs. "Hardly subtle enough for assassination, but I make a marvelous executioner." She leans close and her next words are only a whisper against my ear. "And as the years go by, you will too."

I press my fingers against my eyelids. The horror of my future stretches out in front of me like an endless desert— living forever trapped in a prison of poison. Killing the Nagaraja's enemies and demanding more life for myself as payment to help other girls become killers. I'd rather die tomorrow than live a thousand years like that. "No," I say. "I won't become you. It doesn't matter if I'm the only *visha kanya*. I'm still done."

Kadru steps toward me and drags a scarlet nail down the side of my face. "No, my sweet. You will never be done. Gopal is a snake worshiper—a loyal member of the Naga. When the Nagaraja chose you as his princess, you became an object of worship for them. And they will never, ever let you go. They will hunt you, chase you, follow you to the ends of the earth. Like it or not, you belong to them."

All the air leaves my lungs. Princess. *Rajakumari*. It's what Gopal has called me all my life—she's telling me the truth. I think of the snake tattoos coiled around Gopal's arms and I feel sick. I've been so stupid thinking I was nobly serving the kingdom.

"Go back to Gopal," Kadru says. "Apologize. Promise to be a good little killer. *Rajakumari* or not, the Naga aren't afraid of meting out punishment." She searches my face. "But you probably already know that."

"Who was I killing?" I ask. "All this time, who was I killing?"

Kadru shrugs. "Many in Sundari don't care for the Naga. You've been killing those who are actively trying to stop us."

"Why would they want to stop us?" I ask, and then cringe at the word *us*. I don't want to be one of them. I won't.

"They don't approve of some of our practices," she says evasively.

"Such as?"

Her eyes slide away and she strokes the head of a snake hanging nearby. "The Nagaraja must be fed," she says lightly. "Sundari would like for us to stop feeding him humans."

• •

The walk back through the market feels like a dream. I'm vaguely aware of crowds—of bustling people pushing past me, brushing against my shoulders, pressing into my side, of children clinging to their parents or skipping away, of carts bumping along the cobblestones. But the images are like scattered pieces of broken glass, disconnected and confusing. Everything sounds muffled and I am numb inside.

My head is heavy with all that Kadru told me, with all the lies that Gopal made me believe. I feel as if I've stepped into a nightmare—one filled with cults of snake worshipers and brothers who die and sisters who kill—and I'm longing to wake up. But worst of all, I'm returning empty-handed.

I can't save Mani, just like I couldn't save Deven. They are both in danger because of me, and I haven't been able to help either one of them. I hoped to return with an antidote so that Mani and I could escape together. But now I'll need to get him to safety and keep searching until I find a way to heal him. But the thought of being without him fills me with an aching emptiness.

I walk past vendors calling out enticements—waving bright scarves and bits of meat for sampling. An old man with gnarled fingers shakes a small bag of herbs in front of my face. "Remedies, remedies," he calls. "Remedies for broken hearts and broken bones. Remedies for every ailment." I stop for a moment and gape at his booth. Hundreds of bags line the shelves behind him, and dried herbs swing from the wooden rafters. He sees me watching him. "What's your trouble, miss? I've got cures for everything." Deep lines carve through his face, and his shoulders are curved with age. He grins at me, revealing two rows of yellowed teeth.

"Do you have a cure for *vish bimari*?" I ask, not daring to hope. His smile evaporates and he takes a step back.

"My condolences, miss." He turns his back and doesn't speak again until I start walking away. I hear his voice call out behind me, "Remedies, remedies." I swallow a lump in my throat. Things are so bad for Mani that even charlatans don't dare to promise relief.

Suddenly the urge to be as far away from Bala City as possible overwhelms me. I need to get Mani to the Widows' Village while he still has the energy to travel. If I think beyond that to what comes next, to how I'll find an antidote—to *if* I'll find one—I'll be too paralyzed to move. Instead I focus on Mani's future. Think about how he'll live with a grandmotherly woman who will spoil him. About how he'll fall asleep feeling safe and wake up with sunlight on his face.

One foot in front of the other. One step at a time until I'm finally back to Gali Street. The bookshop is stuffy with afternoon heat. Dust motes dance in the sunlight that streams through the windows. This is always a quiet time of day for business. Japa calls it the midday lull, when the sun renders the customers too drowsy for shopping. But it's even more silent than usual, and it makes my arms break out in gooseflesh. And then I notice that the bells that are usually attached to the door are lying on the floor and I stop breathing.

I race around the corner to the safe room and my blood runs cold. The bookcase is pulled away from the wall, splintered into chunks as if it's been attacked with an axe. A sob tears from my throat as I see Japa lying facedown at the top of the stairs. His cheek rests in a crimson puddle and his head is split open. Dried blood is crusted in his silver hair. Scattered on the floor near his head are a handful of coins. They look Sundarian, with one major difference—three members of the Raksaka are missing. These coins feature only the Snake King.

"Mani!" I scream. "Mani!"

I scramble past Japa toward where I left Mani sleeping only a few hours ago, but I slip and slam my elbows into the floor. I try to claw my way to my feet, but the stairs are slick with fluid and I can't get purchase. I half crawl, half stumble down to the safe room. Blood covers my hands and knees, and I'm terrified that it's not just Japa's blood.

"Mani!" I shove boxes out of the way, sending them flying to the ground smeared with bloody stripes from my stained fingers. Maybe he's hiding. Maybe he saw Gopal coming, got scared and hid somewhere in this room. Maybe there's still a shred of hope. But no matter how many boxes fall to the ground, I can't find him. I tear through the rest of the bookshop calling Mani's name, but only sickening silence answers.

CHAPTER FOURTEEN

I can't stop staring at Japa. I don't know how long I've been here, sitting on the floor of the bookshop with my knees pulled to my chest. It feels like hours, but I don't know for sure because time seems twisted out of shape by the fear pulsing through me, by my worry for Mani.

I long to squeeze my eyes shut, to block out the image of Japa's prostrate body. Of his once-kind face now frozen in an expression of perpetual shock that makes him look like a stranger. But my eyes won't obey me. They stay fixed on him, as if looking away will force me to acknowledge that it's real—that Japa met the same fate as every other man who has gotten too close to me. That Mani is really gone.

But the longer I sit here, the more my panic and grief fade away, and cold calm comes over me. Iyla was right; my love for Mani made it effortless to control me. I've been so desperate to protect him that I would do anything, *be* anything, to keep my brother safe. But by taking Mani, Gopal has twisted that love into something far more powerful.

Now it will be the weapon I use to destroy him.

I stand up and slide Japa's eyes closed with my fingertips. It feels wrong to leave him here all alone, but I have no choice. I have to find out where the Naga took my brother. And to do that I have to find out what Deven did that made them want him dead.

*   *

This time I don't hesitate outside Deven's flat. There's something liberating about knowing he already hates me, about realizing I don't need to measure my words. I climb his steps and pound on the door with the flat side of my fist.

He doesn't answer right away, and a shiver of fear snakes down my spine at the thought that the Naga might have gotten here first. I pound harder.

"Deven?" I shout. "Open up."

The door opens just a crack. "Did you come to finish me off?"

The question should enrage me, but I'm flooded with stupid relief at the sound of his voice. He's alive. There's still a chance of saving someone today.

"If I wanted to kill you, you'd already be dead. I need information, but first we need to leave. I'll ask you questions on the way."

He snorts. "Do you honestly think I'd go anywhere with you? Leave, Marinda. I can take care of myself."

"Japa is dead."

The door swings wide and the horror on Deven's face sends a fresh wave of pain through me. "What?" He takes in my tearstained face, and his gaze drifts down the length of my body, lingers on my hands. Suddenly I realize I'm still covered in Japa's blood. It's smeared across my sari, caked under my fingernails.

Deven presses the back of his hand to his mouth. "Did you . . ."

I don't wait for him to finish the question—that he would even need to ask if I hurt Japa stings like a slap. "They took Mani," I tell him, and my chest aches at the thought of my tiny brother suffering at Gopal's hands. "They'll be coming for you next. We need to leave *now*."

He doesn't say anything, and for a moment I worry that he'll refuse to come with me. But then he gives a resigned sigh. "Come in while I get a bag ready." I follow him into the house and he reaches around me to push the door closed. My nose is filled with the scent of him—wood carvings and cinnamon and indifference. It's hard to breathe. Without my permission, my fingers reach to stroke the cricket in my pocket.

The inside of Deven's house looks completely different than I pictured it. While Iyla's living space was filled with oversized chairs, glossy dark wood and sumptuous fabrics,

Deven's is barely furnished at all. Directly to my left is a threadbare sofa, and on the far side of the room sits a rickety table flanked by two chairs. Other than that, the room is empty. It scarcely looks lived in. I stand awkwardly in front of the door while Deven pulls a bag from a shelf in the closet and starts filling it with supplies.

"Where are we going?" he asks.

"I don't know yet," I say. "We just need to get as far away as possible."

He sighs and slings the bag over his shoulder. "I know a place," he says. "Let's go."

He doesn't wait for me before jogging down the steps and taking a sharp left. I scramble to follow, but when I catch up to him, breathless, he doesn't acknowledge me. We weave through back alleys and side streets without speaking. I glance over my shoulder every so often to make sure we're not being followed. Kadru's warning that the Naga will never let me go thrums at the back of my mind, and a shiver goes through me as I think about being hunted like an animal.

"Are you cold?" Deven asks, and before I can stop myself, I give a bitter laugh. He looks hurt. "What's funny?"

"Just that you can't help but be a gentleman even when you think I've been trying to kill you."

He scowls at me. "I only asked a question. I didn't say I was going to do anything about it."

"Fair enough."

"I don't even have a wrap to offer you," he says

impatiently. "So obviously I wasn't being a gentleman." He shoves his hands into his pockets.

"It doesn't matter," I say. "I'm not cold."

"Good."

We walk in silence for several minutes and then Deven says, "What do you mean I *think* you've been trying to kill me?"

I sigh. "Like I said before, if I wanted to kill you, you'd already be dead."

"So you were poisoning me for fun?" His sarcastic tone crawls under my skin, and I stop walking After a moment, he spins to face me.

"I wasn't *poisoning* you!" I shout. "I was trying to make you immune."

Several people stop to stare and I feel my cheeks flame. I put my head down and hurry forward, pushing past strangers, desperate to put distance between me and . . . and I don't know what. Because it's impossible to run from your own mistakes. Deven catches up and falls in step with me but doesn't speak. Which is a good thing, because I'm fuming. I know that I have no right to anger. I realize that Deven is the wronged party, not me. But my mind can't convince the rest of my body. My stomach is boiling with rage; my heart is on fire with it.

It takes twenty minutes of silence for me to calm down. Deven doesn't speak the entire time, and whether he is giving me space to be angry, or whether he is angry himself, I can't tell. But either way I can't afford to let my pride jeopardize Mani's safety. I need information from Deven, and so I will let him say whatever he needs to say, no matter how the words slice through me.

Once my heartbeat steadies, I clear my throat. "I wasn't the one making Mani sick," I say. I don't know why this feels like the most urgent thing to explain. Maybe because of all the things he believes about me, this one cuts the deepest. That I would hurt Mani. "I never even considered Mani might have *vish bimari* until yesterday when you said . . ." I shift uncomfortably as I remember the look on his face when he said what I had done was disgusting. "When you said what you said. I would never poison Mani, and I thought that I must be making him sick just by being near him, but then—"

"Wait," Deven says. "Just by being near him? How is that even possible?"

My mouth goes dry. "I'm a *visha kanya*," I say, and the disbelief on his face morphs into shock. He opens his mouth, but I keep talking before he has the chance to say something hurtful again. "Japa said people think they are only legends, but here I am. The people I work for—used to work for—made me this way as a baby. When I kiss people"—I can't look at him anymore, so I shift my gaze to the floor—"they die. So if I'd wanted to kill you, I wouldn't have needed to poison your drink."

He doesn't say anything for a moment. "As a baby?" he says finally. It's the last question I expect. I nod and he holds my gaze for a moment. There's something in his expression that I can't read, and I'm not sure if he believes me or not. I decide to keep talking. "Gopal—my handler—he's been poisoning Mani. I thought the breathing treatments were to help his lungs, but I should have known better. Japa said there might be an antidote, and so this morning I went to the person who made me a *visha kanya,* but she couldn't help. And when I came back, Mani was gone and Japa was . . ." I swallow the words as an image of Japa's body assaults me.

"I know how to get the antidote," Deven says softly.

My head snaps up. "You do?"

He gives me a long look before he answers. "It's the maraka fruit."

"That doesn't make any sense," I say. "How can a fruit be an antidote?"

"My father grows them in his orchard," Deven says. "They took years to perfect, but they work."

Mani did feel better every time he ate them. I think of all the grapes and pears I've forced on him over the past week, assuming that it was more fruit in general that he needed instead of realizing that what Deven had offered was special. The irony slams into me—finding a cure when it's too late, when I've already lost Mani.

"You've been trying to help him all along," I say. A wave of affection washes over me. Deven still cares about Mani, even though he despises me. I've been wrong about so many things that it feels good to be right about this one.

"What kind of a person would I be if I didn't?"

There's so much I want to say to him—about how he is exactly as good as I suspected and about how I'm not quite as bad as he thinks—but I can't find the words for any of it. And right now it doesn't matter. The most important thing is finding Mani.

"Now it's time for you to start talking," I say. "Why would your father need to spend years perfecting an antidote to snake venom?"

Instead of answering, Deven steers us into a tiny passageway between two buildings, and at first I think he's stopping to give us some privacy so that he can answer my question. But then he pulls a key from his pocket. "We're here."

CHAPTER FIFTEEN

I'm not sure where *here* is, since we're surrounded by walls on three sides.

Deven rests one hand against the side of the building as he slides the key into a small opening, and I watch wide-eyed as a door-shaped portion of the wall swings inward. I throw him a questioning look, but he just puts a hand on the small of my back and pushes me forward. I step into a small flat not that different from the one I shared with Mani. Three freshly made beds are pressed against one wall, and a table is wedged into a corner. Several chairs are scattered throughout the room. It looks more lived in than Deven's house, but not by much.

"Where are we?" I ask.

Deven sits heavily on the side of one of the beds. "It's a safe house," he tells me.

"I can't stay here," I tell him. "You have to tell me what you know and then I have to find Mani." I move toward the door, but Deven catches my hand.

"We'll talk," he says. "And we'll find him. But why don't you go clean up first?"

I look down at the front of my sari, soaked with Japa's blood. It's all over my hands, arms and elbows—red streaks, little pieces of Japa. Now that some time has passed, the sight of it makes me want to gag, but there's nothing in my stomach. I can't remember the last time I ate anything. I can't imagine ever wanting to eat again. Deven stands up and rests a hand on my shoulder.

"There's a shower in the back," he says. "And we keep extra clothes here. I'll find something in your size."

I look at him blankly. I have so many questions, but a shower isn't such a bad idea. I numbly follow Deven to the washroom and accept the towel he gives me. "I'll be right out here," he says. I nod and close the door. I turn the shower all the way to hot and climb in still fully dressed. The scalding water flows over me, sending rivulets of red swirling around my ankles. Blood is caked under my fingernails, and my hair is stiff with it. When the water finally runs clear, I turn down the heat and strip off my wet clothes. Then I stand under the water and scrub my skin until it's raw.

Deven has slipped a stack of clean clothes inside the door—a black linen tunic with matching black pants. Simple and comfortable. I towel off, dress quickly and wrap the towel around my dripping hair. I scoop up my wet sandals and return to the main room of the flat. Deven is sitting on the bed with his head in his hands. He looks up when he hears my footsteps and I'm startled to see that his eyes are red-rimmed and swollen. I've been so focused on myself, on Mani, that I didn't think about how hard it would be for Deven to hear about Japa's death—Deven knew him longer than I did, loved him more.

"I'm so sorry," I say.

He just nods. I wish I could wrap my arms around him, to try to comfort him, but we both know that this is my fault. If I hadn't left Mani behind . . . if I hadn't gone to Japa in the first place. Every decision I make turns ugly. If Deven hated me before, I can't imagine what he feels now. I sit on the bed farthest from Deven and tuck my legs underneath me.

"I wish I didn't have to ask," I say. "But can you tell me more about why the Naga want to kill you? It might give me some idea why this mission is so important to them. Or where they would take Mani."

"Shouldn't you know why they want me dead? You're the one who works for them."

"They've never given me much detail. I only found out about the Naga this morning."

Deven slams his fist against his thigh. "Stop it, Marinda. I can't help you if you keep lying to me."

"It's the truth," I shoot back. "Gopal—my handler—always told me I worked for the Raja."

He gives a humorless bark of laughter. "The Raja? You thought you were killing men for the Raja?"

My cheeks grow hot. When I hear it said back to me, I can see how I must look either foolish or deceitful. I tug on the hem of my sleeve. "I know it sounds stupid. But it's what I believed my whole life until today. If I'd had any idea I was serving the Nagaraja, I would never have . . ." But the lie dies on my lips. Because I would have done anything to save Mani.

His eyes narrow and I can tell he's deciding how much to trust me. I hold his gaze and hope it's at least a little.

"Look, I know you might not believe me. But do you care about Mani?"

His expression softens a fraction. "Do you?" I press.

"Of course I do," he says.

"Then help me find him."

"That's the problem," Deven says. "I don't know how to do that." He sighs and pulls on the back of his neck. "I wish Iyla were here." The statement makes me feel like I've been slapped.

"Well, I'm sorry that your girlfriend can't be here to spare you from dealing with me," I shoot back. "But I'm all you've got."

He studies me with a furrowed brow. "Iyla's not my girlfriend," he says. "I wish she were here because she might know where the Naga would hide Mani."

"Now look who's lying," I say, and I can't quite keep the bitterness out of my voice.

He raises one eyebrow in the maddening way that he does. "You're saying you know for a fact that I have a girl-friend that I'm not aware I have?"

"I saw you kiss her," I say.

"When?"

"About a week ago. You were standing outside her house and it looked like the two of you were saying goodbye."

Deven's eyes narrow. "And where were you?"

My cheeks heat. "Hiding behind a topiary elephant."

"Why?"

"Don't change the subject."

He sighs. "Iyla works with me," he says. "I thought you would have figured that out by now." I swallow hard. Is that the story she fed him? That she was helping him in some way?

"No," I say. "I'm sorry that she lied to you, but Iyla works with me."

He shakes his head and it makes my pulse spike with anger. He's so sure he has all the answers.

"Iyla grew up with me," I say. "We've worked together since we were small. Are you suggesting that I'm so delusional I imagined it?"

"Of course not." He stands up and goes to the kitchen. I hop off the bed and follow him.

"What, then?"

Deven opens one of the cabinets, pulls out a glass and fills it with water. "Iyla decided to leave the Naga two years ago. She came to our group—"

"What group?" I interrupt. I don't believe that Iyla was really working with Deven—she was tasked with helping me kill him, after all—but maybe if he keeps talking, I'll be able to make sense of what she *was* doing.

He hesitates. "We're spies for the Raja," Deven says. *Spies for the Raja.* Suddenly all the pieces fall into place—the whispered conversations with Japa, the comments about being loyal to the kingdom, Deven's knowledge about how the Widows' Village came to be.

And my orders to kill him.

Deven is serving the master I grew up believing *I* was serving. He searches my face and then continues. "We call ourselves the Pakshi," he says. *Pakshi.* Bird.

"Is that why you like Garuda?" I say, remembering his tattoo. And—my stomach twists—Iyla's earrings.

Deven takes a long drink of water before answering. "We don't just like Garuda. We believe that Garuda is the key to stopping the Naga." *The key to stopping the Naga?*

"You don't mean that the whole Raksaka lives? That they're all more than legend?"

Deven gives me a curious look, and then understanding dawns on his face. "Your handlers didn't teach you from the histories," he says. It's not a question.

I bite my lip. I hate the sense of powerlessness that comes from ignorance. "No," I say. "They didn't."

Something shifts in his expression, and for the first time in days he's not looking at me like I'm a liar. "Okay," he says. "What do you know?"

"That there are four members of the Raksaka," I say. "That they are the protectors of Sundari."

"Is that all?"

I play with the hem of my sleeve. "That they are on our coins and our flags," I say. "And the uniforms of Sundari's soldiers." I try to think if there is anything else I know, but I can't come up with anything. My cheeks are warm.

Deven doesn't speak for a moment. He just watches me, a dozen emotions flickering across his face. Finally he clears his throat. "The Raksaka was composed of four members. The bird, Garuda, to rule the skies, the tiger to rule the land, the crocodile to rule the waters, and the snake to rule the underground. For years they lived in perfect balance, no animal more powerful than the other. But the snake wanted more power. He craved it." Deven leans against the counter and folds his arms across his chest. "The only way for a member of the Raksaka to gain power was to gain followers, and so the snake began to search for humans who wanted power too—humans who would be willing to follow the snake, and the snake alone. As the snake gained supporters, he grew."

I swallow. "His power grew, you mean?"

Deven nods. "His power, yes. But also his body. As the balance of power shifted, the snake physically grew. He grew massive."

Gooseflesh races across my skin. "And the other animals?"

"Got smaller," Deven says. "Eventually the snake

learned how to transfer some of his power to humans, and they began to kill the followers of the rest of the Raksaka." I press the back of my hand to my mouth. Humans like me. Humans who killed on command. "Which, of course, only made the snake's power stronger.

"When the snake was strong enough," Deven continues, "he came up from the underground and set fire to the world." With a lurch I remember the illustration from the ancient book Japa showed me—the villagers running from a snake with fire bursting from its mouth.

"The Dark Days," I breathe.

"Yes," Deven says. "The Dark Days. The tiger and the crocodile disappeared. Most people assume they were killed off—they had grown small and weak and were easy targets. But Garuda . . . Garuda could fly." He unfolds his arms and leans forward. "She had shrunken to the size of a hummingbird, but still the snake couldn't destroy her. The people of Sundari were desperate for relief, and so Garuda's followers grew and grew until she was big enough to blot out the sun. Big enough to force the Nagaraja underground again."

"So where is she now?" I ask.

Deven shrugs. "We don't know. Once Sundari was safe again, most of Garuda's followers grew complacent and she disappeared. We hope that if her followers grow, she will show herself again. But the Naga are growing far faster than the Pakshi, and the Snake King is becoming more and more powerful."

A wave of nausea rolls over me. This is what I've spent my life doing. Helping a monster grow large enough, powerful enough, to steal Mani. I rest my forehead in my palms. It's so much to take in.

"So Iyla was helping you?" I ask. Did she know all of this? Why didn't she ever tell me?

"Yes," Deven says. "Iyla asked if we would help her leave the Naga in exchange for information, and we agreed. She's only been pretending to work with you."

I feel like I've swallowed a brick of ice. "That's not possible," I say. "I've killed based on her information. Recently."

"Not necessarily."

I slam my palm against my thigh. "Stop that. Stop telling me what I have and haven't done. I kissed those boys. I killed them. They're dead and it's all my fault."

He sighs. "I'm not saying that you didn't kiss them. Only that they didn't die."

"You don't understand. *Everyone* I kiss dies."

His gaze is steady. "Not if they're immune." My breath sticks in my throat. I didn't think anyone was immune except Gopal and Kadru. And me.

"But . . ." It doesn't make any sense. Why wouldn't Iyla tell me? She knew how miserable I was. She knew I would have helped her.

"I'm telling you the truth," Deven says. "The Pakshi have been trying to infiltrate the Naga for years. Iyla was the perfect way in. She has been feeding them false information and setting up false kills since she's been with us.

The boys you kissed—we made sure they were immune before Iyla set up the meetings. We hoped it would give us a chance to see how the Naga work, without anyone having to die." If what he's saying is true, then there was no use being sad about Iyla's empty house. She left me a long time ago.

And if Deven knew who Iyla was all along, did he know who I was too? It touches something raw inside me, the thought that he was pretending when he took me on that hike. When he showed me the waterfall and the Widows' Village. When he held my hand. A yawning emptiness opens up in my chest. At least I haven't killed in a long time.

"So none of the boys died? Not for two years?"

"Well . . . we're not entirely sure that none of them died." My heart sinks—my redemption lasted only a few seconds. Deven rubs his palms against his legs like he's nervous, like there's something he doesn't want to tell me. "Iyla may have been working both sides. It's possible she set up kills we weren't aware of."

"What makes you think that?"

He bites his lip. "One of Iyla's primary missions was to reveal the identities of the *vish kanya*. We knew there were dozens, but we hadn't ever been able to locate any of them, and every time we sent spies to witness the false kills, to be there to capture the *visha kanya*, they ended up dead."

My mouth goes dry. He still thinks there are many *vish kanya*, that Gopal has a network of assassins. Deven doesn't realize that the people he works for were only trying to capture me. I take slow, deep breaths and try to regain my composure. "What do you mean they ended up dead?"

He sighs. "We'd find them later at the location of the kill, their throats slit, gone before they'd had a chance to report back to their handlers. The Naga have spies for our spies, and they always seem to be one step ahead." A chill scurries down my spine. Gopal always warned me I might be followed, but I didn't know I was being trailed by multiple sides.

"What about the targets? If they survived, couldn't they give a description?"

He rubs a hand over his face. "Not a good enough one—they expected the girls to be followed and captured, and so they didn't pay attention to details. The descriptions were vague. Always girls between sixteen and twenty. Always alone. It wasn't enough."

I think of the way Gopal made sure I looked different for every assignment—*The boy will prefer the hair down, rajakumari* or *Today we'll cover your hair with a scarf, rajakumari.* Was he aware I was being watched? Did he want me to look older sometimes and younger others? Was I playing the part of a dozen different *vish kanya*?

Deven sighs. "And then there was you."

My breath lodges at the base of my throat. "What about me?"

"You were supposed to kill me, right?"

I swallow hard. It's painful to hear him say it out loud. "Yes."

"Well, we didn't know that. When Iyla showed up with a black eye and told me that you'd had her beaten—well, the story didn't add up. She hadn't told me that you worked with the Naga before then, and she should have. That's when I realized she'd been playing us. That maybe we could never discover any of the Naga's secrets because she didn't want us to."

My heart squeezes at the thought that maybe some of my time with Deven was real. "But wait," I say, "if Iyla told you I was a *visha kanya*, why did you seem so surprised when I told you earlier?"

Deven shakes his head. "See, that's the thing. She didn't tell me that. She told me that you worked for the Naga and that you were trying to kill me by poisoning my drinks. She always claimed she needed more time to find the *vish kanya*. That she had no idea where the Naga were keeping them."

I stare at my hands as I try to decide what it means that Iyla gave Deven only a half-truth. What it means that she only partially betrayed me. Was that for my benefit? For hers?

Deven clears his throat. "Do *you* know where the others are?" he asks.

I swallow hard. I should tell him that I'm the only one, but the fact that Iyla didn't makes me nervous. She must have had some reason to withhold that information. What did she know that I don't?

But I owe him some kind of answer. "My handlers never let me meet the others," I say. "They said it kept us all safer if we didn't know each other." It's the closest thing to the truth I have to offer.

"Basic tradecraft," Deven says. "I thought as much, but I had to ask."

"I wish I knew more," I say, grateful he believes me.

And then a thought occurs to me that sends butterflies dancing in my stomach. "Are you immune?"

The corner of his mouth ticks up. "Yes."

My first thought is that I gave away five years of my life for nothing. And the second is this: I could have kissed him.

I still could.

Neither of us speaks for a moment, and I stare at my feet while I wait for my cheeks to cool. It doesn't matter if Deven is immune or not; he would never want to kiss me. And I have more important things to think about, like helping Mani. But still, my train of thought leads me to one more question.

"If Iyla was never your girlfriend, then why did you kiss her?"

He frowns. "Her cover was that I was a mark she was trying to woo. In public places she made sure to be thorough."

CHAPTER SIXTEEN

My head is heavy with new information, but none of it points toward where the Naga might have taken Mani. I stand up and pull on my sandals. They're still damp from when I rinsed them in the shower. I can't just sit here. I have to start searching.

"What are you doing?" Deven asks.

"I'm going to find my brother."

He raises an eyebrow. "And how do you plan to do that?"

"I'm going to start with the girls' home. It's where I was raised. Where they kept all of the *vish kanya* and spies."

He chews his lip. "I doubt they would keep him somewhere so obvious, but it's worth a try. We can at least have a look around and see if we find some more clues."

"We?" I ask. "You're coming with me?"

He reaches out and circles my wrist with his fingers,

and my breath catches in my throat. I forgot to replace my bracelets after I showered. Deven's eyes widen as his thumb brushes against the scars.

"What did they do to you?" His voice is husky with emotion.

"They're snakebites," I tell him. I can't bear to see the naked pity on his face, so I drop my gaze.

He grabs my other wrist and turns both of my hands over in his own, examining them from every angle. "Oh, Marinda," he breathes. "There are so many."

I don't tell him that these are only half of my scars. That my ankles are just as ravaged, but that no one gets close enough to my feet for me to bother concealing them.

Instead I swallow the lump in my throat and pull away from him. "We have to go," I say.

Deven drops my hands and it takes him a moment to find his voice. "Let's wait until dark," he says. "And then I promise I'll help you find Mani and get him to safety."

I shake my head. "No. We have to go now. It's been hours. He must be terrified."

"I'm sure he is," Deven says. "But we're not even certain where they're keeping him, and it won't do Mani any good for you to get yourself killed."

"They won't kill me," I say.

"Won't they?" he asks softly, his gaze traveling to my wrists and then back to my face. "Isn't that exactly what they did to Japa? And he didn't betray them, Marinda. You did."

I press a palm to my forehead and squeeze my eyes closed. I don't want to think about what they did to Japa, what they could be doing to Mani. But I know I can't sit here and do nothing while we wait for the sun to disappear. I go to the wall where the door is and lean against it.

"How do I get out of here?"

"We have a better chance of saving him if we wait," Deven says. "I care about him too."

My stomach clenches and I fall heavily into a chair. "You don't know Gopal like I do. You don't know what he's capable of. If we go now, I can promise to stay with him in exchange for Mani. That's a trade I know Gopal will make. He doesn't care about Mani—I'm what he wants. And then you can take Mani and get him far away from here."

"No. I'm not willing to do that."

"But you said you cared about him."

"And I do," Deven says. "But I'm not exchanging you for him."

"Why not? You hate me and you care about Mani, so it seems like an easy decision."

"I don't hate you." He rakes his fingers through his hair. "My feelings about you are complicated. I'm angry with you—but I'm not angry enough to leave you with a monster."

"I *deserve* to be with a monster," I say. "Mani doesn't."

Deven shakes his head. "No one deserves that, Marinda. Not even you."

"It doesn't look much like a home," Deven says. We've been creeping through dark alleys for over an hour, and finally we're standing in front of a charmless box of a building. The windows are dark and the front yard is a wild tangle—the weeds have choked the life from every other plant.

But until a few years ago, it was the only home I'd ever known, and I still feel a pull toward it, like if I just stare hard enough, I might see something different.

It doesn't look like anyone is staying here, and yet I'm still praying to the ancestors that Mani is inside. And if he is—I don't care what Deven says—I will offer to stay in his place. Even if I never see either of them again, it will be worth it to know that Mani is safe.

We try the front door first, but it's locked. I reach toward my head for a pin but realize that I left my hair down and I don't have one. "Is there another way in?" Deven asks. I look at him in confusion. "A side entrance? A loose window?"

"I don't know," I say.

He sighs. "Didn't you spend most of your life here?"

I swallow. "Yes, but I was only ever allowed in a few of the rooms and almost never outside."

A long silence stretches between us. It's so dark that I can't clearly make out his expression, but I feel like I've disappointed him. "I'm sorry," I say. "If you have something to pick the lock, I can try that."

"I don't," he says. He shrugs and his shoulder brushes against mine. "We'll find a way."

We steal around the side of the building, and Deven pulls on each window, looking for one that is loose or open, but all of them are sealed tight. The night is inky black and I brush my hand against the side of the wall to keep my footing. Deven is nothing more than a dark shape in front of me. I follow him around the corner to the back of the building.

"Found a way in," he says softly. I hurry to catch up and nearly run into him. He's standing next to a door with a glass window in the top half. Steel rods crisscross the window, forming dozens of diamond shapes.

"Is it unlocked?"

"No," he says. "But I can get it open." He pulls a blanket from his bag and wraps it several times around his fist. Then he punches through the glass diamond in the bottom left corner. The sound of breaking glass shatters the silence. I flinch, but no lights go on and no one comes running. Deven tosses the blanket to me and then reaches his hand through the opening and unlocks the door. We step into the kitchen.

The smell of ginger tea envelops me and I'm suddenly five years old again, curled on Gita's lap listening to her whisper folktales against my ear. Deven lights a candle, but I already know what I'll see in the flickering light. A yellow teapot painted with red elephants, a single matching teacup with a chip in the handle and the dregs of the pale tea Gita favors glued to the bottom. Gita has been here. Recently. My throat is thick with the memories I can't swallow.

"Marinda?"

"She was here," I say.

"Who?" Deven swings the candle so that the light dances between us.

"Gita," I say. "She's . . ." Suddenly I realize I don't know what to call her. My fill-in mother? One of my handlers? The woman who dried my tears when Gopal beat me, but never stopped him from hurting me in the first place? "She's one of them."

If Gita is here, Mani could be too. I race into the dining room, where Iyla, Mani and I would sometimes be allowed to eat together. But large sheets are draped over the tables and chairs, and the moonlight streaming through the windows makes them look like huge, hulking beasts. I let go of Deven and run my hand along the fabric. My fingers come away coated in dust. No one has used this room in a long time—at least months, maybe years.

I run down the long hallway where my bedroom used to be, flinging doors open as I go. All the rooms are dark, cold and empty. When I get to the room that used to be mine, I pause with my hand on the doorknob. Please let him be here. Please. I open the door and it is cold and dark, just like the others. But not empty. My old bed is still here, draped in a gray sheet that might have been white once. Mani's bed is here too. And shoved in the corner, bathed in moonlight, is his tiny baby cradle. It's not covered in anything but dust, as if it wasn't worth protecting. As if it will never be needed again. I'm overcome with a sudden wave of nostalgia. Mani became my brother in this room. For months I woke several times a night to feed him, change him and sing him back to sleep. It was so much responsibility for a ten-year-old. As I stand here, the full weight of my life with Mani comes rushing in on me. Both the burden and the blessing of it.

Deven finds me standing in the middle of the room with my hands pressed to my cheeks. He squeezes my shoulder.

"Mani's not here, Marinda. Time to go."

"Maybe he's in the other wing?"

Deven lifts an eyebrow. "What other wing?"

"On the other side of the dining room. I've never been there, but . . ." And then the realization washes over me. It's where Gopal said the other girls lived, through the dining-room door, which was always kept locked. I always pictured a hallway full of rooms, full of friends that I would never meet. I hurry to the forbidden door and turn the knob. It's not another wing—just a bedroom, the only room in the whole building that looks lived in. Another wing exists no more than the other *vish kanya* do.

"Forget it," I say. "Let's go." I wipe at my eyes. How will we ever find Mani?

We leave through the front door. There's no reason to sneak now, no one to hide from. We cross to the other side of the street and start back the way we came. We've gone only a few steps before I stop.

"Wait," I say, "we can't leave yet."

"What? But he wasn't there, Marinda. I checked every room."

"Gita will be back." And as I say it out loud, I'm certain it's true. Since I was little, Gita has had the same routine: a cup of ginger tea in the evening, followed by a long walk. Then she returns to reheat the pot and have a final cup before bedtime. If she had left for good, she would have washed the teapot, dried it, put it away. Gita can't bear loose ends. She is walking through the neighborhood right now—I know it like I know the feel of my hand in hers, like I know that her skin smells like jasmine.

We wait crouched behind a tree for more than an hour. My eyes stay fixed on the girls' home, but the darkness deepens and there's no sign of Gita. With every moment my despair grows. I'm about to suggest giving up, when I see a dark shape emerge from the shadows. I would know that gait anywhere.

Before I can even think about it, I'm racing across the street toward her. She looks up and freezes. "Where is he?" I shout. Her eyes widen and she takes a step back. For a moment I half expect her to turn and run. Instead she fixes me with a steely gaze.

"I warned you, Marinda," she says. "I told you not to push Gopal any further."

I grab her arm and dig my fingers into her flesh. "Where is he?" Deven comes to my side and puts a hand on my back.

"I think you'd better answer her question," Deven says. He says it softly, but there's an edge to his voice that sends a shiver down my spine.

Gita looks back and forth between us. "I don't know."

Rage floods through me. I won't get this close to finding Mani only to have Gita lie to me yet again. I squeeze her arm harder. "If you don't tell me where he is, I will have Deven hold you down while I plant a loving kiss full on your lips. You'll be dead within the hour."

"Marinda," she says reproachfully. "Don't do this. You aren't this girl." The maternal quality to her voice makes my stomach turn. She has no right.

"I am *exactly* this girl. I became exactly what you raised me to be. And if you don't tell me where my brother is, I promise I *will* kill you."

Gita blanches. "Gopal didn't tell me where they are keeping him," she says.

"What did he tell you?" I ask.

She slides her gaze away and I shake her. "What did he tell you?"

When she lifts her head again, I can see tears glinting in her eyes. "Gopal thinks you will be able to focus better once Mani is gone," she says. I suck in a sharp breath.

"What do you mean when he's gone?"

Teardrops tumble from her lashes. "Gopal is planning on taking Mani to the Raja," Gita says. Anger boils in my stomach that she's still saying "*the Raja,*" that she's still lying even now.

"You mean the *Nagaraja*?"

Gita nods. And then suddenly I remember something Kadru said, and horror wells in my chest.

"What is Gopal going to do?" I whisper.

Gita wipes at her eyes. "It will be better for you without him," she says. "You can fulfill your purpose without distraction."

I slap her hard across the face. "What is he going to do?"

Gita presses her palm against her cheek. "I'm sorry, Marinda. But the Nagaraja must be fed."

CHAPTER SEVENTEEN

Deven sweeps his foot under Gita and has her flat on her back in an instant. She lets out a yelp of surprise, which Deven silences with a hand at her throat. "When?" he asks. "When are the Naga planning to feed the Snake King?" Gita struggles, but Deven is too strong for her. When she finally stops moving, he releases the pressure at her neck.

She gasps for air and then begins coughing. Deven's face is impassive as he waits for her to catch her breath. "When?" he asks again when she falls silent. She doesn't answer right away, and so he moves his hand back toward her throat.

"Wait," she gasps. His hand freezes inches above her neck. "At the full moon," she says. "The Nagaraja always eats on the first night of a full moon."

I look up at the sky. The moon is a waxing gibbous, well over half full. We have perhaps four days.

"Where?" I ask.

Gita's eyes flick to Deven and then back to me. "The Snake Temple," she says. I don't know what she means, but I see a flicker of recognition pass over Deven's features.

"Where is it?" I ask. "Where is the Snake Temple?"

"I don't know," Gita whispers. "I swear I don't."

"Go ahead, Marinda," Deven says.

At first I'm confused by what he means, but then I understand. He's holding Gita in place so that I can kiss her. So I can end her life. I look down at Gita, who is watching me in wide-eyed terror, and suddenly my mind flashes through a handful of vivid memories: an image of Gita spreading out a blanket for a picnic, Mani giggling as he tosses a green rubber ball to her, Gita pressing a cold cloth to my head when I was sick with a fever.

And I can't do it.

I bite my bottom lip and shake my head. Gita doesn't deserve mercy, but I can't bring myself to mete out justice.

Deven studies me for a moment. "It's okay," he says. "But I can't let her follow us." He pulls Gita into a sitting position and then strikes the back of her neck with the flat side of his hand. She slumps over without a sound. I let out a startled cry. "She's not dead," Deven says as he climbs to his feet. "She'll have a terrible headache when she wakes up, but she'll live."

I nod, but as long as I'm not the one to kill her, I'm not sure I care.

● ●

By the time we make it back to the safe house, I am faint with hunger, exhaustion and grief. I don't bother to undress before I collapse on one of the beds and pull my knees to my chest, but my mind is too hectic for sleep. The need to find Mani is like a grating noise in my head. I could go to Kadru—she'll know what the Snake Temple is, *where* it is. But she's as likely to turn me over to the Naga as to help me, and I can't risk being captured, not when I have less than four days to find Mani. I think of Deven's face when Gita mentioned the Snake Temple. He's heard of it before, I'm sure of it.

"Deven?" I whisper into the darkness.

But his breath is deep and even, and my eyelids are so heavy—I'll ask him in the morning.

• •

I wake to the tangy aroma of dosa batter, and before I'm fully awake, I sigh appreciatively. And then reality comes rushing back to me and I feel terrible. It seems wrong to want to eat when Mani is somewhere scared and in danger because of me. But my traitorous stomach doesn't understand the finer points of loyalty and betrays me by grumbling loudly.

Deven pokes his head around the corner. "Hungry?"

"Not really," I lie. There are no windows in the safe house, so it's impossible to know what the hour is, but it feels like I slept for a long time.

"You need to eat something," he says. "You'll need your

energy." This seems an acceptable trade-off—to eat so that I have energy to search for Mani, to save him if I can. I sit up and stretch. Deven brings me a plate of folded dosas with a dish of coconut chutney on the side. As soon as I take the first bite, I realize that I am famished, and I have to work to slow down so I don't make myself sick.

"Do you know where the Snake Temple is?" I say between bites. "You seemed to recognize it last night when Gita said that's where the Naga were taking Mani."

He sighs and sits on the end of my bed. "I don't know exactly," he says. "I've just heard it mentioned in meetings."

"Mentioned by whom?"

He swallows and fixes his gaze on his plate. "The Raja's men."

Hope springs up in my chest. "Then that's where I'll go next."

Deven raises an eyebrow. "To Colapi City?"

"Can you think of a better plan?"

"But they aren't just going to let you walk into the palace and demand an audience with the Raja," Deven says.

"Maybe they will if I tell them who I am. Didn't you say you've been gathering information about the Naga for years? I'm sure the Raja would want to hear from someone who's lived with them as long as I have."

"But didn't you say that you hardly know anything? That the Naga never shared details with you?"

"Yes, but I still have information. We know they are preparing to make a human sacrifice in a few days. And maybe I know other things that they would find helpful. It can't hurt to try."

Deven doesn't say anything for a moment. He bites his lip and stares off into the distance, lost in thought. Then he shakes his head and sighs. "It's not a terrible plan," he says. "I'll come with you."

It's exactly what I hoped he'd say—I'll have a much better chance of speaking with the Raja if one of his spies is with me—but I try to keep the joy from showing on my face. I shrug. "If you're sure that's what you want."

He holds my gaze a beat longer than necessary and heat creeps into my cheeks. "I'm sure."

* *

It will take us at least two full days on foot to get to the Raja's palace in Colapi City. That will leave us only two days to find Mani—assuming we get the information we need. And I'm not ready to assume anything.

"If we hired an elephant, we'd get there so much faster," I say as Deven and I trudge through the back alleys leading away from the safe house. I'm grateful that Deven was able to find me clothing that was more appropriate for our journey—pants and soft leather hiking boots. The boots are slightly too big but far better than my sandals would have been.

"The Naga are likely searching for you. An elephant is a little conspicuous, don't you think?"

"A donkey?" I offer.

Deven shakes his head. "Sorry. Walking is the only option." He glances sidelong at me. He must see the disappointment on my face, because he says, "Don't worry. We'll get there in time. I promise."

I only nod. As we walk, I wonder, not for the first time, about the identities of the rest of the members of the Naga. How many are there? I know of only Gopal, Gita and Kadru, but the way Deven talks about them makes it seem like there must be hundreds. I wonder how many of them know who I am. Would they all make the same choices that Gopal has? Are any of them decent enough to help Mani?

I'm so lost in thought that I trip over a large rock in the road and almost go down. But Deven catches me around the waist before I fall.

"Are you okay?" he asks. He's close enough that his breath dances across my neck. I close my eyes and feel a flood of warmth rush through me. Ever since I found out Deven is immune, I've been far too aware of him. The exact distance between his hand and mine as we walk, precisely how far I would have to reach to intertwine my fingers with his. The way he licks his bottom lip right before he's about to speak. How he taps his middle finger and thumb together when he's lost in thought. Now having him this close with his arms around my waist is almost too much.

"I'm fine," I manage to choke out. "Just clumsy."

"Okay." He lets go of me and I feel the loss like blankets ripped off on a chilly morning. But at least I can breathe again.

We walk all morning, stopping only long enough to eat the dried fruit and flatbread that we packed in our satchels. My feet ache and I can feel a blister forming on my right heel. I open my mouth several times to complain, but then Mani's face pops into my mind and I snap it closed again. Any amount of pain is worth it to get to him. I can't think about Mani too much, though, because if I imagine how scared he must be, the despair makes it impossible to keep moving. Maybe that's why I keep noticing the shape of Deven's arms underneath his white shirt.

We're between towns when it's time to eat again. Deven finds us a place to sit in a copse of trees on a hill overlooking a rice field. The setting sun has turned the sky vermilion, and it is startlingly beautiful against the bright green rows of rice. Deven passes me a loaf of flatbread and I eat, but I don't taste anything. I drain most of the water left in my canteen. I'm so tired that I feel numb.

"I know another safe house in the next town," Deven says. "We'll stop and sleep for a few hours before we go on." I want to argue with him, insist that we keep moving toward Colapi City, but I don't think I can go much farther without a break.

"Thank you," I say.

"You're welcome." He touches the middle of my back for just a moment and then drops his hand like he's changed his mind.

By the time we start moving again, I can see the moon. It's a sliver fuller than last night—one day closer to Mani's death. It makes me walk a little faster. A few hours later we arrive at the safe house. It is nearly identical to the last one.

"How many safe houses are there?" I ask as I sit on one of the beds and pull off my boots.

"Dozens," he says. "Dotted all across Sundari."

"Have you stayed in all of them?"

He sits in a chair across from me and rubs his eyes with his thumb and forefinger. It makes me realize that my eyes feel gritty too.

"Nearly," he says. "I haven't made it to one or two yet."

"What made you want to become a spy?" I ask him. It's a question that's been itching at the back of my mind since yesterday. Who would choose this kind of life without being forced? Deven looks up then and waits a beat too long to answer. His gaze slides away from me, and I realize I've made him uncomfortable.

"I'm sorry," I say. "You don't have to—"

But he surprises me by answering. "I had an older brother," he says. "He was killed by one of the *vish kanya*, and so once I was old enough, nothing seemed more important than destroying the Naga."

All the air leaves my lungs and Kadru's words reverberate in my mind: *There are no other* vish kanya, *Marinda. The Nagaraja chooses only one.*

I killed Deven's brother.

CHAPTER EIGHTEEN

My chin is quivering. With shock. With guilt. "I'm so sorry," I manage to say.

Deven gives me a sad smile. "It was a long time ago." He goes in the back to change into sleeping clothes, but I sit motionless, too stunned to move. Each time I think I've found a shred of humanity, it is snatched away with more evidence of my atrocities. I don't want to be this person, this girl who spends time with the brother of someone she once killed. The girl who leaves her brother alone to be kidnapped, to be taken by people who want to hurt him. The kind of girl who gets Japa killed. But the trouble is, it's the only kind of girl I know how to be.

Deven returns from the washroom. "All yours," he says. I smile wanly and head to the back of the flat. My fingers are stiff and it takes me longer than usual to change. My throat aches, but I have no tears. I am hollowed out.

I return to the main room and climb into one of the empty beds, the one farthest from Deven. "Good night," I say over my shoulder.

"Night."

I curl up on my side and close my eyes, but it's a long time before sleep claims me.

＊　＊

The next day brings more walking. We traipse through bigger cities and smaller towns, and Deven always seems to know which route will give us the most privacy. Silence hangs heavily between us—my worry about Mani is all-encompassing, and if it leaves my mind even for an instant, Deven's brother is there to make sure I don't have a moment of peace. I haven't made eye contact with Deven all day, but he doesn't seem to notice. He's lost in thought too. We walk for hours, and by the time we reach the outskirts of Colapi City, my feet are screaming for relief.

"Not much farther," Deven says. He reaches for my hand as we climb a small hill. When we get to the top, the palace comes into view for the first time. I pull in a sharp breath. It's the most spectacular thing I've ever seen. Colapi Mahal is vast—at least four stories high and the size of a small village. The facade is smooth gray granite broken up by hundreds of windows. Towers on all sides of the palace soar high into the air and are topped with bulbous red domes and golden finials. The main entrance has a grand arch flanked by two smaller ones. It's breathtaking. I glance over at Deven and see that he is watching me with a small smile playing on his lips, like he built the palace himself.

"What do you think?" he asks.

"I've never seen anything like it." This answer seems to please him. We stand together for a few moments in companionable silence. The sun is low in the sky and bathing the palace in soft pink light. It's so beautiful it's hard to look away.

"We probably should get going," Deven says a few minutes later. "We still have about an hour to walk."

I groan. "That long?"

"It looks deceptively close, doesn't it?" Everything in my life is deceptively close. Especially Deven.

As we walk, we pass small clusters of bungalows. Deven explains that they are occupied by the workers who serve at the palace and their families. Some of them are outside, pulling weeds from gardens, sweeping wide porches, chatting and laughing with neighbors. But as we pass, they fall silent, whispering to each other and pointing at us. It doesn't faze Deven in the least; he doesn't even break stride. But I feel like I've been turned inside out, and I wish I had a wrap to pull tightly around myself, or even better, something to shield my face.

The walk to the front of the palace feels like a day instead of an hour, and by the time we get there, my nerves are jumpy. A wide path paved in white stones leads to the grand arches, and it is flanked on either side by dozens of palace guards. They wear red tunics with black linen pants, and their hair is styled identically—slicked away from the forehead and braided in the back. Swords hang at their hips.

My heart jumps into my throat. I hope Deven's connections at the palace are as good as he claims. I'm tired and I have no desire to be on the misunderstood end of a sword.

"What now?" I ask Deven.

"Just follow my lead," he answers.

We start down the path and the guards don't move. They continue to stare straight ahead, as if we pose no threat at all. Either the Raja's soldiers are completely inept or Deven has been here many times before.

We pass through the grand arches and come to an enormous set of golden double doors inlaid with silver-etched birds. Two guards standing on either side of the doors pull them open and Deven nods his thanks. He puts a hand on the small of my back and guides me forward, down a white marble staircase that opens up into a huge octagonal pavilion. I thought the outside of the palace was spectacular, but it doesn't even compare to the beauty of this room. Pale green fluted columns rise to support golden scalloped arches that soar all the way to the domed stained-glass ceiling. I look down and see that the floor is just as stunning— white marble inlaid with semiprecious stones.

My boots are filthy.

"Should we be here?" I ask, and then startle at how loud

my voice sounds in such a cavernous space. But there's no one to hear me. The palace seems utterly empty.

"We have as much right to be here as anyone," Deven says. "Follow me." He leads me around several corners, twisting and turning so often that I lose track of whether we're heading east or west. Finally we end up in a long walkway lined with ornately gilded columns and Gothic vaulted ceilings. The floor is gleaming hardwood and I flinch at the click of my boots with every step.

At the end of the walkway are huge, intricately carved rosewood doors. Guards are positioned on either side and they show no alarm at our approach. When we reach the doors, one of the guards dips his head slightly. "Master Deven," he says as he swings the door open. I shoot Deven a questioning look, but he's not watching me. He's completely focused on the person on the other side of the door. The Raja sits in the middle of the room on a golden throne. He wears a deep-blue tunic and a white crown. He doesn't notice us right away because his head is dipped toward what appears to be one of his advisers. They are deep in conversation.

Deven clears his throat. The Raja looks up and his face registers surprise and then delight. He breaks into a wide grin.

"Deven," he says affectionately. "How wonderful to see you." Deven is smiling too.

"Hello, Father."

CHAPTER NINETEEN

The word takes a moment to register. *Father.* But when it does, dread chokes my throat.

Deven lied to me. Just like Gopal and Gita and Iyla lied to me. Just like I lied to Deven. Well, he didn't lie exactly—he never told me that he *wasn't* the son of the Raja. But it has the same effect. Why wouldn't he tell me this?

Deven turns toward me, and he must see the distress on my face, because his eyes go soft. He circles my wrist with his fingers and pulls me forward. "It's okay," he says. But it isn't. If Deven is a prince, then his brother—the one I killed—is a prince too. And that makes me an assassin *and* a traitor.

"Father, this is Marinda," Deven says. "Marinda, this is my father." His introduction is casual, as if I'm the girl next door and his father is a merchant. My heart is beating so loudly that I'm afraid the entire room can hear it.

"Nice to meet you, Your Highness," I say when I've finally found my manners.

The Raja smiles warmly at me. "It's always nice to meet a friend of Deven's," he says. I flinch at this and hope that he doesn't notice. I've dreamed about meeting the Raja for years. But that's when I thought I worked for him. When I thought he'd be pleased with all I'd done. Now I'm resisting the urge to run.

"We came to ask a favor," Deven says. "Marinda's younger brother has been taken by the Naga. We were hoping you could help us find them."

The Raja's face hardens. He shakes his head. "Is there no limit to what these swine will do?"

At the mention of Mani, the pressure in my chest grows. There are no windows in the throne room, but the moon must have risen by now. And it will be fuller than last night. We're running out of time.

The Raja sees my face, and his angry expression melts away. "How old is your brother?"

I killed your son, I think as I look into his kind eyes. "He's seven." He flies to his feet so quickly that I worry his throne will tumble off its dais. The two advisers in the room raise their eyebrows but don't move.

"Seven?" His face is scarlet, and his lips are moving but no sound is coming out. He takes a deep breath and then steps down to join us. "What would they want with a little boy?" He says it more to himself than to me, like he doesn't expect an answer. Which is fortunate because I'm not sure I can speak. I just stare dumbly at him. Now that he is closer, I can see the resemblance to Deven. The Raja has deep creases around his eyes in the same places Deven's eyes crinkle when he laughs. The two of them are nearly the same height, and their eyes are the same rich brown color. And I've betrayed them both.

"I'm so sorry," the Raja says. It startles me for a moment that he should be apologizing to me when . . . *I killed your son.* But then I realize he's only expressing sympathy.

Deven puts a reassuring hand on my back. "Can you help?" he asks his father.

"I think so, yes," the Raja says. He glances at one of his advisers. "Will you please inform Hitesh that I need to see him immediately?"

"Certainly, Your Majesty," the adviser says, then leaves the room.

Deven leans toward me and whispers, "Hitesh is the head of Sundari intelligence."

The Raja turns toward us. "Deven, why don't you take your friend to the Blue Room, where you'll both be more comfortable? I'll meet you there shortly."

Panic beats inside my chest like a caged bird. I don't want to go anywhere. I want to hear every word from Sundari intelligence and not have it filtered through someone else. I want to find Mani now. But I don't have that option. I'm not bold enough to argue with the Raja, and Deven already has his hand on my elbow, ready to lead me away.

"Thank you, Father," he says.

The Raja leans forward and kisses him on his right cheek and then his left. "You're welcome."

We leave the throne room and I numbly let Deven lead me down the corridor and around the corner to yet another set of double doors. They open into a large sitting room decorated in dozens of shades of blue. The room is aptly named.

"Are you okay?" Deven asks as we sink onto a cerulean sofa. The question strikes me as absurd. Of course I'm not okay. My brother is missing, and my only hope for finding him lies with people I've unwittingly betrayed. And Deven lied to me—misled me at least—but I can't say that. It would be the height of hypocrisy after our history. I want to say it, though. Badly.

"I'm fine," I say instead.

He touches my knee. "Are you sure?" I stare at my hands and refuse to meet his gaze. "I wanted to tell you," he says. "So many times. But no one knows who I really am. It's the only way to help the cause. No one would tell me anything if they knew."

"So you pose as—as what? A bookshop delivery boy with a rich father?"

"Marinda." The way he says my name—halfway between a plea and a rebuke—almost does me in. It's tender and familiar and not at all the way he would speak to me if he knew the truth—that there aren't dozens of *vish kanya,* like he thinks. Only me. I press my fingers to my temples. A headache is building behind my eyes, and my stomach feels unsettled. I need to get to Mani. My chest aches with it.

"You could help us," Deven says. "It's why I agreed to bring you here. You could help us take them down. You've lived with them. You have information we won't be able to get anywhere else."

Nothing would make me happier than to see the Naga suffer, but I have a thousand questions and not enough answers.

"Were you here?" I ask. Deven raises his eyebrows in a question. "Last week you disappeared for several days. Were you here?"

"Yes," he says.

"So Iyla knows who you are?"

"No." He shakes his head. "She doesn't. Why would you say that?"

"She knew you were gone. She said I wouldn't be able to find you."

His brow furrows and he chews his lip thoughtfully. "She must have been guessing. She only knows I've been working to stop the Naga. Not who I am."

I'm not so sure about that. I remember what Iyla told me when Gopal gave her the assignment—that the target was someone important, someone big. Who is bigger than the prince of Sundari? But it doesn't matter now. All that matters is finding Mani.

"Did Japa know?" I ask after a moment. A pained look crosses Deven's face that makes me wish I hadn't said anything. It's a wound too raw.

"No," Deven says, his voice cracking. "He didn't."

"He disappeared too," I say. "During the same few days as you."

He gives a tight laugh. "Were you keeping track of everyone?"

"No. I just . . ." My face heats as I remember why I was looking for both of them that day. To poison Deven, to protect him. "Forget it." I reach into my pocket and stroke the cricket there.

"Japa thought I worked at the palace, but he didn't know I was the prince. He often traveled to help pass information for us. Books are perfect for disguising messages."

"Oh." Japa feels like a presence in the room, as if saying his name has summoned his essence. My chest feels tight as I think of his easy smile and kind face. Deven and I sit quietly for a few minutes, lost in thought.

Then Deven looks sidelong at me. "What do you have there?"

I'm pulled out of my reverie by the question and look up, disoriented. "What?"

"Every time you're anxious, you reach into your pocket. What are you keeping in there?" My cheeks flame. Why does he have to notice everything? I can't say the words, and so I pull the cricket out and show him. He tilts his head to the side. When he speaks, his voice is soft. "You kept it."

I shove the cricket back into my pocket. "Of course I kept it."

He reaches forward and brushes a lock of hair out of my face. I stop breathing. His lips are only inches from mine; I could lean forward and kiss him without fear of him dying. I wonder what it would be like to kiss him slowly, sweetly. To linger. To run my fingers through his hair. His eyes are bright and his cheeks are flushed. He hasn't moved his gaze from my face, and my heart is beating as fast as humming-bird wings.

The double doors open and we fly apart. It feels like coming up from underwater and I suck in a sharp breath. The Raja strides into the room, and as soon as I see him, my anticipation drains away. I killed his son. Deven's brother. I will never be able to kiss Deven, immune or not.

Following the Raja are a spindly man with silver hair, who I assume is Hitesh, and a serving girl carrying a tray of tea. Both Deven and I stand. The girl slides the tea onto a round table surrounded by sapphire-colored chairs.

"Will there be anything else, Your Highness?" she asks.

The Raja smiles. "No. That's all. Thank you."

The maid bows and slips out of the room. Two guards enter and stand on either side of the doors. They are dressed in red and black, just like the guards outside the palace, and they both have the same faraway gaze; they stare straight ahead at the wall on the opposite side of the room as if there were nothing to see but that.

"Come," the Raja says, motioning for us to join him at

the table. "Sit." He makes quick introductions, but I fidget impatiently. I don't care who Hitesh is and I doubt he cares about meeting me. I just want to find Mani.

"Hitesh has been tracking the Naga for many years," the Raja says. "He knows more about them than anyone else outside their circle."

"Do you know where they might have taken my brother?" I ask.

Hitesh clears his throat. "The Naga operate from many different locations, and unless I know what they have planned for him, I'm afraid I can't say for certain. But we can make some guesses."

"I know what they have planned." My voice comes out shaky and raw. Hitesh puts his elbows on the table, his hands clasped tightly together, his chin balanced on his index fingers.

"And what is that?"

"They want to sacrifice him," I say. "To the Nagaraja."

Hitesh drops his hands, palms down, onto the table. "The Naga don't typically sacrifice children," he says. "Do you have a reason to believe that's true?"

Deven answers before I have a chance. "One of their operatives told me." He makes it sound like I wasn't there at all, like he got the information from his duties as a spy. But maybe he's only trying to lend the statement credibility.

Hitesh sighs deeply. "Very well. We believe that the sacrifices take place in the Snake Temple. It's only about thirty miles from here, underground in a cave. We've tried to catch the Naga during one of these ritual sacrifices for years, but our intelligence is always faulty. We know that they happen, but not when. We arrive either too early and find nothing or too late and find only . . ." He stops short, and my stomach clenches while I wait for the word I know is coming. "Remains," he finishes softly. I place a hand over my mouth. "Our informants, as it turns out, are not very accurate when it comes to anything that would actually stop the Naga. We've even tried placing soldiers at the Snake Temple for weeks at a stretch but they disappear. The Naga outsmart us every time."

"It's the moon," I say. "They are planning on sacrificing Mani on the first night of the full moon."

Hitesh's eyes widen with interest. He looks at Deven, who confirms what I've said with a short nod. "We haven't tried paying attention to the moon. Thank you, Marinda."

"How do we get there?" I ask. Hitesh glances at the Raja.

"I don't see the harm in telling her," he says.

Hitesh turns toward me. "Due west is a mountain range with a small footpath at the base. It starts out as one trail but then forks off many times until there are dozens of different paths. The trail that leads to the Snake Temple follows a pattern of right twice, then left twice, repeated all the way to the cave. You'll know you're in the right place by the rather unpleasant odor. It's impossible to miss." I know the smell he's talking about—musky, reptilian. The smell of snakes.

"Now, Marinda," the Raja says. "May we ask you a few questions?"

"Of course." My palms start to sweat and I dry them on my pants.

"Do you know why the Naga would take your brother?"

"Yes," I say, suddenly thirsty. I take a sip of my tea and then trace the rim of the cup with my finger. Deven squeezes my knee under the table, and I'm not sure if he's providing support or trying to send me a message, but I don't dare look at him.

"And why is that?" The Raja's voice is gentle.

"They are trying to punish me," I explain. "I used to work for them, and when I stopped, they took my brother to try to coerce me." Deven lets out a breath and moves his hand from my knee. He seems relieved. He must have been trying to encourage me to tell the truth.

The Raja leans forward and puts a hand on my forearm. "I'm so sorry, Marinda. Were you one of their spies?" I go stiff. I'm not sure what to say. I want to look at Deven, but the Raja is maintaining eye contact, and to look away would appear dishonest. Iyla taught me that much. The Raja's eyes are kind. He searches my face while he waits for an answer, and just for a moment he reminds me of Japa. How Japa always seemed to see more of me than I intended to show him. How he always seemed to care even when I tried to keep him at arm's length. And my mind is made up. I'm tired of lies. Mine and everyone else's.

"I'm a *visha kanya*," I say softly. Hitesh lets out a small gasp, but my gaze is focused on the Raja. His face falls and he closes his eyes, as if he was bracing for this answer all along but is still disappointed to have it. And then he opens his eyes and pats my arm.

"I appreciate your honesty," he says. "I really do." He makes a motion toward the doors and I swivel to see the guards approaching us.

One of them is holding manacles.

CHAPTER TWENTY

Suddenly the room is in chaos.

Deven is on his feet shouting, "Father, no!" I'm struggling against the guards, kicking and screaming, but they are too strong for me, and before I know it, my hands are restrained in front of me, my wrists bound by manacles. The guards each hold one of my elbows. I'm sweating and my heartbeat is roaring in my ears.

"Please," I say. "Mani is only seven and he's done nothing wrong. Please."

"My son was only seventeen," the Raja says. "That may sound much older to you, but to my wife and me it seemed but a few days older than seven."

I have no response to that. Because he's right—I deserve to be locked up and punished. But Mani doesn't. The Raja puts an arm around Deven's shoulders.

"Thank you, son. Thank you for bringing us a *visha kanya* and correcting the wrong that was done to our family."

Deven pushes his father's arm away. "I thought you would help her," he said. "I never would have . . ." His eyes find mine and they are pleading with me to believe him.

The guards are dragging me toward the door. "Deven," I cry. "Help Mani. Please."

The Raja holds up a hand and the guards stop. "My first priority is finding and detaining the Naga. If the boy is still alive after that, we will see what can be done to help him." I try to catch Deven's gaze, to see if he will honor my request, but I can't tell what he's thinking. His expression is stunned, as if he's suddenly found himself in a room he never entered.

With a flick of his hand, the Raja dismisses the guards and they drag me through the double doors. Once we're in the corridor, I stop struggling. There's no one to help me now. I'm so panicked that I don't pay attention to where we're headed until we reach a flight of stairs, and then my legs start to shake. This is not like the elegant, curving marble staircase in the foyer; these stairs are plain and narrow. And they descend into darkness.

One of the guards plucks a torch from a sconce on the wall. "Follow me," he says. We move down the stairs in a single line with one guard in front of me and one behind. I wish I could trail my fingers along the stone wall; I feel unsteady with my hands bound in front of me. Defenseless.

Every step downward feels like a death sentence for Mani. My mind is racing for a way to escape. I could push the guard in front of me with my shoulder and hope he's incapacitated as he falls, but that doesn't help with the guard behind me. I might be able to turn quickly and kiss the man behind me before he could retreat, but my poison doesn't work fast enough. It's a bitter irony that my whole life I've felt like I'm too deadly to find happiness. But now, when it really counts, I'm not nearly deadly enough.

We reach the bottom of the staircase and my breath feels trapped in my chest. Rows of cells separated only by iron bars line either side of a narrow walkway. It's chilly and damp, and an unpleasant musty smell fills the air. The flickering light from the torch doesn't allow me to see much, only huddled shapes behind the bars. But I can hear them. A man muttering to himself. A woman humming an off-key tune. A child crying. I shiver. What kind of person imprisons a child? It gives me even less hope that the Raja will help Mani.

The guard behind me takes my elbow and leads me to an empty cell at the back of the dungeon. The other guard holds the torch so that his comrade can see to unlock the huge metal padlock. And then they both escort me inside. The cell is small, with a stone floor and a single blanket folded in the corner. Water drips from the ceiling, forming a puddle in the center of the room. I'll have to sleep pressed against the wall to avoid getting wet.

"We're going to take these off now," one of the men

tells me, pointing to my wrists. "Don't do anything foolish." I hold out my hands, but before he touches me, the other guard steps forward and holds the torch off to one side, careful to keep it between my face and both of theirs. They obviously overheard my confession in the Blue Room and know exactly what a *visha kanya* can do. My heart sinks. For the first time I see the appeal in being as deadly as Kadru. If I were two hundred years older, both of the guards would be dead already and I wouldn't be powerless to save Mani.

Once the manacles are removed, the guards back slowly out of the cell, as if I might charge forward at any moment. They secure the padlock and then retreat back down the path without a word. The torchlight disappears and I am plunged into darkness.

"A flicker and gone!" one of the prisoners yells. "A flicker and gone." He sounds like he's in a cell across from me, but I can't tell for sure.

"Hush," says another voice, a woman's. "Go to sleep."

"A flicker and gone!" the man shouts again. The woman yells back and the two start trading insults—hers make sense and his don't.

I press my back against the wall and sit with my knees drawn up to my chest. My wrists are tender from where the manacles dug into my flesh, but it's nothing compared with the pain I feel at failing Mani. Why did Deven bring me here? Did he know his father would imprison me? Was that the plan all along? I feel sick at the thought that I walked into the palace and confessed. That I allowed myself to be taken.

Gopal always worried about me being captured. He taught me never to trust anyone, never to say more than what was absolutely necessary, never to ask him questions and above all never to answer questions from anyone else. Not with the truth, anyway.

It's basic tradecraft that the person with the most information has the most power. How foolish of me to trust the Raja enough to tell him the truth. I should have been more careful. I should have traded information for Mani's safety and not given anything away until they led me to the Snake Temple, until Mani was back in my arms. I rest my forehead on my knees and let the tears soak through the thin fabric of my pants.

The other prisoners finally fall silent, and the only noises are the constant *drip, drip* from the ceiling and the sound of my own breathing. And I have nothing left to focus on but despair.

• •

I wake up to the creak of a door. I'm slumped over in an awkward position and my neck is so kinked that it screams in pain when I try to straighten it. It takes a moment to sort out where I am, for my mind to arrange all the unfamiliar smells and sounds into a memory of the previous day. But then it all comes rushing back—the Raja, the Snake Temple, the dungeon—and I wish I hadn't woken up at all.

Flickering light dances at the far end of the walkway, and I hear footfalls and the low hum of whispered conversation. And then a loud voice ricochets through the dungeon. "Wake up!" It's a man's voice, probably one of the guards. He takes something metal and scrapes it along the bars of the cells as he walks back and forth. It makes a horrible screeching noise, and suddenly the dungeon is filled with groans. He laughs. "Breakfast time."

Another guard lights torches all along the passageway. It barely illuminates the space, but compared with the blackness of last night it feels like stepping out into full sun. The guards are sliding metal trays to each prisoner through a small slot near the floor. I scramble forward to examine the opening, but it's too small for even my head, let alone my whole body. When the guard approaches my cell, I recognize him from the Blue Room. He slides the tray forward and water sloshes over the side of the cup, soaking the small loaf of bread.

"Wait," I say. He pauses but doesn't look at me. "Could you give me any information about my brother?" He shakes his head slightly and starts to move away.

"Please," I say. "You were in that room yesterday. I know you heard everything. He's only a little boy." The guard keeps moving down the corridor, sliding trays to prisoners. I'm the only one even attempting conversation. "Could you tell me if anyone has left yet for the Snake Temple?" I shout. "Is Deven still here in the palace?" Only silence as an answer.

The guard finishes distributing the trays, and as he passes my cell again, I try one more time. *"Please,* tell me something." He pauses and turns his face toward me, his expression conflicted.

For a moment I think he will answer me, but then he looks away. "I'm sorry," he whispers. My stomach pitches forward. Sorry for what? Sorry that he can't tell me? Or sorry that the Raja tried but couldn't save Mani? But I don't have a chance to ask because he's already gone.

I sink to my knees, but I have no tears left to cry. Mani will be fed to the Nagaraja in less than two days and I'm trapped here. I want to believe that Deven will help him, but the image of Deven's stunned face as the guards placed the manacles around my wrists haunts me. He did nothing to help me. What if he does nothing to help Mani?

I scoot forward and shake the bars of my cell, but they are solid. The guards didn't take my boots, though, and maybe with enough effort . . . I sit down and press my feet to the bars and push as hard as I can. They don't budge. I kick at them until sweat trickles down my back.

"Are you finished?" It's a small voice and it sounds so much like Mani that I leap to my feet. Maybe they've already rescued him. Maybe they brought him here last night and I never noticed. I press my face to the bars of the neighboring cell. But the eyes staring back at me aren't Mani's. This boy is a few years older, his hair is a shade darker, and his eyes have a haunted look. "Are you finished?" he asks again.

"I—yes, I guess I am," I say. "I'm sorry if I scared you."

"No, not finished with your tantrum," the boy says. "Finished with your breakfast. I'm still a bit hungry."

"Oh." I look over at my tray. I don't think I could eat right now even if I wanted to. I scoop up the loaf of bread and pass it through the bars. "I'm afraid it's a little soggy," I tell him.

"S'okay," he answers through a mouthful of bread. I wait until he's swallowed and then pass him what's left of the water.

"What is such a little boy doing in a dungeon?" I ask. He looks offended and I feel a pang in my chest. He reminds me so much of Mani. "Sorry. Young man," I correct myself. "What's a young man doing here?"

He shrugs and takes another bite. "In trouble for telling the truth," he says. "How about you?"

"Same."

I sit down with my shoulders against the bars, and the boy mimics me. We sit like that for a long time—him finishing his bread, me berating myself for not being a better sister, a better person.

"What's your name?" I ask him finally.

"Kavi," he says. Kavi. Mani. They aren't so different. My throat aches.

"What's your name?" he asks.

"Marinda."

I look over at my tray and the porridge still sitting there untouched. I can't fit the bowl between the bars, but we could pass the spoon back and forth. "Are you still hungry?" I ask. "I have some porridge."

"Nah," Kavi says. "I'm okay. But I feel like I should give you something in return for the bread."

I laugh. "And what could you possibly have to give me?"

He turns and looks at me earnestly. "I could give you some wisdom."

My blood runs cold and I scoot away from the bars. "I know you," I say. "I saw you on Gali Street." He was the boy selling wisdom, the boy Mani thought could give us hope.

"I saw you too," he says. He shakes his head sadly. "But it looks like you didn't listen to me." The hair on the back of my neck prickles to life.

"Stop," I say. "You don't know anything about me."

"You shared your bread with me," he says. "That tells me a lot. And you love your brother. That tells me something too."

And I kill people. What does that say about me, you strange little child?

"You really look like you could use some wisdom," Kavi says.

"Stop talking," I say. "Just leave me alone." I don't know what it is about this boy that unsettles me so much.

He just shrugs. "Let me know if you change your mind."

I snatch the blanket from the floor and retreat to the far side of my cell, where I lie down and pull the blanket over my head. Water continues to drip from the ceiling, so I have to smash myself against the wall to stay dry. It's an uncomfortable position, but not as uncomfortable as being turned inside out by a little boy who talks too much.

* *

I attempt to sleep away the rest of the day, and from what little I can see, most of the other prisoners do the same. There isn't anything else to pass the time.

The guards don't return with another meal until evening, and by then I'm famished. It's a different man distributing trays this time, and when he approaches my cell, I try asking about Mani again. But I get even less of a response than before. He acts as if he can't hear me, and when I repeat my question, he begins humming and moves along to the next prisoner.

I curl up in the corner and start on my dinner—a thick stew, a mug of water and two small loaves of bread. I can hear Kavi in the next cell loudly slurping his stew, and again I'm forcefully reminded of Mani. With every bite I grow more unsettled. I was unkind earlier. To a child. I don't know what it is about Kavi that makes my stomach churn. Maybe it's the culture he comes from—the fortune-telling and snake charming. It ruined my life, and maybe I'm taking it out on a little boy because I can't reach the Naga.

I stand up and move to where Kavi sits with his back against the bars. "I have some extra bread," I tell him.

He glances up. "But you didn't eat breakfast."

I smile at him. "I'll be fine. I don't eat that much."

He shrugs and takes the bread. "Thank you."

"Sure." I take a deep breath and force the next words out. "What is the wisdom you wanted to share? Maybe I need it after all."

"Really?" he asks, and the hopefulness in his voice sends a pang through me.

"Really."

Kavi closes his eyes and his whole face relaxes. He sits like that for several minutes and then snaps his eyes open. "It's better when I write it down," he says apologetically. "But here it is: Suspicion is the only defense against betrayal."

I roll my eyes. "That's exactly the same thing you told me last time."

"Is it?"

I laugh. "Yes, it is." I can't believe I let Kavi get to me. He really is just an innocent child pretending to be grown up. "Let me guess. You tell the same thing to all of your customers?"

"No," he says indignantly. "Of course not."

"No? Then tell me. What does it mean?"

Kavi purses his lips. "Usually I don't know," he says. "But this time I have a pretty good idea."

"And what is that?"

"Well, I think it means that the guards should be more suspicious of little boys with sticky fingers." He pulls a key from his pocket and shakes it at me. "And then they would avoid being betrayed."

CHAPTER TWENTY-ONE

I gasp. "Is that—"

"Shh!" Kavi holds a finger to his lips. "Yes, it is."

My heart starts pounding. He's holding the key to my freedom, to Mani's. "Will you help me?" I ask. "My brother is in trouble and I have to get to him."

Kavi nods slowly as he says, "He who has a full belly has a big heart." I wish there weren't bars between us so that I could grab him and hug him close. He's an odd little boy, but if he can help me escape, I will forever be in his debt.

He presses the key into my palm. "The guards will come in a few hours to put out the torches. You can leave then."

"Aren't you going to come with me?"

"Nah," he says. "They never keep me for very long. Just a few days now and then to teach me a lesson. I'll be out in no time."

"What lesson are they trying to teach you?" I ask.

He sighs. "That a person will more easily believe a sweet lie than a bitter truth." He scratches his head. "And that I shouldn't sell either one."

I reach through the bars and touch his cheek. "Thank you, Kavi. You have no idea how much this means to me."

He grins at me. "You have no idea how much the bread means to me." It seems that a loaf of bread and a boy's life can't compare, but I'm grateful for Kavi's help.

The next few hours are some of the slowest of my entire life. I pace circles around my tiny cell until a woman shouts out, "Hold still, girl! You're making me jumpy." The last thing I need right now is to draw attention to myself, and so I sit and pull my knees to my chest. I run my fingers along the smooth metal of the key. The hope I had earlier is draining away. I don't know how I will get out of here, or if I can find Mani, or how I can possibly overcome the Naga if I do. I wish I at least had Deven to make the journey with me. But I don't know anymore if he's trustworthy or if he only pretended to help me so that I would end up here, locked in the dungeon to pay for my crimes. What will the Raja do to me if I'm caught trying to escape?

Finally the door at the top of the stairway creaks open and the guards come to put out the torches. As soon as the prisoners hear them approaching, the dungeon bursts into a cacophony of noise. The woman who yelled at me earlier begins chanting at the top of her voice, several of the men start arguing with one another, one man mutters as he slams his head against the bars. Kavi bursts into tears.

The guards ignore the whole scene and dispassionately walk down the corridor extinguishing each torch with large metal cones. When all the flames are out, they make their way back to the staircase. Once their handheld torch disappears up the stairs, the dungeon is plunged into darkness. Panic fills my chest. How will I get the lock open if I can't see?

Once the door clicks closed, the theatrics of the prisoners die down. I press my face against the bars of Kavi's cell.

"Are you all right?" I whisper.

"Of course I am," he says without a trace of sadness in his voice.

"You were crying pretty hard."

"It's good to remind them that I'm only a child," he says. "It gets me released sooner." With the way Kavi talks, I think I need reminding that he is a child. "Good luck tonight," he says.

I sigh. "I'm not sure I can get the lock open in the dark."

"Give your eyes a few minutes to adjust," he tells me. "But even if you can't see, it will be okay. I can usually do it by feel."

My mouth drops open. "Usually? You've done this before?"

"Yep. I stole the key when I was here the time before last," he tells me. "I like to go exploring at night."

"Exploring?" I say incredulously.

"Quit yakking over there!" someone shouts. "Some of us are trying to sleep."

Kavi lowers his voice to a whisper, but I can still hear his indignation. "I told you before. I get hungry."

"But why not just leave if you have a key?"

He doesn't answer for a moment. "It makes them feel better to think they control me," he finally says. "If they thought that I had outsmarted them, they would try harder." I sit with that for a while. It makes me think of Iyla. I wonder if that's how she felt—wanting to let the Naga think that they controlled her, but playing by her own rules. Voluntarily staying in a prison she knew she could leave whenever she wanted. I wonder where she is and if she's happy. Even after everything, there's a part of me that still cares about her.

"You'd better go," Kavi says. "The guards are changing shifts right now, so you don't have to worry about them checking for a while."

My fingers are trembling as I slide my hand through the bars and grope in the darkness for the padlock. I'm holding the key so tightly that my fingers ache; I'm terrified I'll drop it and send it clattering to the stone floor and my hope of escape will be gone. I try several times, but I can't twist my wrist at the right angle to get the key into the lock. Beads of sweat have broken out on my forehead.

"Marinda," Kavi whispers. "Give me the key." I pass the key through the bars to him and wait for the sound of him opening his own lock, but I don't hear anything. My heart starts to pound—maybe he changed his mind and plans to keep the key after all. Then—the tiniest creak as the bars to my cell slide open. Kavi touches my elbow and I clap my hand over my mouth to avoid yelping. He pulls on my arm so that he can whisper in my ear. "Don't say a word."

He takes my hand and leads me carefully through the dark. We turn left, which means we're headed in the opposite direction of the staircase. The only sound I hear is the blood rushing through my ears. We make it to what seems like the end of the walkway, but then Kavi squeezes my hand, turns to the right and pulls me downward. We duck through an opening in the wall only half as high as a proper door. As soon as we're around the corner, the space opens up and I can see a small amount of light coming from somewhere farther down the passageway.

"This is a secret entrance," Kavi tells me once we're far enough away that we won't be overheard by the other prisoners. "It's a way for the guards to check on us without making any noise." He leads me forward. "They keep some weapons in that little room there," he says, pointing to the left, "in case the prisoners get out of control. And the kitchen is around the corner and up the stairs. I recommend the sweet bread."

"Thank you," I say. My voice is trembling and my knees feel weak. I'm not sure I can do this.

"Okay," Kavi says. "Gotta go." He puts one arm around my waist and gives me a quick hug. "Remember," he says.

"Fear is the fuel of bravery." And then he scampers off back down the pathway and into the dungeon.

I lean my head against the stone wall and take deep breaths. I'm out of my cell, but I have no idea what to do next. I don't know how to get out of the palace, let alone how to find the Naga. I try to remember Hitesh's directions. Due west. Path up the mountain. Snake Temple. But even if I find them, I don't know what to expect. Will they try to kill me? Will they let Mani go if I promise to stay?

The sound of footsteps somewhere above startles me into action. I creep along the wall toward the staircase, intending to head straight for the kitchen. But then I pause in front of the weapons room. The door is slightly ajar, and a weapon of some kind could prove useful. I glance into the room to make sure it's empty and then I slip through the doorway. The room is considerably dimmer than the corridor, and it takes a moment for my eyes to adjust. Dozens of weapons hang on the walls: curved swords, battle-axes, a large mace, several spears. I heft one of the swords from the wall and immediately realize that carrying it will be impossible. It's too heavy for me even to lift, let alone use properly. Or carry for thirty miles.

I experiment with several other weapons before settling on a small dagger. It's not much, but it's the most I can manage. I squeeze back through the doorway and continue down the path. When I round the corner, I stop short. I'm at the bottom of the staircase that Kavi said led to the kitchen, but that's exactly where the light is coming from. The last thing I want is to walk headlong into a room full of people when I smell like the dungeon. But I don't have time to wait for the lights to go out either. I move up the staircase one step at a time, careful to make as little noise as possible.

When I reach the top of the staircase, I peer into the room, but I don't see anyone. Several rows of freshly baked rolls are cooling on the countertop. I'm just about to step into the room, when a maid breezes into the kitchen, humming softly. I flatten myself against the wall and hold my breath. The maid starts packing rolls—a dozen or so at a time—into canvas bags. I wonder if one of those rolls will end up on Kavi's breakfast tray in the morning. After the bread is packed away, she starts cleaning the kitchen—scrubbing down the work surfaces with soapy water from a large wooden bucket. My calves are on fire from being pressed against the wall on my tiptoes, but I don't dare move.

After several minutes the maid disappears from view, and moments later I hear a door open. A breeze races past me and I hear the slosh and splash of water being tossed from the bucket. My heart leaps. There's a door to the outside from the kitchen. It's more than I could have hoped for. The maid continues working for what seems like an eternity, and by the time the lights finally go out in the kitchen, my whole body aches. I lower my heels to the floor and roll my shoulders, but I wait a few minutes before leaving the stairway.

At last, when I'm convinced the maid isn't returning, I

dart from my hiding place and grab one of the canvas bags. I feel guilty taking so much bread—I don't need all of it—but I most definitely need the bag and I don't want to take the time to relocate the rolls. I look for something with a lid to carry water, but the only thing I can easily find is a metal mug. Hopefully, there will be a spring nearby. I toss both the mug and the dagger into the bag with the bread and slip out the door into the night.

● ●

The mountain range looks close enough to touch, but I jog for at least two hours before I reach the trail Hitesh described. By then I am gasping for breath and my mouth is gritty with thirst. The nearly full moon is a grim reminder that I have less than a day to find Mani and still twenty miles to hike with no water and no plan. My head is pounding and I feel unsteady on my feet.

I need to find water before I can do anything else. I wander along the path, looking for animal tracks, mud or any sign of a stream. When the trail forks, I choose a path at random and keep searching. The path branches off several more times before I finally hear the gurgling of flowing water. I run toward the sound and find a small stream full of large boulders. The water turns white as it spills over the rocks.

I pull the mug from my bag and fill it at the edge of the stream. The water is ice cold and I'm certain nothing has ever tasted better. My thirst is satisfied after draining the mug once, but I fill it twice more anyway. I don't know when I'll find water again. I pull some bread from my bag and take small bites, forcing myself to chew and swallow. I'm not even a little bit hungry, but I can't hike for twenty miles on an empty stomach.

Once I'm back on the trail, I realize I'm hopelessly lost. I can't remember how many times the path broke off or which way I turned. Finally I realize that there's no choice but to go back to the base of the trail and follow Hitesh's directions. My jaw is tight as I hike back down the mountain. I should have paid closer attention to where I was going, and now I have no idea how much time I've wasted. As I walk, it occurs to me that Hitesh could have lied about the location of the Snake Temple. The thought sends a wave of nausea over me, but I push it away. It's the only information I have, and so it's follow this trail or nothing. The Raja couldn't have known I would escape, so what would be the point in telling Hitesh to lie? I need to hold on to the hope of seeing Mani again if I'm ever going to make it up this mountain.

When I'm close enough to the bottom that I can see the head of the trail leading straight down, I turn and quickly begin jogging back up the mountain. But my energy doesn't last long and soon I can only manage a fast walk. At the first fork in the path, I turn right. And then right again. And then left. I walk all through the night, forcing myself to put one foot in front of the other, slowly plodding along. I find another stream—or maybe the same stream higher up—and fill my mug again. Then I continue hiking. Right twice. Left twice. Right twice.

The darkness gradually recedes and the sky turns indigo and then violet. If I don't hurry, this will be Mani's final sunrise. But my legs are so tired they feel like jelly and I can barely keep my eyes open. Maybe if I rest for a few minutes, I can move faster and make up the time. I move off the trail and find a place to sit with my back against a large tree. My eyelids are heavy. It won't hurt to close them for just a moment and then I can—

I wake with my head slumped forward and a line of drool dangling from my lips. The sky is blue and clear; I must have slept for hours. Panic floods through me and I scramble to my feet. And then I hear voices and I go stiff. That must have been what woke me—the low hum of conversation. I peer around the tree toward the trail and see Sundari soldiers—dozens of them—traipsing up the path. These must be the men the Raja has sent to capture the Naga. It's both good and bad news for me. Good because it must mean I'm headed in the right direction. Bad because now I have to worry about being discovered and hauled back down the mountain to the dungeon. Surely the Raja's guards have informed him of my disappearance by now, and I can't be certain he hasn't alerted his soldiers. Especially since this is exactly where he would expect me to be.

I wait for the soldiers to pass, and then I start hiking

again, keeping a safe distance behind them. The boot prints in the path make them easy to follow, but I still keep track of my turns. Left, left. Right, right. They seem to be following the same path I planned on. But somewhere around midday their path turns in the opposite direction. I stare at the boot prints on the trail—turning down a right path when we were due for a left—and wonder which direction to choose. Do I trust what Hitesh told me? Or do I trust the soldiers that the Raja actually sent to deal with the Naga?

I'm still staring at the dirt when I hear footfalls. I dive off the trail and press myself against a tree. The entire group of soldiers marches down the path, and they take a left now instead of a right. It seems sloppy to make such a basic mistake. Too sloppy. The only explanation is that there must have been a reason to go that way first. And then I see one of the men drinking from a canteen. Water. There must be a water source up there. I wait behind the tree until the group passes and they are far enough away that they won't hear me. Then I follow the boot prints up the path to the right. Sure enough, a stream bubbles up from the rocks. It's small, but it's sufficient. I drink as much as I dare and then splash some water on my face and neck. My legs ache with exhaustion, but I keep picturing Mani, keep talking to him in my mind. *I'm coming, monkey. Hang on, I'm coming.*

I fall into a rhythm with the Raja's men, following their footprints up the right trails and up the wrong ones too, where there's always water waiting for me. My hike becomes so mechanical that I'm barely thinking anymore—right turn, right turn, left turn, left turn—and so I nearly walk headlong into where the soldiers have stopped to make camp. They are fanned out on either side of the trail, and I spot them just in time to hide before they see me. My heart is pounding in my chest. Why are they stopping? It's nearly nightfall. Are they not planning on confronting the Naga after all? The wind rushes through the trees above me and that's when I smell it.

The unmistakable odor of snake.

CHAPTER TWENTY-TWO

"The Naga are due to arrive at dusk."

I'm hiding in a copse of trees, listening to an older soldier talk to a younger one. For perhaps the first time in my life, I'm grateful to Gopal for teaching me to be invisible, to see without being seen.

"But won't they see us as they pass?" the young soldier asks.

"No. Greffi's group has spotted them coming from the other side of the mountain. They'll enter the temple from there."

My heart pinches at the thought of Mani trudging up this mountain to his own death, and I long to run to him. It's all I can do to hold myself here and wait for an opportunity to slip past the soldiers. They're too close right now—at least these two are. I'm holding my muscles so taut that they are trembling, but I'm afraid if I move an inch, if the soldiers hear so much as the rustle of a leaf, they will find me and kill me before I can get to Mani. The soldiers keep talking, and the conversation turns mundane—weapons, food, women—and I have to draw in slow, deliberate breaths to withstand the pain of keeping still.

But then my ears are filled with the thundering of footsteps, someone running toward the camp, and I can't help it, I turn my head. A boy dressed in mottled clothing stops near the camp. His cheeks are bright red and he's gasping for breath. All the soldiers are immediately on their feet, and at first I think they mean the boy harm. But, no. They stop short and wait for him to speak.

"They're here!" the boy shouts. He puts his hands on his knees and sucks in a deep breath before he continues. "Somehow they got to the temple without us seeing them. The Naga are already here."

I'm on my feet and running before I hear another word. I don't even bother with the trail; I just scramble up the mountain, underbrush cutting into my calves and branches scratching my cheeks. The musky smell grows stronger the higher I climb, and I follow my nose all the way to the mouth of a cave. The reptilian stench curls from the opening and I clap my hand over my nose and mouth, but it's too late. I fall to my knees and retch until my stomach is empty and then stand up and wipe my mouth on the back of my sleeve. I can hear the soldiers behind me, racing up the trail. I pull the dagger from my bag and tuck it into my waistband. I will kill any one of them who tries to stop me.

The cave opening is small and I have to stoop to get inside. Huge rocks litter the path and I carefully pick my way across them. The farther I get into the cave, the more the ceiling slopes downward. Eventually the only way through is on my hands and knees. Sharp stones cut into my palms and tear through my pants. I can hear the sound of water rushing somewhere beneath me and fear claws at my insides. Am I in the wrong cave? The musky smell has nearly vanished, and I don't know if my nose has adjusted or if the odor really is gone. The cave is so dark I can't even see my hands in front of me.

A spray of rocks tumbles past. It must be the soldiers, though they will have to enter the cave one at a time. But now I don't know if they are chasing me or the Naga. I crawl faster. I can feel blood trickling from my palms. After what seems like an eternity, the path beneath me starts to smooth out and becomes moist and slippery. I reach a hand above me and find only air, so I try standing. The cave has finally opened up and now I can walk upright without bumping against the ceiling. I trail the fingers of one hand along the wall and hold the other hand out for balance. The sound of rushing grows louder and I feel a stab of worry that I'm about to walk headlong into swiftly moving water.

Finally I see light ahead and I speed up, moving as fast as I dare, keeping my fingers on the wall to steady me. As I get closer to the light, the sound grows too, reverberating off the walls and filling the cave. With a start I realize it isn't water.

It's chanting.

I hurry forward and step into a cavernous space with a soaring ceiling. Hundreds of candles are scattered throughout the room, casting flickering shadows on the walls of the cave. I take a step back so I can survey the area without being seen, so I can search for Mani. The Naga—perhaps twenty of them—sit in a semicircle, holding hands and chanting words I don't understand. They are wearing hooded cloaks made to look like snake scales—copper-colored and gleaming in the candlelight. A shiver races up my spine. It's impossible to see their faces, but none of them is small enough to be Mani. My eyes scan the room again and it's all I can do not to cry out his name.

And then I see him.

In the center of the semicircle is a stone altar. Mani sits on top, his hands and feet bound, fat tears crawling down his cheeks. I launch myself toward him, trampling over one of the Naga to make my way into the circle. The chanting dies away and the room breaks into confusion. I'm almost there. Mani sees me and relief floods his face, which only makes him cry harder. I get to him and pull on the rope tied around his wrists. I've almost got it loose when an arm circles my waist and drags me away from the altar. Mani screams, and it echoes through the cavern.

"Marinda, stop this instant." Gopal's lips are against my ear. I stop for a moment, and then when he relaxes his grip, I elbow him hard in the stomach. He lets go and I race toward Mani again, but I'm too slow. Gopal wrenches my arm so hard I'm afraid he's broken it. I cry out and stop struggling.

"That's a good girl," Gopal whispers. And then he raises his voice and addresses the group. "My apologies," he says. "This is our *visha kanya* and she's feeling a little feisty today." A few nervous laughs come from the circle. "I'm afraid she's gotten rather fond of our sacrifice and now thinks she can keep it," he says, and then squeezes both of my shoulders affectionately. "Entirely my fault. I've pampered her a little too much."

Rage flies through me. I try to kick Gopal, but he twists my arm again and pain shoots from my wrist to my shoulder. Where are the Raja's soldiers? Why aren't they here apprehending the Naga? The others in the circle start to whisper to each other, and for a moment I have some hope that they might oppose Gopal, that they might let Mani and me go. But then Gopal clears his throat, and the cavern falls silent except for Mani's sobbing.

"Have no doubt," he says loudly, "that our dear Marinda will behave herself once the sacrifice is finished."

"Don't you dare touch him!"

"Silly girl. He was nothing but an experiment. Unfortunately, he can't hold his poison as well as you can, my dear." Gopal must see the horror on my face, because he laughs. "We had hoped to have someone the Naga could count on to kill our female enemies, but alas, the boys all seem to die eventually."

I flail around, but I can't seem to land a blow. Gopal just holds me tighter and whispers in my ear—*Shh, shh*—like I'm a baby who needs comforting.

"This child is the last thing keeping Marinda from being fully in our midst," he tells the Naga. "Once he is gone, she will embrace us as family."

"I will *never* become one of you," I say through clenched teeth. "Never."

"We'll see," he says softly. He turns back to the group. "Let us continue summoning the Nagaraja. I will restrain the girl." The Naga begin chanting again and panic blooms in my chest. Gopal's grip on me is like a vise, and no matter how I struggle, I can't get away. And then I remember the dagger in my waistband. I stop fighting and let my body go limp. "Good girl," Gopal says. Beyond the altar, from a round hole in the floor of the cavern, smoke begins to rise, and with it the musky smell of snake. The chanting grows louder, more urgent. Gopal's grip relaxes as he begins to chant along with the other Naga. I twist my body slightly, pretending that I am as transfixed by the ritual as he is. I use my uninjured hand to reach for the dagger. Gopal looks at me, but I keep my eyes trained on the smoke.

"See?" he says. "Isn't it wonderful?"

"I'm so sorry," I tell him.

His eyes soften. "Oh, Marinda," he says, his voice full of love. Because he thinks I am apologizing for resisting him, for not wanting the life he gave me, for loving Mani.

I give my body one last twist and plunge the dagger into

Gopal's heart. His eyes go wide with shock and betrayal as he stumbles backward. He touches his chest, and his fingers come away soaked in blood. He holds them up to his face and stares at them like he can't quite make sense of what's happening.

He reaches out a hand toward me, and I can't tell if he's beckoning me to come closer or pointing a finger of accusation. His mouth opens and closes, fishlike, but he's not making a sound. He continues to stagger back until he's pressed against the cave wall, until it's the only thing holding him in place. His gaze lands on my face and stays fastened there.

My heart gives one slow beat and a moment of clarity shivers between us—the realization that, despite everything, he was only human and just as easily killed as any other man.

And then he slumps to the ground.

I run toward Mani and untie his hands. He throws his arms around my neck. "I love you," he says.

I bury my face in the soft skin of his neck. "I love you too, monkey. I love you so much."

I hear a collective gasp behind me and whip my head toward the smoke.

The Snake King has arrived.

My entire body goes rigid.

The Nagaraja makes even Kadru's largest snake look no bigger than an earthworm. As he slinks from the hole in the rock, his head skims the top of the cavern—and that's with at least half of his body still submerged beneath the ground.

Fully stretched out, he must be at least as tall as the palace. His skin is snow white and his beady black eyes are the size of human fists. He seems to survey the crowd, until his gaze fixes on me and Mani. The Nagaraja lets out a hiss that makes my blood run cold. Huge droplets of yellow venom drip from his fangs and splat on the ground.

I'm vaguely aware of a commotion behind me, but I'm frozen in place with fear. The Nagaraja sways his head back and forth, dancelike, until our faces are level. His eyes are so shiny I can see my own reflection—all the terror and awe of it. And then a voice comes into my mind as clearly as if it were spoken out loud.

Daughter.

The weight of the word burrows into my mind and I can feel everything else slipping away, until there is nothing left but the Nagaraja.

I have been waiting for you.

My mind is foggy and I think maybe I've been waiting for him too. Or maybe I came here to find him?

I see you, Marinda.

And I feel him there in my mind. Looking, searching. He shakes his head and I can feel his disappointment.

You want all the wrong things. You desire love . . . but love only makes us stupid.

Love. The word nearly brings a face to my mind, and I turn my head—a young boy crying. An older boy nearby shouting my name. I feel like I should—

Look at me. My gaze swivels back to the Nagaraja and there I am again, reflected in his eyes.

You feel powerless.

Memories flood into my mind—finding out I killed the man with the balloon, watching my friend die after Gopal forced me to kiss him, lying helplessly in Kadru's arms as the snakes infused me with their venom. No one has ever understood before, but I can feel the Nagaraja there in my mind sharing my pain. Yes. He does see me. He knows. He understands.

You are not powerless, Marinda. The blood of my children runs through your veins. If you serve me, I can make you more powerful than you ever dreamed possible. If you want love, I can make people love you. If you want money, you can have all you wish. Come to me and I will give you the world.

A vision fills my mind of all my life could be. I see myself sitting on a throne, dripping in jewels, surrounded by people who live to serve me. Power. Wealth. Love.

Get the dagger, Marinda.

I go to the man slumped in the corner and pull the dagger from his heart. It makes a sucking sound as it leaves his body. I return to the Snake King, fist clenched around the weapon, my palm sticky with fresh blood, and wait for him to show me what to do.

The Nagaraja laughs. *I know you can use this. I watched you. It is a pity. Gopal was a loyal servant. But if you don't care for him, then it is good that he is dead.*

A vague memory tugs at me—did I stab someone? I'm not sure if it's a real memory or a dream. I have the urge to turn toward the man in the corner, to try to place him, but I don't want the Nagaraja to stop talking to me. I can't look away.

You must do something for me, Marinda.

I blink. I'm ready to do anything he asks if he will keep talking to me, keep seeing me.

You must kill him. Kill the boy and we will feast on him together.

My nose is filled with the mouthwatering scent of human flesh. I turn back to the boy on the altar. He is shivering and his eyes are puffy and red. There's something familiar about him, something just at the edges of my memory, but I can't quite reach it.

Do it now. Kill him. The Nagaraja's voice cuts through my mind, sharp and demanding. I raise the dagger.

"Marinda?" Mani's voice washes over me like sunshine. He is cowering, his face full of fear. I lower the dagger back to my side. Horror wells in my chest.

But then the Nagaraja's voice is back in my mind, pressing with a force I can't withstand. *Kill the boy!* And I know what I must do—now, before I change my mind.

I raise the dagger high above my head and with all the force I can muster, I turn and stab the Nagaraja.

CHAPTER TWENTY-THREE

A howl pierces through my mind so painfully that I stumble backward. I scan the length of the Nagaraja's body for the wound I'm sure will be there, but I have made a huge miscalculation. My tiny dagger was not enough to kill him—not even enough to injure him. Only enough to infuriate him.

I start untying the knots at Mani's ankles. I have to get him away from here.

Out of nowhere I hear Deven's voice. "Marinda, watch out!" I whip around just in time to see the Nagaraja's head plunging toward me. His voice is back in my head. An instant, shrill command: *kill him, kill him, kill him.* I almost fall under the snake's spell again, but Mani is calling my name—his is the only voice that keeps the Nagaraja at bay, the only voice stronger than the killer in my head. I remind myself who I am, who I love. It works, but the moment of hesitation was too long.

The snake clamps his jaw down on Mani's arm, sinking his fangs deep into Mani's flesh. Mani's screams turn my blood to ice. I can feel the Nagaraja's pleasure in biting him, and he doesn't intend to stop there. I know now that I have no chance of killing the snake, and my mind is scrambling for how to get him away from Mani. Deven charges forward with a sword. He tries to stab the Nagaraja, but the snake is too fast. He twists his body right before Deven can land a blow. Deven pitches forward and falls to the floor. Mani's screams fade away as he loses consciousness. He's dying.

Rage explodes in my chest.

I lift the dagger and plunge it into the center of the Nagaraja's shiny eye.

Pain blasts through my head and black spots dance in my vision. I grope at my face, searching for the sharp tip of metal I can feel there, but I can't find it. I press a palm to my eye to stem the bleeding and my hand comes away dry. Panic swallows me in a single gulp. I'll never be able to defeat the Nagaraja if hurting him means hurting myself. Mani's head lolls to one side, and my stomach lurches forward. I have to do something. If I feel the Nagaraja's pain, maybe I can force him to feel mine. I let all my anguish come to the surface, not just from this moment, but from years and years of terror wrought by the Nagaraja's subjects. I focus all my pain until it is as sharp as the tip of a sword, and then I shove it toward the snake and try to invade his mind like he took over mine.

The Nagaraja shrieks and rears back, releasing his grip on Mani. The dagger is still lodged in his eye, and thick rivulets of blood gush from the wound. My own head is throbbing too. I scoop Mani into my arms. Pain shoots through my shoulder, but I push it away. My injuries are nothing compared with Mani's. I run with him to the far end of the cavern. His face is pale and his breathing is shallow. I risk a glance at his arm and bile rises in my throat—it looks like ground meat. And there's so much blood. I lay him on the ground and put pressure on his arm with both of my hands to try to stop the bleeding, but it's not working. His arm is torn up in too many places. Soon my hands are soaked in red, and blood is oozing through my fingers.

"Stay with me, Mani. Stay with me."

Deven runs up beside me. He kneels down, yanks the sleeve from his shirt and wraps it tightly just above Mani's elbow. Gradually the blood stops flowing. A sob escapes my lips. "Thank you," I say. Mani is so pale. I can't lose him. I lay my head on his chest.

"Please," I whisper. "Please don't die."

Deven lays a hand on my shoulder. "Marinda, you need to go now."

My head snaps up. "I'm not leaving him."

"If my father finds you—"

"I'm not leaving him!"

Deven nods and sits back on his heels.

"I'm surprised you bothered to come," I say. I smooth the hair from Mani's forehead.

"Of course I came," he says. "But I was too late. We all were." And I would have been too if I hadn't escaped. The Raja may have cost Mani his life. Deven touches my shoulder and I shrug him away.

The Raja's soldiers are swarming through the cavern, detaining the few Naga that haven't scattered. Gita is several paces away from me, her hands shackled in front of her, her face pinched with worry. Our eyes meet and the door in my heart that I used to let her walk through slams shut. I wonder if she feels it too—the loss of who we used to be to each other. The cavern looks utterly ordinary now. The Nagaraja has disappeared along with the smoke. For a moment I let myself hope that he might be dead, that the Raja's men succeeded in killing him when I couldn't. But I know it's not true. There's a corner of my mind that still feels the snake's fury. His frustration. His hunger.

He's still alive.

"Marinda," Deven says. His voice is low and urgent. "I promise I will take care of Mani, but you have to go." I open my mouth to protest, but he shakes his head. "You'll go back to the dungeon when these soldiers realize who you are. You'll probably hang. Mani will never forgive you if you leave him."

I chew on my lip. I don't know which is worse: to leave Mani when he is so badly injured or to risk never seeing him again. A sudden vision of his face as I held the dagger above him flashes through my mind, and I think I might be sick. I don't want that to be his last image of me.

"Where would I go?"

Deven exhales forcefully, as if he's been holding his breath. "There's a place you can stay in the Widows' Village." His eyes flick up. "Iyla can take you there."

"Iyla? She's here?"

"I'm here," Iyla says softly behind me.

I spin around and relief floods through me. She's here. She didn't leave Mani to die at the hands of the Naga. Her expression is guarded and unreadable, but I'm so happy to see her. Deven shoots a worried glance at the soldiers.

"Time to go," he says. I feel like I'm being ripped in half.

I press my lips against the top of Mani's head and my tears dribble down his cheeks. "I can't leave him," I say.

Deven lays a hand on my arm. "I'll bring him to you when he is well. I promise." He scoops Mani into his arms and my heart breaks. If I lose Mani, nothing else matters.

"Please," I say, grabbing a fistful of Mani's shirt and burying my face against his chest. I don't know if I'm pleading with Mani to live or with Deven to take care of him, but I can't stop saying it—"Please, please, please."

"Marinda," Deven says, "I need to get him out of here. You have to go. *Now.*" Deven shoves me toward Iyla. "Don't forget what I said," he tells her. His voice has an edge to it— maybe from the exertion of lifting Mani. He holds her gaze until Iyla nods.

"I'll see you soon," he says to both of us. "Now go."

Iyla grabs my arm and drags me into the dark passageway. I can hear the echo of Deven's voice across the cavern. "We need to get this boy to a physician now!" I wipe the tears from my eyes as we make our way out of the cavern.

And I leave the only person I love behind me.

* *

We are nearly to the Widows' Village when I spot the cloak peeking out from Iyla's bag. The coppery scales glint in the waning sunlight, and the sight of them sends my stomach spinning. I stop walking.

"You didn't come to the Snake Temple to help. You were there with the Naga." I can see from the expression on her face that I'm right.

She sighs. "It's complicated."

"No," I say. "It's really not." She turns her back and keeps walking as if I haven't spoken.

"So what now?" I ask. "You betray me again? Tell the Naga where I am so that they can capture me?"

"Of course not." Her voice is flat and unemotional. Something about her refusal to argue enrages me.

"He is a little boy, Iyla! And you were ready to let them take his life!"

She spins to face me. "You weren't so concerned with life when Kadru was taking mine and giving it to you."

I suck in a sharp breath. Years of visits to Kadru unspool in my mind—the fear, the pain, the torture. And Iyla was there every time. Those were the only times I ever saw her visibly afraid. Kadru's voice, when she told me what Gopal had done, echoes in my memory: *It was someone else's life in the bargain, but those are his secrets to share.*

"It was you? She drained the life from you?" I feel like I've swallowed a brick of ice.

Iyla rubs her forehead. "Over and over. In Gopal's mind my life was valuable only if it sustained yours. My job was to make sure that *your* jobs were safe. He didn't care how endangered I was. From the very beginning everything was about you. 'The Nagaraja chose Marinda. Marinda is special. Marinda must be protected at all costs.' "

"Wait," I say. "You've known we were serving the Nagaraja since we were *children*?" A pit opens in my stomach. I assumed that she sought out Deven because she found out who we were really working for, but I can tell by the heavy silence and the expression on her face that I was wrong.

"Why?" I'm practically shouting now. "Why would you let me think I was killing for the good of Sundari when you knew those men were innocent?"

"Why do you think?" Iyla shouts back. "Gopal has broken my bones, Marinda. He has held a blade to my throat and whipped me until I bled. What do you think he would have done if I'd told you the truth?"

"I would have protected you," I say. "We could have come up with a plan together."

"No," she says, her voice raw with pain. "You've never been able to protect me, and we stopped making plans together a long time ago."

"Gopal was cruel to me too—" I start.

But Iyla cuts me off. "He was cruel to you by being cruel to me. I paid a heavy price for your friendship."

My heart clenches. Mani paid a heavy price too. And Japa. "I'm sorry," I say. "I never knew." But that hardly seems an adequate excuse. "You must hate me."

"Yeah," Iyla says. "I kind of do." She stares at her feet, nudges a stone with her toe. "But I care about you too."

I think of Gita. I know all about hating and loving someone at the same time.

"When I met Deven," Iyla continues, "I thought I'd finally found a way out. But then you stole that too."

My mouth drops open. "That's not fair. I didn't steal anything."

Iyla pinches the bridge of her nose. "Deven was going to get me out. He was going to protect me. You were supposed to kiss him, Marinda, and then I planned to tell him who you were, what you'd tried to do, so that he would take you down with all of the rest of the Naga. Instead you made him fall in love with you and ruined everything."

"You wanted him to hate me," I say.

She fixes me with a cold stare. "Someone should."

My hands curl into fists. "Is that why you lied to him and told him I had you beaten?"

Her face is stony. "That wasn't a lie." I feel like she's slapped me. She blames me for every time Gopal punished her, even though he was the one holding the whip. Maybe she's right. Maybe I should have done more to protect her.

But then the full realization of what she's done settles over me and sweeps away my guilt. She's planned this for months—to escape at my expense. To have me captured by the Naga's enemies and be . . . who knows what? Tortured? Killed?

The betrayal tastes bitter at the back of my throat. "Do you hate me so much that you wanted me dead?"

"Of course not," Iyla says. And then after a beat, "Maybe. I don't know." She sighs. "It doesn't matter anymore. I tried to turn Deven against you and it didn't work. He loves you. And now you'll be living in the house that was meant for me."

I press a hand to my forehead. Of course. That's why Deven had such a quick solution for my escape. He'd already prepared a place for Iyla in the Widows' Village.

I don't know what to say and so we keep walking in silence. It's astonishing, really, that her hate for me was as strong as my love for her. My heart feels heavy with loss today. Worry about Mani is pressing at the forefront of my mind. And when I saw Iyla in the cavern earlier, I was so relieved—I thought she would help me cope. I thought I'd found my best friend again. But it turns out I lost her long before I knew I had.

"Deven doesn't love me," I say after a few minutes, because it's true and because I think it will make her feel better.

She laughs humorlessly. "Yes, he does. When he saw me in the circle of Naga, he pulled me aside and told me to shove the cloak in my bag. I thought that he was trying to protect me from being discovered by the soldiers. I thought it was proof that he cared about me. But, no. He threatened that if I didn't help you escape, he would let the Raja know that I was Naga and I would be executed. Once again, my life matters only if it can save yours." Her voice breaks. She loves Deven. It didn't occur to me until this moment that any of her feelings might be real. I think of seeing her kiss him that day in front of her house. I was so worried that he loved her, and now she's afraid he loves me. But she doesn't need to worry. Deven is only thinking of Mani. When he finds out that I killed his brother, he will want nothing to do with me.

"Why did you come back?" I ask her after a few minutes.

Her eyebrows draw together. "Come back from where?"

"From wherever you went when you ran. I went to your house. All of your things were gone." I can't quite keep the bitterness out of my voice. "You escaped without me."

"I didn't escape. Gopal moved me. He hoped it would draw you out. He thought that you'd come to him panicked and ask for help finding me. But you never did." A look of hurt crosses her face. "I really thought you would, but you never did."

Her comment makes me wonder how much of our anger toward each other is because we've been looking through a window in the dark instead of in daylight—we thought we were seeing each other, but it turns out we were only seeing ourselves.

CHAPTER TWENTY-FOUR

Iyla and I name our cottage the Blue House, even though every other house in the village is blue too. It amuses us, and there is so little to be amused about anymore. Over the next few days we settle into a routine. Iyla cooks, and I do the dishes. The jobs suit us. Iyla can make even the most boring ingredients desirable, and I can't get enough of plunging my hands into soapy water and watching the stains lift away. Washing dishes is like witnessing redemption over and over again.

The cottage is cozy—not as lavish as Iyla's old house, but not as spare as the flat I shared with Mani.

When Iyla and I stumbled through the mountain pass, the widows greeted us with open arms and a conspicuous absence of questions. "You're safe now," one of them whispered as she led us to the cottage, and I wondered if we weren't the first ones to seek refuge here. The women have taken us under their wings—spoiling us with home-baked treats, teaching us how to mend ripped saris and boil fruit with sugar to make a spread for chapati.

It's like having three dozen grandmothers and is so far removed from my life as a *visha kanya* that it feels like a dream. The women say it's good to have young people in the village, which always pinches my heart because it makes me think of Mani. They would love Mani. I examine their faces and try to figure out which one of them is Deven's grandmother, which woman shares his crooked nose, or his dark eyes, or his chin. But age has erased their features and made them all look alike. I don't dare ask questions. Even here, it isn't safe to draw attention.

One of the younger widows, Vara, is teaching us how to grow our own food—how to plant the brinjal seeds two knuckles deep, how to water just enough to nourish but not to drown, and how the things that sprout first and most easily are the very things that, if not eliminated quickly, will destroy our efforts. More and more Iyla and I find ourselves out here with Vara, our hands buried wrist-deep in the soil, luxuriating in the silence. It such a hopeful thing—gardening—the faith that we'll be around long enough to enjoy the harvest.

I'm holding a handful of earth in my palm when I hear the rumble of a caravan coming through the mountain pass. My fist tightens around the dark soil, but the harder I squeeze, the more it slips through my fingers. Iyla's gaze finds mine and together we turn toward the south and the cloud of dust that is rolling into the valley. My first thought is of Mani—I haven't heard from Deven since we got here, and so my mind is preoccupied with my brother every moment. There's an empty space in my middle that aches like only emptiness can.

But the dust cloud belongs to a group too large to be Deven and Mani, which means it's likely the Raja's men.

I scramble to my feet and brush my palms against my sari. My chest constricts at the rush of disappointment and then fear. Iyla and I need to make a decision. Do we run? Or do we stand and face our fate?

Iyla's eyes are wide as she fumbles for my hand—even after everything that has happened, we still reach for each other when fear tugs at us—but she's intercepted by Vara, who pulls both of us into her arms. "It's only a supply caravan, girls. Don't be frightened."

"A supply caravan?" I ask. "But couldn't it be the Raja? Or his men?"

Vara shakes her head. "The Raja doesn't visit here, *janu*. And neither do his men. But we do need deliveries of fabric and meat"—she dips her head toward our gardening supplies—"and seeds. You are safe here. I hope one day you'll come to believe that and find some peace."

But I'm not convinced that the Raja won't come looking for us one day. And even if he doesn't, I'm not sure peace is enough anymore.

I know I should be happy here, tucked away far from

anything resembling my old life. A year ago I would have been. Escape would have been enough. More than enough. But something restless is stirring inside me, and every so often it sits up and stretches and I feel as trapped as ever. Now I long for freedom.

Weeks pass without word from Deven and I start to worry that he'll never bring Mani back to me. And maybe he shouldn't. Maybe Mani is safer without me. After what happened in the cave, I'm not sure my brother ever wants to see me again.

On my worst days I worry that Mani didn't survive and Deven doesn't know how to tell me. The thought makes me ill, and so I try to push it away, to think of Mani as vibrant and happy and living in the palace like a prince. It's a big upgrade from his purple cushion in the bookshop. The bookshop. I think of Japa often too.

Reminders of the Naga are everywhere—a glint of copper in sunlight, the hiss of the wind through the trees. And just today Iyla found a silver hair sprouting from the top of her scalp, long and shiny against the velvet black of the rest of her hair. She plucked it out and held it in her trembling palm. We both stared at it, wordless. Years and years of her life gone and we both blame me.

And so I decide to take Iyla to the first place I ever glimpsed what a different kind of life might look like. The first place I ever felt hope. I take her to the waterfall. The air is cooler than it was when Deven and I hiked here so long ago, and the trees are alive with hues of orange and red. I rub my arms for warmth.

"How much farther?" Iyla asks.

"I think we're close," I tell her. "Last time I came from the opposite direction, so I'm not exactly sure. . . ." Just then we round a bend and there it is, every bit as beautiful as I remember.

Iyla and I sit on a grassy area near the edge of the water. This time it's too cold to lie back with the sun in our faces, so we pull our knees to our chests to stay warm and I tell Iyla the legend of the waterfall. When I get to the end, where the maiden and the prince are in love but never see each other again because they are both too stubborn, Iyla sighs.

"It's so sad," she says.

When Deven told the story, I didn't think it was sad. I thought it was romantic. But now I agree with Iyla. I think it's the saddest story I've ever heard, and I'm not sure why I liked it so much. We sit in silence for a while, and I wonder if I'll ever see Deven again. And I wonder if that's what Iyla is wondering too.

• •

I'm dozing on the sofa after our hike when I hear a knock.

"No more sweets!" Iyla shouts from the other room. Because we both know that is what awaits us on the other side of the door—a widow with *jalebi* or *sandesh* or sweet flour dumplings. I get up from the couch and stretch. I'm still rubbing my eyes when I swing the door open. And then my heart leaps in my chest.

It's Deven.

And he's brought Mani.

First I squeal. And then I cry. I gather Mani into my arms and hold him close to me. He's crying too, and then he's laughing, and I can't imagine how we must sound to the neighbors. It's not until I let go of him that I see it: his left arm is missing below the elbow. Mani sees me notice and I can feel him studying my face, measuring my reaction. I smile. "I'm so glad you're all right."

He smiles back shyly, but there's something guarded in his expression that wasn't there before and it's a splinter in my heart. "I'm getting used to it," he says, lifting up what's left of his arm. "I can do lots of stuff I couldn't do a few weeks ago."

My eyes are teary. "I'm sure you can, monkey." I ruffle his hair. His complexion looks better than it has in a year. His cheeks are rosy and his breathing is effortless, just like breathing is supposed to be. "You look so healthy." I pull him to me for another hug. "I missed you."

Deven clears his throat. "I'm sorry it took so long," he says. "He was pretty sick for a while there."

Mani makes a face. "Deven made me eat maraka fruit at every meal. He even told the cook to add it to my *bread*."

My eyes flick up to Deven. "Thank you," I mouth. He nods.

Iyla steps into the room, and for an awkward moment

no one says anything. It's Mani who moves first, who circles his good arm around her waist and wraps her in a hug. My heart swells at his compassion. He had to have seen her in the circle that night in the cave, and even before that he was never very fond of her. I wonder if he sees her differently now that he's witnessed the worst I have to offer. Iyla stiffens at first, and then a sob rips from her, a scratchy, feral thing that sounds like it's been waiting years to escape. She hugs him back, her whole body shaking with sobs. It's the first time I've ever seen her cry. "I'm sorry, Mani. I'm so, so sorry," she says.

"I know," Mani tells her.

I prepare a thick stew for dinner, and we eat and talk. Mani tells us about his recovery and about all the new friends he's made at the palace. Iyla and I fill the boys in on the village and our never-ending supply of dessert. Finally Mani's eyelids start to droop, and so I take him upstairs and tuck him into bed. His eyes are closed before I make it to the door.

When I get back to the kitchen, Iyla has already gone to bed. And just like that, Deven and I are alone. He stands up and wraps his arms around my waist. "I missed you," he says. And I missed him too, but there's a lie between us and I can't pretend there isn't. I put a hand against his chest and gently push him away.

"There's something I need to tell you."

He bites the corner of his lip. "Okay . . ."

I hold out my hand. "Come and sit on the sofa with me."

He slides his palm against mine and I try to memorize the feel of it, the warmth of his skin, the shape of his fingers. He sits on one side of the sofa and I sit on the other. I tuck my legs underneath me and stare at my hands while I try to find the words.

"What's wrong?" he asks.

I gaze at his face for a moment before I answer. I want to see him one more time when he looks like this—all boyish and kind—before hate twists his features. And then I gather my courage and clear my throat. "Kadru—she's the woman who made me a *visha kanya*—she told me something the last time I visited her that I think you should know." His eyebrows pull together, but he just waits for me to continue. I wipe my palms on my thighs. I nearly tell him that I'm the only *visha kanya,* but the words stick in my throat. It's dangerous information to risk the Raja discovering, that he could have stripped the Nagaraja of his biggest advantage just by killing me.

Not that I don't trust Deven; I do. But he didn't stop his father from imprisoning me, and the image of him standing there, horrified, as they took me away in chains still haunts me. I swallow hard and frame the thought as a question instead.

"What if I'm the one who killed your brother?" I stare at my hands so that I don't have to see his face.

There's a long silence, and I think he may have left. Then he asks softly, "Is that why you won't let me touch you?"

I meet his gaze, and my eyes fill with tears. I can't speak, and so I only nod. Deven shakes his head. "You didn't kill my brother, Marinda."

"But I must have. Kadru said—"

"He was fifteen years older than me. I was only two when he died. You weren't kissing boys as a baby, were you?"

"No," I say. "I wasn't."

For a moment I just sit there. It's a new sensation, discovering my innocence instead of my guilt, and I'm not sure where to put that knowledge—where it fits or what it means. Of all the horrible things I've done, I didn't do this one. Some of the heaviness that's been pressing on my chest for months lifts away. It's not everything, but it's something.

"I didn't kill him," I say, as if the words will make it true.

"No," Deven says. "You didn't. And you didn't kill me either. You could have, and you didn't."

"No," I say, "I really couldn't have."

Deven scoots closer to me and lays a hand on my cheek. "I'm going to kiss you now," he says. "And then I'm going to continue living and so are you."

My heart skitters forward. Deven brushes his lips softly against mine and then pulls away and searches my face like he's making an important decision. My cheeks are warm and all my limbs feel heavy and loose. Deven strokes my cheek with the backs of his fingers, then he takes my face in his hands and kisses me again. And this time the kiss is passionate and soft and all-consuming. Something inside me trembles and then splits wide open.

I have kissed dozens of boys, but I have never *been* kissed. Until this moment I didn't know there was a difference. I didn't know kissing could be like this—like creating instead of destroying, like beginnings and not endings. Like melting. Like love.

The restlessness I've been feeling for months wriggles and expands in my chest. It takes shape—and it is hard and courageous and defiant.

Deven pulls away and trails his fingers down my neck.

"I want a meeting with the Raja," I tell him.

Deven's eyes widen as if that was the last thing he ever expected me to say. "I'm not sure that's a good idea," he starts. But he must see something in my expression, something where the fear used to be. "Okay," he says. "When?"

I lay my head on his shoulder. "Soon," I say. "Tomorrow." But for tonight I just want to stay right here—curled up in Deven's arms and basking in the feeling of being loved, of Mani being safe, of being free.

It's likely the last bit of peace I'll have for a long time.

◆ ◆

This time when I enter the Raja's throne room, I'm wearing Iyla's cloak. I took it from her satchel months ago, when we first arrived at the blue cottage. If she noticed it was missing, she never said anything. I don't know why I did it. Only that it felt like it belonged to me and I was tired of people taking the things that were mine.

Deven warned me that wearing it to the meeting with his father was a bad idea. He was right, of course. When the Raja sees me, his face goes white with rage.

"How dare you?" he says. His hands are fists at his sides. "You escape from my prison, undermine my plans to apprehend the Naga with a half-baked rescue effort, and then have the nerve to show up here wearing a cloak of scales?" He motions to the guards. "Put her in chains," he says.

But Deven holds up a hand. "Stop," he says. The guards hesitate and look uncertainly between father and son. "Hear her out, Father."

The Raja's mouth twists. "You will not defend her," he says. "You know what the Naga are, what they do."

"But Marinda is not—"

This time the Raja's words are a roar. "You will. Not. Defend her!"

"You need me." I say it softly, but the room falls silent and every head swivels in my direction. I lift the hood of the cloak and let it drop behind me. "If you're going to take down the Naga, you need me."

The Raja's mouth pinches. A vein bulges at his temple, throbbing in time with his rapid heartbeat. But he doesn't speak. I take his silence as an invitation.

"The Naga have taken everything from me," I tell him. "They have robbed me of parents, of friends, of freedom. They have beaten me and tortured me and attempted to kill my brother." I swallow. "They have turned me into a killer. I want what you want. I want to destroy the Naga."

The Raja's eyes narrow. "And yet"—he waves his hand in my direction—"you come to me dressed like this."

"The Nagaraja gave me a gift," I say. "If I don't use it the way he intended, is it any less mine?"

The Raja temples his fingers under his chin and stares off into the distance. His breathing evens out, and when he turns back to me, his expression is drained of anger. His eyes are sharp, calculating. "What do you propose?"

Breath rushes out of me in a long exhale. The guards recede to their posts.

"I go back to the Naga," I say. "I pretend loyalty and I pass you the information that you need."

"You become my spy?"

"Yes," I say. "For a price."

The Raja bristles. "You haven't earned the right to ask me for favors."

"Fine," I say, holding out my wrists. "Then throw me back in your dungeon. And best of luck finding another *visha kanya* willing to do your bidding."

He narrows his eyes and holds my gaze. I refuse to look away. "What are your terms?"

"You protect Mani," I say. "You allow him to live here at the palace and make sure no harm comes to him. You give me the training and the information I need to take down the Naga. And when they have been eliminated, you give me my freedom."

"That is all?"

"Yes," I say. "That is all."

His brows lift. "You ask for so little."

"My freedom is no small thing," I tell him.

The Raja nods. "Indeed," he says. He doesn't speak for a long time, and I watch the emotions play across his face, watch him measure his hatred of me against the desire for an ally on the inside. In the end it's not a difficult choice. Not for a man who loves his kingdom. "We have a deal," he says. "But you would do well to remember that you are at my mercy."

"Yes, Your Majesty," I say. "And you would do well to remember that you are at mine."

I hear a sharp intake of breath from one of the guards. The Raja's eyes flash, but he stays silent, and I feel as if I've won something, as if we finally understand each other. "What do you need?" he asks.

"For starters, I need to know where you are holding the Naga prisoners. And a key so I can free them."

• •

Two weeks later Gita and I arrive back at the girls' home under cover of a purple darkness. The rest of the Naga have gone their separate ways—back to their posts to plot the destruction of the Pakshi, to find new targets for me to kill.

My feet ache from the hours of walking, and my throat is raw from talking, scratchy with all the lies I've coughed up.

"The Raja threw me in the dungeon," I said.

"He has Mani," I told them.

And this is how I will do it, wrap up the lies in slippery truths so that they will slide down easier. Just like Gopal used to lie to me.

Gita twists a key in the lock and pushes the door open. She wraps her arm around my shoulders and kisses my cheek. "Welcome home, Marinda," she says.

My stomach is swimming with dread. But I smile at her anyway, because this is the only way to get what I want.

That's the thing about poison. The deadliest ones always come from the inside.

A NOTE FROM THE AUTHOR

Story ideas come from all kinds of unlikely places, and *Poison's Kiss* is no different. Several years ago, I was listening to a lecture series on espionage and covert operations. In one of the early episodes, the professor discussed different civilizations and their views on and myths about spies and assassins. He mentioned a legendary figure in Indian folklore—the poison damsel, a woman fed poisons from childhood so that she gradually becomes immune but is toxic to any man she lures as her lover.

It was one sentence in an eighteen-hour course, but my mind caught on the idea. Forty minutes later, I realized I hadn't heard a single word since "poison damsel." Most assassins and spies are recruited as adults, so I was fascinated by the thought of making such a monumental choice for a child. I wondered what would happen to a girl who was poisoned but wasn't cut out to be a killer. How would the fact that she was deadly shape her? How would it break her?

The idea wouldn't leave me alone. I started researching

the legends of the *visha kanya* (Sanskrit for "poison maiden"), as well as mithridatism, which is the process of slowly becoming immune to a poison by ingesting it in ever-increasing doses.

Gradually, the idea for *Poison's Kiss* took shape. I knew I wanted the story to take place in a world other than our own, but I also wanted to be true to the origins of the *visha kanya* and create a setting that looked and felt like the place where the myth was born. So although Sundari is not India, it is influenced by that culture and its mythology.

I read dozens of Indian folktales, and bits of those legends made it into *Poison's Kiss*. I knew I needed a mechanism for obtaining the poison that would make Marinda deadly, and I couldn't think of anything more terrifying than snakes. I had already made the decision that Marinda would be poisoned by snake venom when I stumbled across a mention of the Nagaraja in my research. Anciently, this "king of the serpents" was worshipped as a deity in northern India, while in southern India the serpent cult included worship of live snakes. I thought it would be fascinating to explore how a blend of these two elements—the *visha kanya* and the Nagaraja—could be shaped into something new that would provide a context for Marinda, a reason she had been turned into an assassin.

I read everything I could find on snake worship and came across numerous references to the Naga. In some stories, the Naga are serpentine beings who live under the sea and are considered deities. Other tales cast the Naga as a human tribe of snake worshipers. My imagination took off as additional pieces of the puzzle fell into place.

Another nod to Indian mythology in *Poison's Kiss* is Garuda, a giant birdlike creature (sometimes depicted as half bird, half human) who appears in both Hinduism and Buddhism. Garuda in these myths is always male, but I've taken creative license and made my Garuda female.

The other members of the Raksaka (as well as the concept of the Raksaka itself) are my own invention.

Sundari's belief system differs from those found in India as well. Although reincarnation is a central tenet of Hinduism, and the concept of rebirth is found in Buddhism, the characters in *Poison's Kiss* believe in a limit of ten lives, a notion that isn't found in either religion.

My goal in *Poison's Kiss* was to create a unique world, with its own history and culture, while paying homage to the origins of the *visha kanya* myth. I hope you've enjoyed reading it as much as I loved writing it.

ACKNOWLEDGMENTS

It's a strange thing to work with words all day and then suddenly be unable to locate the right ones and put them in the correct order for something as important as saying "thank you."

But I'm told that an acknowledgments page filled with nothing but kisses and hearts isn't going to cut it, so words it is.

This book would not have been possible without a whole host of amazing people. First, to my brilliant agent, Kathleen Rushall, for believing in this story right from the beginning and for being not only a great advocate but also a great friend.

A million thanks go to my exceptional editor, Caroline Abbey, for asking all the right questions and for being such an enthusiastic champion of this book. I can't wait to work with you again on the next one!

I'm so grateful to the entire team at Random House: Nicole de las Heras and Martha Rago, for the gorgeous cover design; Barbara Bakowski and the copyediting team.

My heartfelt thanks to my mom, Sharon Berrett, who saved everything I ever wrote, convinced it was brilliant (even when it wasn't), and who laughs at my jokes even when they aren't funny (and occasionally when they aren't jokes). Thank you for filling my childhood with books and my life with laughter.

I'm indebted to my dad, Dan Berrett, for encouraging me to take out my teenage angst on the page instead of in real life. ("Feel free to name the villain Dan Vader," you told me once when I was in a particularly bad mood.) And then, in the years that followed, for always asking how the writing was coming along. You never forgot where I was going, and you always had faith I'd eventually get there. I hope it's not too disappointing that you get to be a hero instead of a villain.

To Britnee Landerman, who read this story in less than twenty-four hours and then texted at 3:00 a.m. to gush. You have no idea how much that meant to me. You may claim to be the World's Okayest Sister, but we both know it doesn't get any better than you.

To Cameron Berrett, who read my writing (in the form of letters) every single week for two years and who almost always wrote back. Thank you for teaching me not to take myself too seriously.

To Derek Berrett, who shares my love of all things reading and writing and who will have his own name on a book cover one day. Marinda only knew how to love Mani so much because of how much I love you.

To Don and Ginny Shields, my wonderful parents-in-law, for all your love and support over the years and for raising such a fantastic son. And thanks also go to Steve and Christy Shields, for making sure their brother grew up with a high tolerance for teasing and excellent taste in movies. (Where there's a whip, there's a way.)

To Stephen Beck, who taught me to use strong verbs, colorful nouns, and crisp prose. I'm still taking your writing advice all these years later.

My deepest appreciation to all my fellow writer friends (you know who you are) who have offered encouragement and advice along the way.

Others who read this book (in whole or in part) at various stages and offered valuable feedback and encouragement: Elizabeth Briggs, Krista Van Dolzer, Caroline Richmond, David Landerman, Keaton Landerman, Kaiser Landerman, Danica Landerman and Jill Shields.

Everlasting hugs and kisses to my children, Ben, Jacob and Isabella, for your love, your enthusiasm and your endless supply of great ideas. You are the kind of people I would choose as friends if I weren't lucky enough to call you family. It is the great privilege of my life to be your mom.

And finally, most important, to Justin, my best friend and the love of my life, for your unwavering faith and support. You are my partner in crime, my sounding board and my safe harbor. This book is just as much yours as it is mine. (Well, it's a *little* more mine, but you get the idea. . . .)

WILL MARINDA LIVE AS A SPY . . .
OR DIE A TRAITOR?
READ ON FOR A SNEAK PEEK.

THE TRUTH HAS TWO SIDES

POISON'S
CAGE
BREEANA SHIELDS

CHAPTER ONE

Marinda

It's too beautiful to die today.

Gita and I hike along a slender trail blanketed on either side by glossy green leaves shaped like teardrops. The path isn't steep, but I can hear Gita's breath—the rise and fall of it, the way it catches in her throat each time she speaks.

Her fear is like the moisture trapped in the humid air—hidden, but so heavy I can feel it pressing against my skin.

"Everything will be fine," she says. "Balavan just wants to meet you. I'm sure that's all it is."

"Or maybe he wants to execute me," I say, trailing my fingers across a plant with bright red blossoms. The flowers release a cloying scent and coat my fingers with a filmy residue that feels like drying blood. I snatch my hand away.

"No, Marinda," Gita says. "I won't let that happen." But I can hear the lie in her voice. She couldn't protect me from Gopal, and she won't be able to protect me from Balavan either.

The small palace that serves as Naga headquarters is nestled in a rain forest outside Sundari and far from the prying eyes of the Raja. Far enough that only the tigers and monkeys would hear a girl screaming.

I was a fool to think there was a chance the Naga would allow Gita to continue as my handler, to hope I'd be allowed to remain living on my own in Bala City, to believe that anything would be the same after my betrayal. Today I'll either get a new handler or I'll die for my disloyalty. Judging by the sweaty palm marks pressed on the middle of Gita's sari, she thinks it's the latter.

"Tell me about him," I say when I can't stand the silence any longer. We walk under a canopy of trees that provides shelter from the sun. Monkeys squeak and twitter above us like gossiping ladies.

"What do you want to know?"

"I want to know what to expect," I say. "Tell me something that might save my life."

Gita shakes her head. "I wish I could," she says. "But Balavan is unpredictable. Sometimes he is charming and personable. And sometimes . . ." She presses her eyes closed as if blocking out a memory. "He can be cruel."

She reaches for my hand and I resist the urge to flinch. Most days it takes all the restraint I have to look at her without grimacing, to touch her without wrapping my hands around her neck and shaking her like a rag doll. But if I want to bring the Naga down, I have to swallow all of my anger and play the part of the compliant follower.

Gita squeezes my fingers. "You must convince Balavan of your loyalty," she says. "You must tell him what you told me. How the Raja is holding your brother captive, how he beat you and imprisoned you. It's important that Balavan feels your hatred for the Raja. That he knows you will be loyal to the Snake King. Just tell him the truth."

Dread twists my stomach into a tight knot. Because it's not the truth that will save me today. It's how well I'm able to lie.

I curl my fingers into my palms. My hands always feel useless now, empty without Mani's tiny fingers threaded through mine. There's a hollow space in the center of my chest that aches with how much I miss him. But, for once, I'm grateful we're not together and that he's tucked away in the Raja's palace in Colapi City. He's safe. If I die today, at least I've given him that much.

Gita and I walk in silence for several minutes until two men emerge from the forest and step onto the path in front of us. Thick tattoos of snakes curl around their muscular forearms, and swords hang at their hips.

I take another step forward to explain why we're here, and in a single fluid motion one of the guards slides his sword from its scabbard and presses it against my neck. The cool metal bites into my skin. My breath gathers at the base of my throat, trapped.

"This is a broad and winding path," the guard says. The sword is heavy on my shoulder, and my spine starts to collapse under the pressure.

"The path that twists like a serpent always is," Gita says behind me, her voice calm and even. The guard lowers the sword and returns it to his side. I press a palm to my neck to check for blood as I try to make sense of the exchange. It must be some kind of password.

"Marinda is the *rajakumari*," Gita says, motioning toward me, and I try not to cringe at the title. I don't want to be anyone's princess, let alone the Nagaraja's. "Balavan has requested a meeting with her."

"Yes," the guard says, raking his gaze along the length of my body. "I bet he did."

"She's the *ra-ja-ku-ma-ri*," Gita repeats, emphasizing every syllable, her eyes blazing.

"For now," the guard says, looking everywhere except at my face. "But maybe not for long. Rumor is she's deadly with a blade."

He's heard, then—how I killed Gopal, how I stabbed the Nagaraja in the eye to save Mani. The memory makes bile rise in the back of my throat. That and the way this man is looking at me like I'm a piece of ripe fruit.

"See something you like?" I ask.

He grins wickedly. "I see a lot I like."

I step toward him and put a palm on his chest. "That's more like it," he says, throwing one arm around my waist and pulling me close. I stand on my tiptoes so that my lips are just inches from his. "Didn't you hear?" I ask, running my fingers through his thick hair. "I don't need a blade to be deadly."

I see the flash of realization in his eyes as he remembers the rest of my story—how I can kill a man with only a kiss as a weapon. He wrenches away from me so fast that he nearly tumbles over. The other guard rushes forward with one hand on the hilt of his sword. "Leave that where it is," I say.

He clears his throat and drops his gaze to his boots. "Of course," he says, stepping off the path. "Forgive me."

We pass the guards and continue on the path. "I'm not sure that was necessary," Gita says once we're out of hearing range.

"Of course it was," I tell her. "If I'm going to die today, it won't be after letting some man look at me like I'm a rabbit roasting on a spit."

"It's better if he thinks you're about to kill him?"

I fix her with a hard gaze. "Yes," I tell her. "It's better."

I'm about to say more, but the Naga headquarters materializes in front of us and my words die on my lips. I understand why Gita has been calling it the palace.

It's a pyramid-shaped building made entirely of dark gray granite. Pillars carved with snakes, birds, tigers and crocodiles circle the perimeter like sentinels. It looks both majestic and like it's part of the landscape, as if it could have sprouted from the ground right alongside the bamboo and the soaring fig trees.

Gita reaches for my hand, and even though I hate when she touches me, I let her take it. Because I need to feel tethered to the earth. I need to feel the reassuring press of another human heartbeat against my wrist to remind me that I'm alive, that I'm not alone.

We climb the sheer staircase that leads from the bottom of the forest floor to the entrance of the palace. My heart slams against my rib cage, and I tell myself that it's from the exertion and not because I'm worried about what will happen once we reach the top.

The moment our feet touch the final step, a monkey off in the distance howls a single shrill note and the door swings wide. A chill races down my spine.

Gita gives my hand a squeeze that I think is meant to be reassuring, but it feels more like a warning. I let go of her as I step over the threshold.

It takes a few moments for my eyes to adjust to dimmer light, but when they do, my astonishment overtakes my fear.

I'm not sure what I was expecting—something more like the caves near Colapi City. A shelter made from the earth, thick with the musty scent of reptile and lit only by flickering candlelight. But this. This is something else entirely.

The palace is dripping with splendor.

My gaze sweeps over the walls, inlaid with gemstones in intricate mosaics that stretch from floor to ceiling. Millions upon millions of winking jewels—sapphires, rubies, emeralds, amethysts. The walls are literally made from treasure. The furniture is finely carved and gilded, and the floor is gleaming black marble, so shiny I can see my own reflection.

In the center of the room is a rug shaped like a huge white snake. But when I look more closely, I see that it's made not of fabric but of living flowers. Creamy magnolias—so many that the entire chamber is filled with the sweet, lemony scent of them.

"Do you approve?" I startle at the voice and spin around to face a woman dressed in a green-and-gold sari. Her hair is braided in half a dozen loops, and gold disks hang from her earlobes. She's several years older than I am. Maybe in her midtwenties. Her hand still rests on the doorknob, and she gives me an easy smile.

"It's breathtaking," I tell her.

"The Nagaraja would be pleased to hear it," she says, and my sense of wonder vanishes.

I think of the last time I saw the Nagaraja—his jaw clamped down on Mani's arm, his anger at my escape like a hot knife in my head—and I know that he wouldn't be pleased to hear anything from me right now.

The woman must see something shift in my face, because her smile fades and she clears her throat. "I'm Amoli," she says, pressing her palms together and dipping her head. "Balavan is waiting for you."

She motions for me to follow, but before I do, I glance once more around the room to commit it to memory, along with all the other scraps of information I've gathered today: the Naga headquarters is roughly 14,842 steps from the entrance to the rain forest; the path is manned by armed guards who require a password; the entrance to the headquarters faces west. The lavish main foyer has only two visible exits—the one I just walked through and the one Amoli is headed toward.

Both Gita and I fall in step behind her, but a few moments later she turns and shakes her head. "I'm sorry," she says. "He only asked for the *rajakumari*." She gives Gita a forced smile. "You can wait here, and I'll let you know when it's finished."

When *what* is finished? My gaze flits to Gita, but the panic swimming in her eyes is no comfort.

I take a deep breath and square my shoulders. I can't afford to look weak or scared. This is the moment I've been preparing for. The moment I prove to the Naga that they can trust me again, that I'm one of them.

It's the moment I either live as a spy or die as a traitor.

CHAPTER TWO

Marinda

Balavan is the highest-ranking member of the Naga, save the Snake King himself, so as Amoli leads me down the long corridor, our sandaled footsteps echoing off the polished marble, I'm expecting her to escort me to a throne room.

Instead she opens the door to a bedchamber.

Against the far wall is a low mahogany bed covered in scarlet silk and piled with sumptuous, jewel-toned cushions in all shapes and sizes. A table sits off to one side, burdened with honey-drizzled wedges of pale cheese, a stack of flatbread, and a silver bowl filled with mangoes, apricots and pears.

A breeze blows in from the open window, carrying the delicate scent of earth. Climbing vines creep up the side of the building toward the sky.

I frown. "I thought you were taking me to meet Balavan," I say.

Amoli's gaze deliberately sweeps from my feet to my face. "You've been traveling," she says.

"I'm not tired," I tell her. "I'm ready to meet with him now."

She shakes her head. "You misunderstand," she says. "He won't want to see you in this state."

I open my mouth to argue, but then the voice of the Raja's spymaster, Hitesh, echoes in my memory. *You must be a vision of compliance, Marinda. Loyal followers of the Naga want to please their leaders.*

I swallow my frustration and give Amoli a tired smile. "Of course. Whatever Balavan wants."

"Good," she says. And then after a beat, "May I have your satchel, please?"

My heart stutters, but I keep my face passive, grateful that I listened to Hitesh and didn't load my bag with hollow coins and edible paper. *We'll get you the supplies you need later,* he said. *The Naga won't trust you at first. We can't take the risk.* Now the only things Balavan will find in my possession are a supply of clean saris and an ivory comb. Except for . . . I resist the urge to put my palm to my head and draw attention to the scarf in my hair. It's the one piece of contraband I did bring from the palace. Instead I slide the satchel from my shoulder and hand it to Amoli.

"I'll need your money too," she says.

I shake my head. "I didn't bring . . ."

Amoli reaches into the tiny pocket sewn at the hip of my sari and pulls out the few coins I tucked away. She frowns as she examines them. My palms start to sweat.

"Oh," I say. "I forgot those were there."

But it's not the money that seems to upset her. Her thumb traces the four members of the Raksaka etched on the surface: the Tiger Queen; the Great Bird, Garuda; the Nagaraja; and the Crocodile King. With a start I remember the coins I found in Japa's bookshop on the day he died. Coins that featured the Snake King alone.

Amoli clears her throat and drops the coins into the satchel. Her expression is unreadable. "Rest," she says. "Eat something. I'll be back in a bit to help you prepare."

I sink down onto the bed and rub my eyes. The silence wraps around me like an embrace. Despite my impatience to meet with Balavan and find out what he has planned for me, it feels like a luxury to be alone. Pretending to love Gita requires so much focus, so much tamping down of the hate that simmers in my chest, that it leaves my entire body aching.

I kick off my sandals, lie back against the pillows and close my eyes, but no matter how hard I try, I can't sleep. My gaze skips to the table of food, and my stomach grumbles. I sit up and pull one of the platters onto my lap, but I'm not sure I dare eat. The food could be laced with poison. It would be an elegant way to get rid of me—to serve me tainted food and let me die by my own hungry fingers. But the more I think about it, the more I doubt it's true. The Naga won't waste my death by killing me discreetly. If I'm to die, they'll want to make a spectacle of it.

I pinch a bit of cheese between my fingers and drop it onto my tongue. The flavors explode in my mouth—the sharp and the sweet both more pronounced when married. Just to be sure the food is safe, I wait a full twenty minutes before I take another bite. Then I eat most of the cheese, a loaf of flatbread and a pear before I finally feel less hollowed out.

The feast has made me sleepy, but before I lie down, I pull the scarf from my hair. The blue silk is printed on one side with deep golden stars, moons and suns. On the other side is what looks, at first glance, like a smattering of constellations. Only on close inspection could a person make out the subtle shape of Sundari and the brighter stars that indicate every dead drop in the kingdom—all the places I can leave whatever information I gather for the Raja. I fold the scarf into a small square and nestle it beneath one of the slats under the bed, examining it from every angle to make sure not even a hint of color is visible. When I'm satisfied the map is safe, I lie back and drift off to sleep.

* *

I'm dreaming of Deven when I feel a hand on my cheek. I nearly say his name—it's on the tip of my tongue as I sigh into the touch—but then awareness comes rushing back and my eyes fly wide. Amoli takes a startled step backward.

"I'm sorry," she says. "I didn't mean to frighten you. I called your name several times, but you didn't stir."

I sit up and pull my fingers through my hair. "It's okay," I say. "I must have been more tired than I realized." My head throbs lightly, and I take a deep breath and try to force the fog of disorientation to dissipate. I have to be more careful. What if I'd said Deven's name in my sleep? Am I certain I didn't? If anyone here suspects that I still care about him, both his life and mine will be in danger.

Amoli has a berry-colored sari draped over one arm and a basket full of supplies in the other. "Shall we do a bath first?" she asks, though her tone suggests it's not a question. And she doesn't wait for an answer before she unburdens her arms and makes her way through the open door of the bathing chamber at the far side of the room. She starts the water running and then pulls a vial of oil from her pocket. The room fills with the scent of jasmine.

While her back is turned, I close my eyes and steel myself for what's ahead. *Be compliant,* I remind myself. *Seem eager to please.* But the thought of letting Amoli touch me, when she serves the people who tried to sacrifice Mani, makes my skin crawl.

Amoli shuts off the water and I force my face to go slack, like curtains falling closed. By the time she turns toward me, my mind is empty, and I hope my expression is too.

"All set," she says, motioning toward the tub, where steam curls into the air like warm breath. She shifts away from me to allow at least the illusion of privacy while I disrobe and slip into the bath, but as soon as I'm submerged, she plunges her hands into the water and begins scrubbing at my skin with a rough cloth.

It takes all the self-control I have not to wrench away from her. The pressure on my bare skin is too familiar, too much contact when so few people have ever dared touch me. I bite my lip to keep from crying out.

Amoli freezes, the cloth in her hand hovering above my shoulder blade. "Am I hurting you?"

The question knocks something loose inside me, and tears threaten at the corners of my eyes. But I can't afford to let them fall. Instead I let out a light laugh. "No," I say. "You just seem to be under the impression that I walked here in a cloud of dust. Am I really so dirty?"

"I'm sorry," she says. "I just want you to make a favorable impression on Balavan." But her hands are gentler when she resumes scrubbing.

When every square inch of my body is red and raw, Amoli pours a handful of thick soap into her palm and lathers it into my hair, kneading my scalp with her fingertips. The motion is so relaxing that my eyes flutter closed and I slump deeper into the water. Cleaning my skin felt like an invasion, but this. This feels like the height of luxury.

I'm almost disappointed when Amoli disentangles her fingers from my hair and pours several pitchers of warm water over my head until all the suds are rinsed away.

She holds out a thick, creamy towel, and I wrap myself in its warmth as I step out of the tub. The scent of jasmine wafts from my skin, clings to my hair.

"Sit here," Amoli instructs, pulling up a low stool and placing it in front of a mirror. I want to argue with her, want to tell her to stop ordering me around like I'm a child, but I bite my tongue and follow her instructions.

Amoli uses a wooden comb to untangle my hair, leaving it hanging in a dark curtain around my shoulders. Then she wraps a strand tightly around her fingers and holds it there for a full minute before she unwinds it. She continues working one section at a time until my hair falls down my back in loose curls.

Next Amoli fishes a muslin cloth out of her basket, along with a shallow clay oil lamp and several small containers.

She fills the lamp with castor oil and holds a match to the wick. Flickering light dances across the mirror. She dips a corner of the cloth in one of the containers and then plunges it into the flame. The scent of sandalwood fills the air, and nostalgia overtakes me. *Kajal.* When Iyla and I were little girls, Gita would occasionally line her eyes and color her lips. We thought she looked glamorous and begged to try the cosmetics. "No, my loves," she said. "You are beautiful just as you are." A pang of sadness shoots through me at who I thought Gita was then. I wonder where she is right now. Probably pacing through the corridors, fretting over my fate, when she should be worrying about her own.

Amoli waits for the cloth to cool and then dips it in a pot of ghee and swipes the *kajal* over both my upper and my lower eyelids. Next she mixes powdered fruit rind with a splash of milk and applies it to my cheekbones with her fingertips, blending the paste into my skin in steady, sure circles. But when she dips a tiny brush in the mixture and moves toward my lips, I flinch away.

"Don't worry," she says softly, holding my chin firmly between two fingers. "I'll be careful." The brush is feather soft against my mouth, and the sensation isn't entirely unpleasant, but as Amoli applies layer after layer, my lips start to feel suffocated and I'm reminded of the poisoned lip balm Gopal used to make me wear when I was small and not yet deadly enough on my own. A shiver dances down my spine and finally Amoli pulls away.

Despite myself, I'm mesmerized by my reflection.

It was always Iyla who looked desirable, who smelled

like flowers and had color in her cheeks. Now that it's me, I'm surprised at how powerful it makes me feel.

But then I wonder why I need to look like this to meet Balavan, and my stomach sours. Is this the treatment of an honored guest or the ritualistic body cleansing before I'm put to death and my ashes are flung into the Kinjal River?

"*Rajakumari?*"

My gaze flits to Amoli, who is holding out fresh clothes and studying me with knitted brows. The look on her face suggests this isn't the first time she addressed me.

"Is something wrong?" she asks.

I give her a smile. "Of course not," I say as I wrap the plain end of the sari around my waist and pull the jewel-edged *pallu* over my shoulder. "I was just lost in thought for a moment."

"Do you need a break?" she asks. "I can come back later to finish."

I'm transformed from head to toe. What more could there possibly be left to do? "No," I tell her. "Really, I'm fine."

She searches my face without speaking for a few moments and then nods and motions toward the stool. "Let's start on your hands, then."

"My hands?"

She pulls a slender tube from her basket. "Yes," she says. "I'll be applying *mehndi*."

My breath catches. The intricate henna designs are only used for special occasions. Weddings. Funerals.

"Is he going to kill me?"

Amoli frowns, and it takes her a long time to answer. "I don't know," she says. "But I hope not."

She squeezes the henna paste from the tube with careful, practiced fingers, and soon the backs of my hands are covered in delicate, interlacing lines broken up by flowers and teardrops. It's as if I've slipped on a pair of black lace gloves, and the effect is breathtaking. Amoli applies the design all the way from my fingertips to my elbows and then starts on my feet, decorating them from toe to ankle. The designs conceal the dozens of scars left by years and years of snakebites. By the time she's finished, the sun has slipped beneath the horizon and I'm so captivated by her artistry that I've nearly forgotten why I'm here. But the truth comes crashing back when Amoli stands up and stretches. She pulls a final item from her basket, a ruby teardrop dangling from a golden wire. She fastens it around my forehead so that the jewel rests between my eyebrows.

"You're ready," she says.